LIE OF THE TIGER

WINDY MOUNTAIN
BOOK 1

JOHN MARTIN

ABOUT THE AUTHOR

John Martin is an Australian. He used to be a journalist, now he's free to be frivolous.

FOREWORD

"Great characters. Great fun. Hilarious blend of characters and lies."

Two old scallywags break a silly law to "prove" the extinct Tasmanian Tiger lives on.

This is the first in a 10-book series based on the island of Tasmania at the bottom of Australia. Nine books down, one to go.

CONTENTS

ONE
THE MYSTERY MAN ARRIVES

THE LARGE IRISHMAN rolled down his taxi window and peered out into the gloom.

A flickering streetlight flashed its yellow hue on and off across the deserted building in front of him.

He turned to the shadow next to him. "Are you sure you've brought me to the right place, fella?"

The cab driver flicked on the overhead light.

Jaysus.

The man looked well into his 70s, barely tall enough to see over the steering wheel. His spectacles were patched together with sticking plasters.

The old man took a crumpled piece of paper from his shirt pocket and slowly unfolded it. His tiny hand trembled as he held it inches from his glasses.

He turned, his eyes magnified by the thick lenses.

"Yep, Moose," he said in a reedy voice. "This is where I was told to drop you. The Windy Mountain Tasmanian Tiger Museum."

The Irishman unbuckled his seatbelt. "Look, pops, I haven't got a clue who you think I am, but if you can just open the boot, I'll get out of your way."

The driver stiffened and adopted a fighting pose. Southpaw style.

"How dare you call me 'pops!' I don't care how big you are, Moose. Someone should've taught you some respect long before now."

The Irishman sucked in a deep breath, trying to steady himself and force calm into his voice. "You can just put your fists down, fella. I've never heard of anyone called Moose, let alone be him. I came to Tasmania to escape trouble."

The driver punched the steering wheel, making it vibrate.

"Is this the thanks I get for being the first trainer on the scene when you pulled your hamstring in that footy match 18 years ago, Moose?"

"Cop on!" The Irishman's accent thickened and his voice rose. "You don't tink I'd know dat I was growing up in Dublin 18 years ago?"

"You're not fooling anyone with that phoney accent. I won't be the last person in this town who recognises you. I know for a fact you still owe Oodles and Wish-Wash money." He stared somewhere beyond the windscreen. "Well, one of them. I forget which one."

"You're crazy!"

The Irishman reached back, pulled out his wallet, peeled off a few notes and tossed them into the driver's lap. "Keep the change, you silly old eejit."

"Right, that's it!" The driver's voice became more tremulous. "No one calls me crazy, old and silly, and whatever that other word means."

He launched a punch.

The Irishman ducked sideways just as the old man's fist sailed past his ear and hit the horn on the rebound.

HOOONK!

The Irishman scrambled out on to the footpath.

"Tell you what," he said, leaning back inside. "You pop the boot, I'll grab my luggage, and we'll call this a draw."

The old man leaned over. "You haven't changed, Moose. Just so you know, if you slip in something nasty and pull your hammy again, I won't be coming running with my medical bag this time."

The Irishman closed the door, restraining himself from slamming it.

A faint, cold breeze carried the scent of wet earth.

He glanced at the museum.

None of the lights inside the building appeared to be on — though it was difficult to tell, the strobe-like effect distorting everything. A faint hum came from the faulty streetlight.

The only other sounds were the clicking of the car's engine cooling down and a distant cricket chirping.

Then, suddenly, the boot flew open and the old man fired up the engine, revving it like he was waiting for the chequered flag. Thick smoke spewed from the exhaust.

The Irishman fanned the fumes away as he lifted his suit-cases on to the footpath.

He slammed the boot shut.

The taxi shot away like a rocket, tyres screeching.

The Irishman shook a fist at the disappearing car. "Happy New Year to you too, fella."

Amazing.

The old fella had driven all the way from Launceston Airport like he was transporting wedding cake.

Now he was auditioning for Bathurst.

Here he was, left standing in the dark with only the flick-ering light and a lingering sense of unease.

His ponytail swished around as he looked left and right.

Where was everyone?

He turned when he heard footsteps, but all he saw were two elongated silhouettes on the other side of the road, clip-clopping away with haste.

TWO
POT OF GOLD AT THE END
OF A CRAPPY RAINBOW

HE HAD BEEN LOOKING FORWARD to the New Year's Eve fireworks over Sydney Harbour. But the closest thing to pyrotechnics around here seemed to be that damned flickering streetlight.

He put his suitcases down in front of the big glass door, bent over, and lifted the doormat.

Sure enough, a key glinted back at him.

So much for a welcoming committee!

Jaysus! It wasn't in his nature to lie low like a scared rat. But here he was, stuck in the remote back-blocks of Tasmania, the island at the arse end of Australia.

Joh had insisted this was the best place for him to hide out. No one would ever think to look for him here — and it was only for a while.

"How much do the locals know?" the Irishman had asked.

"Absolutely nothing," Joh had said. "So keep it that way. The less they know, the safer you'll be."

"You must have told them something about me?"

"I had to tell a few little white lies."

"Will someone be waiting for me?"

"Of course. But if they're not, you're to go in and make yourself at home. The key will be under the mat."

"What do I know about running a museum? I know nothing about art."

"You don't have to. This is a different kind of museum. It's called the Windy Mountain Tasmanian Tiger Museum."

"Toigers!" The Irishman gulped. "Are you kidding me?"

"Relax. You'll have two days before your employer calls by. Use that time to look around the place and get yourself up to speed."

"That's easy for you to say. Now I know there are toigers in Tasmania, the speed foremost on my mind will be leg-speed."

———

He flicked the light switch inside the door. Nothing happened. The electricity wasn't even connected!

The bedroom would be upstairs. They always were.

He squinted, trying to make sense of the room in front of him. The flickering yellow streetlight at least provided a strobe effect. He made out a long counter on the far side of the room.

Hoisting his heavy suitcases, he began inching his way across the carpet in rhythm with the pulsing light.

A foul smell distracted him, and as he sniffed left and right, he lost track of the counter. He certainly remembered it when his ribs slammed into its sharp edge. Something on the ledge clattered to the floor, the jangling sound of a landline phone.

Behind the counter, he discovered a spiral staircase.

The suitcases seemed to grow heavier with every turn.

At the top of the stairs, he found a bedroom at the end of the hallway.

It was a long room with windows at either end. There was

a single bed near the door. But up the other end, to his relief, was a much larger bed, illuminated by moonlight and, wouldn't you know it, the poxy, flickering glow from the street.

But it was like the pot of gold at the end of a crappy rainbow.

Crossing the room, he nearly tripped over something soft on the floor but managed to stay upright. With a groan, he dropped his suitcases beside the bed.

Stripping off his clothes, he flopped on to the mattress and passed out like a light.

THREE
TIME FOR REFLECTION
NEW YEAR'S DAY, 2017

THE WARMTH of the morning sun streaming through the window on to his face was probably what awakened him.

He kept his eyes shut as he listened to the sound of the birds chirping outside.

Fuelled by exhaustion, the Irishman had slept like a log in the kingsize bed despite his sore ribs. Not even the flickering light outside had annoyed him once he closed his eyes.

Now he was in that blissful stage of waking fully, and not really wanting the serenity to end. He just wanted to lie here and enjoy it some more. He had nowhere to be, nothing to do in a hurry, no one to see.

But something nasty-smelling crept into his nose.

He sniffed. And sniffed again. Another pong? What was that stink?

He opened his eyes.

His heart skipped a beat. A large, bearded man was looking down at him! He had the type of tattoos that looked like they had been done in a jail cell.

Then he realised they had been.

It was only a reflection of himself from a mirror on the ceiling. Jaysus! Didn't putting mirrors on the ceiling go out of fashion in the 1970s, around about the same time as spiral staircases went arseways.

He threw off the covers and swung his legs to the side of the bed.

The walls were decorated with framed photos of topless women. The floor was a minefield of discarded socks, jocks, shirts and jeans.

Then the horrible smell hit him again.

He grabbed a handful of the sheets, which he raised to his nose. Yuk! He had been too tired to care last night the sheets on the bed had probably already been slept in. Whatever pong he was smelling now had probably been enlivened by the morning sun.

He had to get out of here.

He looked at his watch. It was 7.16am, which meant he hadn't eaten for almost 24 hours.

He bent down to unzip a suitcase and felt a stabbing pain around his ribs. It was a painful reminder of his first night in his hideaway.

He found his mobile phone.

He started checking for messages but realised it was out of credit.

He dressed, bunched his hair together and secured it with a hair tie, and headed down the hall.

The eyesore that was the foyer revealed itself to him as he descended the stairs.

Jaysus!

This large room was in an even bigger mess than the bedroom. How was that even possible?

He picked an old black phone up from the worn, grey carpet near the gate. He raised it to his ear. Nothing. Completely dead.

He placed the phone on the counter and hurried across the room. He really needed to get out of here into the fresh air.

As he approached the glass door, he realised too late a figure backlit by the sun was standing on the other side.

When he opened the door, the unexpected heat of the morning hit him. But it was the man's blue eyes burning into him that really raised the temperature.

The stranger was tall, thin and unsmiling, and he was wearing a white shirt with a blue tie. He switched his clipboard from one side to the other and offered his hand. "Henk Van Gogh . . . I was about to knock."

The Irishman took his hand tentatively. He had no idea who this man was but he relaxed when the man said:

"I'm here to welcome you." He spoke in a deep baritone with the hint of an accent.

He tensed up again, however, when the man on the doorstep added: "Well, I'm here to induct you really. I'm the group manager for Biggs and Sons. The owner of the museum?"

"Um, of course. You'd better come in. Happy New Year."

Van Gogh brushed past. He looked around and shook his head. Then he locked his piercing eyes on to the Irishman again. "You might want to keep that door open."

The Irishman sniffed the air for effect. He could hardly say he hadn't noticed the pong. He followed his nose to the other side of the reception counter and lifted up a milk carton that had solid bits floating inside. "I'll just put it outside."

When he came back in, Van Gogh was still surveying the shambles.

The foyer needed a good scrub, and perhaps a lick of paint. Some of the posters on the walls had come partially unstuck. Some were lying on the carpet. One had fallen on to the reception counter.

"I wasn't expecting you until Tuesday."

"You didn't get my email?" Van Gogh said. "You said in your application you were keen to hit the ground running."

But before the Irishman could reply, Van Gogh said: "I must say I was expecting someone older. When I think of a professor, I think of an *old* guy with a *white* beard. How do you like to be addressed? Professor O'Brien?"

The Irishman wished now he had bothered to look at the job application that had been lodged on his behalf. What had Joh been thinking?

He forced himself to smile. "Just call me Paddy, that's fine."

Van Gogh studied him. "Did you know you look a bit like a young Moose Routley?"

"Not him again!"

"How could you possibly know him?"

"I don't, but I've got a bone to pick with him."

Van Gogh sniffed. "If you don't mind me saying, you smell a bit like him, too."

The big Irishman did mind his lack of tact, actually, but Joh had asked him to be on his best behaviour. So instead of punching him in the face, Paddy raised an arm, which caused him a bolt of pain from his sore ribs, but was worth it because it made the rude Dutchman step back.

"I've been marinating in my own juices on planes and long car rides, and I couldn't have a hot shower when I arrived last night because the power wasn't on!"

Van Gogh tapped a finger on his clipboard. "You didn't read the contract properly. It's the manager's role to ensure the power and phone services are reconnected. You can sign up to both at the town hall."

Van Gogh bent over and picked up one of the posters from the floor. He sighed before screwing it up and throwing it down again. "I fail to see what girls in bikinis have got to do with the Tasmanian Tiger. Do you, Professor?"

Paddy's eyes narrowed. "You should see the mess upstairs. Did the last manager leave in a hurry?"

"Not fugging fast enough for my liking. Luckily for you we haven't got customers beating down the door, which gives you a bit more time to get this place back into shape."

Van Gogh's eyes bore into the Irishman's again. "You say in your application you are interested in studying the Tasmanian Tiger?"

Paddy had no choice now but to bullshit his way out of this. "Do you keep them in a cage at the back?"

Van Gogh frowned. "Keep what?"

"The toigers."

Van Gogh raised an eyebrow. "What university did you say you were from?" he said slowly.

Paddy rubbed his sore spot, mainly to stall for time so he could think of a feasible reply. "I didn't, but, er, you've probably never heard of it. It's one of the smaller campuses in Dublin."

"That might explain it."

"Explain what?"

Van Gogh sighed. "We weren't even going to reopen this place. But when we received your application and you said you'd work for nothing until you could ramp up business, that was the clincher for Mr Biggs."

Paddy blinked. Twice. Did he just say he had agreed to work for *nothing*?

"Of course, you have free use of the flat upstairs."

Van Gogh looked at his watch. "I'll give you a couple of days to get on with the clean-up. I'll be back on Wednesday. 10am sharp?" He looked towards the doors on the other side of the room. "If it's OK with you, I just need to do a quick stocktake in the gallery and then I'll get out of your hair."

Paddy watched the Dutchman head across the foyer.

———

Paddy stomped back upstairs.

Breakfast would just have to wait.

Who did this Van Gogh think he was anyway?

If he liked cold baths so much Paddy would have been happy to hold his head underwater for a bit. It was easy for Joh to tell him to stay out of trouble, he wasn't the one who had to go against his normal inclinations.

Paddy decided to kill time by putting his things away.

But the more he started flinging open drawers and cupboards in his new bedroom, the harder he flung them and the more his ribs stung. Jaysus! All of the drawers were still full.

He stormed into the bathroom. Same result. Shampoo on the side of the bath, a stiff-as-a-board towel hanging over a rail, two-thirds of a roll of toilet paper sitting on the window ledge above the jacks, and half a cake of cracked soap with three strands of pubic hair on the sink. A red electric razor sat in a cradle attached to the wall. Paddy opened a cabinet and found a toothbrush in a mug shaped like another topless woman.

He stormed out of the bathroom and crossed the hall to the other door, which he opened.

What a mess!

It looked like it was the kitchen/lounge room.

Dirty dishes were scattered all along a long white bench that divided the room.

As he stepped further in, he could see more encrusted dishes filled the sink.

A pale yellow phone sat surrounded by dishes on the bench. He lifted the receiver to his ear. Nothing. Just like the phone downstairs, it wasn't connected. It was probably just an extension.

He opened the fridge, and slammed it shut almost immediately. The smell was overpowering, which was surprising considering hardly anything was in there.

He opened the cupboard above the sink. Inside was a stack of saucers and a few stubby holders.

He turned around and found himself looking at six long rows of books along the back wall..

Jaysus! That looked out of place.

He walked across and examined the books. They were all in alphabetical order of author.

Paddy selected one and looked at the cover. It was Jules Verne's *Twenty Thousand Leagues Under the Sea.*

The front door downstair slammed. Van Gogh obviously wasn't happy. Was something missing from the gallery?

Served him right!

The good news was that Paddy could now go and try to find some breakfast.

FOUR
FIRST SIGN OF THE PINSTRIPE SUIT

WHEN HE TURNED to lock the door, his shirt felt sticky against his back. Who knew Tasmania got this hot?

Left and right of him were full length windows, which provided lots of light inside, as well as a brilliant view of the car park out front and the road beyond. But right now the windows were just radiating lots of heat and glare.

Paddy caught a flickering reflection of movement on the street behind him, and spun around.

He was blinded by the sun.

Only when he raised a cupped hand to shield his eyes did he see the little dog on a leash pulling an elderly man past him on the footpath.

The old man was shiny-faced, like he had shaved, then scrubbed his mug, then shaved again in case he had missed a whisker. He was dressed in a neatly pressed grey pinstripe suit, and he carried a little yellow spade and a plastic bag.

Paddy smiled. "Rioght? Grand day. Happy New Year."

But the man just kept walking towards what Paddy assumed was the town centre.

Maybe he hadn't heard him?

He did had large hearing aids protruding from both ears.

The dog stopped and squatted a little further along the footpath, and the old man shakily went down on one knee and held the spade behind the pooch.

Aware he was being watched, he turned and shouted: "FOR GOODNESS SAKE, HAVE YOU NOT SEEN A MAN USING A POOPER-SCOOPER BEFORE?"

He spoke at the decibel level you might employ in a noisy room, with a voice halfway between clipped plum and rusty razor-blade.

He stood back up, funnelled the droppings into his bag, and continued huffily on his way.

FIVE
'MOOSE IS BACK'

CLARRIE NOODLE COULD FEEL his ears burning when the old timber church came into view as he climbed the steps, and the voices grew louder.

He had only hit Bert Whish-Willson twice at the funeral yesterday, but he feared their punch-up would be the red-hot topic of discussion among people milling outside the church waiting for it to open for the 8am mass.

If it had been two young bucks fighting at the gravesite of a beloved dearly-departed citizen, that'd be bad enough.

But the culprits were two elderly blokes who ought to have known better. Their altercation would be regarded as much, much more disrespectful.

At 83, the man everyone called Oodles was the second-oldest person in town and Wish-Wash, at 81, was the third oldest.

Oodles thought it was almost as if the do-gooders thought the more money they put in the plate, the more high and mighty they were allowed to be.

This was a good excuse for him to skip mass today. What he didn't hear couldn't hurt him.

But Oodles had never been one to break a promise.

When he walked around the other side of the church, the hostile, hateful looks he got made him think he was entering the gates of hell.

Oodles grabbed at his tie to loosen it. Maybe this wasn't such a good idea. Perhaps he'd come back for the 10am service?

He turned to go, but he turned around when he heard two clunking sounds behind him.

An overweight woman in a floral dress was climbing on to one of the benches.

Daisy Rowbottom had kicked off her high heels and she was slowly raising herself into a standing position.

"Moose Routley is back!" she said. "I saw him last night."

Meredith Mayweather tightened her grip on her water bottle. "I thought Moose was still in jail."

"So did I," Daisy said. "But I saw him arrive in a taxi around midnight. He went into the Tasmanian Tiger Museum but I didn't see any lights go on, so I think we can safely assume he doesn't want anyone to know he's here."

Bob Gregan said, "He must have come for the reunion. Shouldn't someone warn James Northan?"

Moose had left town in the back of a paddy wagon more than 20 years ago. Unlike most folk, Oodles wasn't terrified of the big bloke. Moose still owed him $20. But it was hardly his fault because he had been arrested the day after borrowing it.

Heads turned towards the museum through the trees.

It was about two or three hefty kicks of a footy away, on the other side of the river.

That area used to be Northan's orchard, now it was the site of an unoccupied building.

Just then, a huge man came out the front, turning to lock the door.

I'll be buggered. So Wish-Wash had been right. They were replacing the manager of the museum? He hadn't suggested it'd be Moose though!

Daisy lowered her head to see beneath the branches.

"Now do you believe me?" Daisy spoke with the voice of confident authority she had honed as head nurse at the Windy Mountain Hospital.

What she was doing wandering around town at midnight was another question.

Oodles could hardly believe his luck they'd found a distraction big enough for him to escape mass condemnation.

They were mistaken though

That bloke certainly did look like Moose Routley.

But what made Mrs Mayweather think he'd still be in jail though? If he had kept his nose clean, Oodles knew he would have been out years ago.

There was something different about the far-away figure that Oodles couldn't put his finger on.

As they gawked, someone else came into view. He was walking a dog, so it could only be one man.

SIX
FIRST SIGNS OF DOG SHITE

PADDY BEGAN WALKING in the same direction as the old man had gone but veered towards a sign that told him the building next door was a pub.

He looked up at the large sign suspended on two posts above a low, yellow stone fence.

If he had looked down, he would have seen the dog excrement right in front of him.

He trod in it and went sliding. It was like slow motion. He tried to recover his balance but couldn't, and realised he was crashing head-first towards the fence. He threw out his hands as he fell.

Next thing he knew, he was spreadeagled on the ground. Dazed. Feeling stupid. What if someone had seen him?

He hadn't actually hit the fence, but it must have been close. His head was almost resting on it.

He ran his fingers over the top of his scalp to check for damage.

He reached up for the top of the fence and slowly hoisted himself up.

Once he was upright, Paddy squinted towards the town centre. Some sort of statue stood in the middle of the wide road. But no people were in sight. No traffic, not even a parked car. Where had the old fart with the dog gone? He deserved a right bollicking for not cleaning up after his dog properly.

He patted himself down. His hands were a bit torn and bloody, his ankle hurt and the tumble hadn't made his ribs any less sore.

He focused back on the sign.

It told him the Applecart Hotel was established in 1861. But it kept the worse news till last and in the smallest type. "We stay true to our traditional roots by only selling apple cider."

What kind of tradition was that?

Paddy removed his left shoe and scraped the dog excrement off his sole on the edge of the gutter.

He re-tied the shoe and started wiping his hands clean on his handkerchief but stopped and turned around when he heard voices.

The noise was coming from one of two churches on either side of the road just beyond a little yellow, stone bridge but he couldn't see any movement through the trees.

He turned around again, put his hanky away in his pocket and started hobbling towards the statue.

The street was lined on both sides with leafy old English Elm trees whose roots had pushed up the footpath here and there — causing yet more tripping hazards if he wasn't careful.

He came to a supermarket, but a sign inside the door said it was closed. Pity. It probably sold milk, possibly even phone cards. He hobbled on.

The closer he got to the statue, the bigger it became and the more it glinted in the sun.

Close up, it was enormous. It was a depiction of a colonial soldier astride a horse that was rearing high up into the air.

He limped across for a better look.

The plaque said it was a bronze likeness of Colonel Richard Northan, who had founded the town in 1841.

Paddy crossed to the other side of the road and started heading back the way he came.

He got his hopes up when he spotted a cafe painted lemon and blue, and looking very out of place among the other buildings, which all appeared to be built from the same yellow stone blocks. But when he tried the door of the cafe, it was locked.

The post office next door looked closed, too. Pity. It might have had a phone inside available for public use.

A bit further on, he came to a shop called Taylor's Takeaway.

It didn't look much chop but at least it was open.

———

The coloured plastic string curtains rustled when Paddy limped through them.

On the other side a young Asian woman with green hair was leaning on the yellow laminate-covered counter.

She looked up, and clutched her heart. "You gave me a fright."

He gave *her* a fright? Bad enough no one had warned him it could be this hot in Tasmania, no one had told him to expect Asian girls with green hair.

The shop's decor screamed 1960s.

The faded yellow paintwork was marked by heat and grease splatters that came from the deep-fryer at the rear, above which hung a sign that said: WASH YOUR HANDS.

The girl was wearing a plastic apron, latex gloves and was chewing gum.

"I was just getting ready for the after-church rush," she said. "I haven't got much food left so you'll get first pick."

"Good. I'm famished. I was beginning to think I wouldn't find *anything* open."

"You must be the new manager at the museum?"

He smiled. "How did you know that?"

"Mum knew you were coming. And we don't get too many Irish strangers in here. No one told me you had a limp though."

Paddy rubbed his leg. "I slipped on the footpath."

Then his face twisted. "So how come your mammy knew I was coming?"

"She's the Mayor."

The town had an Asian mayor? And she knew he was coming? How was he supposed to keep a low profile if people knew about him?

He threw out his hand over the counter. "I'm Paddy O'Brien. Happy New Year, by the way."

The girl just looked at his big mitt.

"Velda Hit. Nice to meet you but I don't shake hands. Even on New Year's Day. Nothing personal. Germs."

"But you're wearing gloves?"

"Germs can burrow. Besides, your hand is bleeding. How would you feel if I served you food with someone's blood on my glove."

Paddy pulled back his hand and examined it. She was right. There was some blood. But only a few specks.

"You've got good eyesight, I'll say that."

"Thanks," she said. "I never thought they'd reopen the museum. It didn't surprise anyone the owners didn't replace Billy Gumboots."

"Who's Billy Gumboots?"

"He used to be the live-in manager. The place has been closed since they found him dead late last year."

"He died!" Paddy tried to lower the pitch of his voice. "Was he an old guy?"

"Pretty old, yeah. About your age, I'd guess."

"My age?" Paddy's voice went up a notch again.

"Will you be taking over Billy's debts? Billy owed a bit of money around town. I know for a fact he never got round to paying my sister for piercing his left nipple."

"People do that?"

She poked out her tongue, revealing a metal ring. "It's called fashion but I wouldn't expect someone of your generation to understand," she said.

"Just how old do you think I am?"

The girl shrugged. "Older than me. Younger than the old blokes who had the fight at the funeral yesterday. So middle-aged, I guess."

"I'm only thirty-three." Then he realised what she had just said and his eyes widened. "Hang on. There was a fight at a funeral?"

She nodded. "Wish-Wash and Oodles had a fist-fight at the gravesite."

"Wish-Wash and Oodles?"

"Bert Whish-Willson and Clarrie Noodle. They're both in their eighties."

"What is it with the feisty old men in this town? The little old taxi driver who dropped me here last night also wanted to fight me!"

"Oh, that'd be Sir Cedric," Velda said.

"He didn't look like a knight. More like a garden gnome. He wore stretchy trousers and red suspenders, and he had a stomach round as a watermelon."

"That's him. People just call him Sir Cedric to annoy him. His real name is Cedric Knightly. He's always calling people out. Mum reckons he suffers from small-man syndrome."

"What can you tell me about the rude old man I just saw walking a dog?"

"That would be my grandfather, the Mayor."

"I thought your mammy was the mayor?"

"That's just what people call him. He's actually the former mayor."

"He didn't look …" Paddy stopped and wondered how to proceed with the question.

Vicki rescued him. "Korean? No, that's because I was adopted as a baby, much to his displeasure."

"He must be over it by now?"

"He barely talks to me. He walks straight past this place every day."

"That so? But how can you be sure this man was even him?"

"I can even tell you the dog's name. Howard. Grandfather never lets anyone else walk him."

Velda pointed to two pies in the glass cabinet. "I'm afraid we had a run on food after the fight. I guess the excitement made the other mourners hungry."

Paddy scowled. "Is that all you have?"

"We turn on the fish'n'chip cookers in a couple of hours if you want to come back."

Paddy sighed. "OK, I'll have the pies, tanks. What kind are they?"

"Meat."

"Yes, but what kind of meat?"

"If people knew where the meat came from for their pies, we probably wouldn't sell many of them."

She used tongs to shovel the pies into a bag, which she then put in to the antique microwave.

Paddy grabbed from the fridge behind him a plastic container of chocolate milk and put in on the counter.

"You know that's got preservatives in?"

"Jaysus, does your boss know about your sales pitch?"

"No, he's too busy running his other business to worry about me."

"What else does he do?"

"Dave's the local undertaker."

The microwave pinged.

Velda put an index finger to her mouth. "It's no secret around here, of course, but, shhhh, I don't think funeral directors are allowed to own food shops."

Paddy smiled weakly.

"I guess Dave could have got Billy's nipple ring back for us," Velda said. "But what was the point? There's not much of a market for second-hand nipple rings — especially ones that come from people who die in their beds."

Paddy's eyeballs nearly popped out. "He died in *his* bed? *My* bed?"

"I assumed someone would have told you. He was dead in the bed for three days before anyone missed him."

Paddy puffed up his cheeks. "I only arrived last night and nobody was around to tell me anything."

"Why does that not surprise me? That place has gone even further downhill since it got new owners."

Paddy raked his hair. "Do you know where I can buy a phone card?"

"You driving?"

"No, walking."

"Good luck then." She pointed. "The nearest newsagency is about 50 clicks that way."

SEVEN
THE THUGS CRAWL OUT OF THEIR HOLES

OODLES WAS WRIGGLING towards the other end of the pew when he heard a noise.

He looked around and saw a scruffy man sliding quickly towards him.

"Hello Oodles. Fancy meeting you here?" Freddy Cuthbert had some momentum up by the time he smacked the old man into the wall.

Freddy smiled. His stubbled face was almost touching Oodles's now. The five or six teeth he had left were yellow with nicotine and he reeked of last night's booze.

"Haven't you got something better to do?" Oodles grabbed at his right shoulder. "You've heard Moose Routley is back in town?"

Freddy just laughed and pushed him harder into the wall. "Nice try. Think he'll come save you?"

Freddy pinched at the fabric on Oodles's free shoulder. "Now you're in the money, I thought you might have splashed out on something new?"

"How'd Birty's funeral go yesterday, anyway?"

Oodles's reply came out as a wheeze. "It went well."

"That's not what I heard." Freddy grinned again. "I heard

you and Wish-Wash got into a bit of biffo. Tut-tut-tut, old people these days! I bet Birty's rolling in his grave, wishing he could come back and re-write his will."

"I'm not expecting *one cent* from Birty's will!"

"No need to shout, old man. You want everyone in the church to know what's going on?"

"I reckon they can see what's happening here?"

"Nonsense." Freddy released the pressure on the old man and put his arm around him. "Far as everyone's concerned, we're just two mates catching up with some boyish hijinks." He looked behind him. "They probably think we're in the same pub trivia team. So be a good old man and keep it down, eh?"

"And what if I blinking don't?"

"You'd only be making it worse for yourself." Freddy smirked. "Did I mention Gordo's outside?"

Oodles tried not to react. He just hoped Freddy couldn't hear his heart beating.

"The thing is, I reckon Birty had a bob or two. And you were his best mate? So who do you think he's going to leave his money to?" The thug laughed. "The dog's home?"

Oodles squeezed his eyes shut.

"Your friendship with Birty makes what you and Wish-Wash did even more disrespectful. Thought it was funny, did you?"

Oodles opened his eyes. "Not that it's any business of yours, but I said sorry to Wish-Wash and he's fine with that."

"And everyone lived happily ever after. Is that what you reckon?"

"Look. I wish it hadn't happened, but it did . . ."

"Which is why Gordo and I want a chat with you after mass."

Oodles had not seen Freddy for ages, and never in church. He knew no love had been lost between him and the dearly departed police sergeant. Freddy was in his sixties and had a well-earned reputation as a nasty drunk. Birty had put him in the clink a few times. He had not held down a job for years, unless you counted burglaries and being a standover man as decent work. His wife had left town long ago. Oodles guessed she finally got tired of telling people she had run into doors.

Freddy had been leading Gordon Bennett astray for years. Gordo had lots of brawn but very little brain. He had a full-time job as chef and co-owner of the Wind Tunnel Cafe and sometime assistant at the local funeral parlour. So thuggery was just a sideline he got sucked into.

"So why are you here so early?" Freddy said. "And so near the front, too? Couldn't you sleep, old man? Or do you just want to be closer to God?"

God was actually the last person Oodles wanted to be close to — well second-last now Freddy had arrived.

Oodles glanced behind him but it confirmed what he already knew. The church, built by convicts long before public health and safety codes had been thought of, only had two double doors and they were at the back. Even if Oodles could get past the oaf next to him, the church was filling up now.

The organ music stopped.

Someone said, "Shall we begin, brethren." Oh, no! Oodles knew that Irish voice. He turned around and sure enough it was Father O'Boring in his green robes up in the pulpit.

———

Father O'Boring was the oldest man in town by a long shot. He was actually retired.

But he filled in whenever the younger Father O'Flaherty had to go away. And this must have been one of those times of need. Again.

Father O'Boring's real name was Father John O'Rourke. You could barely understand the man. *Dis and dat* and *dey* and *den* and *dare* and *darefore*. It was like he was just off the boat, yet he had lived in this country almost forever.

How the nursing home could release him from time to time was an outrage to Oodles.

One time Father O'Rourke had nodded off in the middle of the Gospel according to Luke. He had stopped mid-sentence for a good 20 seconds, which had the members of the congregation exchanging quizzical looks, each of them wondering if someone else was going to go up and check the old boy's pulse. But before anyone moved, Father O'Boring spluttered back into life, cleared his throat, and continued on as if he did not know anything at all had come to an awkward standstill.

The air inside the church today stank of incense, body odour, cheap after-shave and Freddy's alcohol fumes.

The interior was lined with Blackwood beams, floorboards and panelling. But none of the high stained-glass windows opened and do you think the Catholic church would fork out for an air-conditioner for these rare hot days?

Oodles wished now he hadn't dressed in that heavy suit.

He focused on the crucifix above the altar, not wanting to give Freddy the pleasure of turning and looking as scared as he was.

The service went on and on, and on some more. Sweat rolled down Oodles's face and his shirt stuck to his skin. His whole right side ached now as Freddy kept up the pressure.

Even when the mass finally ended, Oodles knew there was no escape. At least 100 people were between Oodles and Freddy, and Gordo outside. The men slid their way along the pew, then they joined the slow line to the exit.

"You look worried, old man?" Freddy was walking side by side and smiling. "What's the matter? Shame Gordo had to wait outside in the heat, eh? Being C of E, he can't risk coming into the opposition's sheds."

"It didn't blinking stop you!"

"Didn't you know I was a Catholic? Regular prodigal son, I am. What's the matter? Sorry you didn't pick a pew near the back? I can relate to that. If it was me in your shoes, I'd want to get this whole thing over and done with as quickly as I could."

"You said you just wanted a talk?"

"I did, didn't I? But I can't speak for Gordo. Do they even believe in the 14 commandments in his church across the road?"

Oodles wanted to shout for help. But he couldn't. Not in a church.

The organist played *God Be with You Till We Meet Again* as they shuffled towards the door and fresh air. She might as well have been playing a death march.

The line spilled outside on to a path that led to the other side of the building.

Freddy was right behind him, with a firm hand on the back of his shoulder as they shuffled forward around towards the narrow set of steps to the front gate and the car park below.

"We'll just stop here," he commanded when they neared to top of the stairs. "Step aside and let these good people past."

As Oodles stood captive, he squeezed his eyes shut and loosened his tie.

He heard the strike of a match and opened his eyes to see a stream of cigarette smoke jetting towards his face.

"Al'right, Oodles?" Freddy's fag bounced up and down on one side of his mouth.

A phone rang somewhere and someone pushed his way up the steps, with a mobile to his ear.

It was Gordo.

He was still wearing his checkered chef's trousers and his white T-shirt was riding up the roll of fat around his midriff.

He handed over the phone, puffing from the sudden exertion. "It's Dutchy."

Freddy pressed the mobile phone against one ear and a hand against the other to block out the chatter around him. Whatever was said wiped the smirk off his face. As soon as he hung up, he turned to Oodles and prodded the old man's chest with a finger.

"You're a lucky old bastard because we've been called away for a meeting. But don't think this ends here?"

The two thugs pushed their way forward and disappeared down the stairs.

EIGHT

FIRST SIGNS OF BIRD SHITE

PADDY STARED down at the bench in disbelief. Some vandal had gouged out a series of notches on almost every available wooden edge.

"I WOULDN'T SIT THERE IF I WERE YOU."

Paddy looked around as the man with the dog walked past. Once again, the man they called the Mayor didn't stop.

Paddy thought about shouting abuse at him but remembered he was supposed to be on his best behaviour.

The bench was right across the road from the museum, and from a distance it had seemed like a good place to flop himself down to collect his thoughts and eat his mystery pies.

But now he was looking down on it again, he was having second thoughts.

It looked important. It carried a metal plaque that said it was the Colonel Richard Northan bench, donated by the Rotary Club of Windy Mountain in 1956 to coincide with the Olympic Games in Melbourne.

But the bird shite splattered on it might be the only thing holding it together. Or were they just flecks of peeling paint? It was hard to tell. In any case, finding a safe place to sit between the protruding nails would be a challenge for someone of his size.

He looked at his watch.

If only he could ring Joh up right now to tell him where to shove this job in this hick town.

It would be doubly satisfying if the lawyer was nursing a New Year's hangover and the phone call added to his displeasure.

But the sad reality was that he had run out of phone credit.

Paddy's stomach emitted a long, echoey rumble.

Who knew they didn't feed you on planes these days? Last time he had flown, an endless stream of food had been delivered to his seat. But now it seemed the user-pays rule operated even above the clouds.

The Irishman had felt like an eejit when the steward had held out his hand for payment for the sandwich he had selected from the trolley. He wanted how much? No way! He gave the sandwich back.

So, yes, he was ravenous.

But as he stood looking dubiously at the bench, with the sun burning on the back of his neck, he realised his priorities had suddenly changed.

Perhaps he'd go back over to the museum and take a cold shower before eating.

Now he knew he had shared the same linen as a three-day old corpse, he felt icky and sticky.

He limped across the road and went inside the museum.

He laughed to himself when he saw the spiral staircase again. That undertaker must have had fun getting Billy's body down around those narrow stairs.

NINE
THE TRUTH ABOUT THE TASMANIAN TIGER

HE LIFTED his head toward the shower-head.

It had been painful with his sore ankle to step over into the bath, but now it seemed worth the effort.

The sprinkle of cold water cooled him down and washed away the stink and the blood from his hands.

It was only after Paddy turned off the taps and drew back the plastic curtain he remembered the only towel in sight was the stiff blue one hanging on the rack.

For feck's sake!

The towel hadn't been fresh and fluffy for a long time, and he had no idea where the clean towels were stored.

Grasping the corner to help his balance, he stepped awkwardly on to the floor dripping water.

He snatched the towel off the rack and dabbed his torso to soak up the worst of the dampness.

Then he used it to mop the floor. That was all it was good for, any fecking way.

Paddy dressed again and crossed into the kitchen/lounge.

He slumped down in an armchair by the bookshelf, placed his brown paper parcel on the wide armrest and ripped it open. The pies didn't stand a chance even though they were now barely warm.

What would a few more crumbs matter in the greater scheme of things?

He finished the pastries, and continued to sit there thinking.

If he could get that phone connected, there really was no urgency for him to get a new phone card. He could ring Joh from the museum, tell him there had been a terrible mistake and he really needed to come home.

But who knew how many days he'd have to be here?

Until then, he had to at least make this place liveable.

First though he needed to take a quick look at the gallery downstairs — to see what the Dutchman had been so upset about.

————

The gallery was a U-shaped room of the foyer, with swinging doors at either end marked IN and OUT.

Inside, the walls near the entrance were lined with historical photos — some showing hunters with their prized Tasmanian Tiger skins hanging from lines, others purportedly showing the tiger in the wild. They didn't look like any tiger Paddy had ever seen.

He came to a series of display cabinets.

He pressed the button of the first one, and it brought up a grainy black and white video of what it said was a tiger pacing up and down in its enclosure in the Hobart zoo.

For feck's sake! Call that a tiger? It looked like a dog with a few stripes, not an orange, majestic big cat killing machine like a Bengal tiger.

But what the display said next really blew his mind.

Shortly afterwards, this poor excuse for a tiger had died. A zookeeper had forgotten to bring it in out of the cold for the night.

It was thought to be the last captive example of the carnivorous marsupial species scientifically called the thylacine.

Despite numerous alleged sightings since, the International Union for Conservation of Nature declared the Tasmanian Tiger extinct in 1982.

Feck me! The whole species gone. Wiped from the face of the earth.

No wonder Van Gogh had looked at him oddly!

Paddy moved on until he came to an empty cabinet.

A sign said it contained a model of a Tasmanian Tiger hunter, but it was nowhere in sight. Bingo. This must have been the missing thing that had so pissed off the Dutchman. But why?

Dozens of newspaper clippings were arranged along the walls near the end of the room. He only gave them a cursory look. Mostly they were reports of sightings, news of study projects and the like.

It had taken him only a few minutes to reach the door out.

Jaysus! He could recognise mediocrity when he saw it.

————

It was hard to know where to start upstairs.

He couldn't put things away until he had turfed out Billy's stuff, and he couldn't start on that till tomorrow when the little supermarket he had seen in the High Street opened and he could buy some plastic bags.

Paddy found some sheets in the hall cupboard, which he used to remake his bed.

He couldn't do much else upstairs, and he didn't feel like getting stuck into cleaning downstairs now. Luckily, Van Gogh had said there was no hurry. Paddy would wait until he could get the power put back on.

He carried the dirty sheets downstairs and threw them on to the foyer floor. He'd look for a rubbish bin tomorrow.

TEN
THE VANDAL

THE NEXT DAY Oodles was back dressed in his comfortable overalls doing what he always did on Monday mornings.

He had his head down vandalising the park bench opposite the Tasmanian Tiger Museum when two shadows loomed up beside him.

"MORNING CLARENCE."

Oodles didn't have to look up. He could smell his sickly, posh aftershave. He had known that voice for years. It had become louder the more deaf James Northan had become.

Trust him to arrive early. He'd want money.

The smaller shadow belonged to James's little dog Howard whom he tied up to the other end of the bench Oodles was carving with his knife.

At 80, James was the fourth-oldest man in town.

He hadn't been mayor for 20 years, but people still called him so, which he hated because he thought it showed disrespect to the actual mayor, who happened to be his daughter Maddie.

Oodles blew away the wood scrapings, and looked up from the bench in time to see Wish-Wash arrive, too.

The big oaf was still wearing the shirt adorned with

pictures of hola dancing girls he had souvenired from the Windy Mountain hotel. What were the odds of a surfer who also had a stomach shaped like a beachball leaving his shirt behind in one of the rooms of The Applecart? Fair dinkum!

"Morning, Jimbo." Wish-Wash looked from the immaculately dressed James, down to Oodles in his workman's clothes. "But you can get stuffed, cobber."

Oodles got to his feet. "I thought you were fine with me saying I was sorry."

"Now I've slept on it, I realise how remarkably lucky I was you didn't kill me!"

"You're kidding me? What's really remarkable is I've resisted so many temptations to kill you before."

"You're just lucky I didn't hit you back."

"I wish you had. A black eye would go some way towards easing my conscience."

"Want me to slug you now?"

Oodles clenched his eyes shut. "You muppet! Haven't you noticed I'm holding a pocketknife? You have to admit you did a lot to provoke me."

Wish-Wash turned to James, who had sat down, pinching the pleats of his grey pinstripe trousers so as not to crease them. "Did you think I provoked him?"

"WHAT?"

Oodles snapped his bone-handled knife shut and put it into his top pocket. "No use asking James, old cock. Can't you see he hasn't got his hearing aids in. He didn't have them on at the funeral on Saturday either, not that he would have heard anything from where he was sitting."

Wish-Wash sighed and leaned over. "You silly old git," he shouted into James's left ear. "PUT . . . YOUR . . . HEARING . . . AIDS . . . IN."

The Mayor pulled a case from his pocket and took out the aids. He adjusted a setting on one of them, which caused it to make a high-pitched whistle, then he plugged them both in.

"CAN . . . YOU . . . HEAR . . . ME . . . NOW?" Wish-Wash said.

James looked like he was in pain as he turned to Oodles. "Why is he talking to me like I am some kind of imbecile?"

"My guess is he's just being his normal self."

Wish-Wash looked daggers at Oodles. "I was just stirring the pot at the funeral. Can't you take a joke?"

"I don't think Freddy Cuthbert saw the funny side when he cornered me at mass yesterday," Oodles said. "He reckons our little to-do showed a lack of respect. Can you believe that? *Him* lecturing *me* about respect!"

Oodles shook his head as he sat down next to the Mayor. "If you had hit me back, he wouldn't have an excuse for wanting to hurt me."

"They let Freddy into church?" Wish-Wash smirked. "It's a wonder Jesus didn't fall off the cross in shock."

"You can laugh, but he had that fat sidekick Gordo with him. Luckily for me, they got called away. I think it's got something to do with Moose Routley allegedly being back."

"Moose!" James bounced to his feet. "He's out of jail?"

"Daisy Rowbottom said she saw a brute of a fella arrive at the museum a couple of nights ago. I saw him, too, from the church yesterday. But I don't think it's him. Moose would never have lost his balance like he did."

James slumped back down into a sitting position and brushed a hand across his forehead. "You are right. It's someone else."

"You're sure it's not him?" Wish-Wash said.

"He's big enough to be," James said. "But he's definitely not Moose. I saw him up close trying to sit on this very bench. He would have crashed right through if I had not warned him."

Wish-Wash scratched his head. "Funny you should mention Freddy and Gordo. When I went into the back bar to buy some fags yesterday, they were there with Dutchy."

"Were they?" Oodles needed some quiet time to try to nut out just what was going on. He pulled out his pocketknife again and opened it. "If you don't mind, fellas, I've still got a bit of work to do."

"So how many notches is that now?" Wish-Wash asked.

Oodles tilted his head skywards. "Fair dinkum, it's one more than I told you last week. You two make a bloody good pair — him with his hearing loss, you with your early dementia."

Wish-Wash's lip quivered. "There's nothing wrong with my memory!"

"No? Maybe it's just the early signs of an oncoming aneurism. Got life insurance, have you?"

Wish-Wash waggled his finger. "Don't even joke about that."

"Why not? You can give it but you can't take it. Is that it?"

"Come on Jimbo, let's go for a walk," Wish-Wash said.

ELEVEN
THE GETTING OF OODLES

OODLES HAD ARRIVED in town in the winter of 1972. He brought his FH Holden across on the Bass Strait ferry, which had bobbed like a cork all night. How the ship ever got past the big waves at the head of the Mersey River in Devonport, he'd never know.

He and his wife stopped for a cuppa at the Wind Tunnel Cafe. He remembered how the wind bit into them as they got out of the car. It was warmer in the cafe and Benny Hill's *Ernie (The Fastest Milkcart in the West)* was blaring from the radio.

Oodles and Madge were on their way to Hobart, but the cafe proprietor, Bill Watley, said a job was going at the local council works depot and an experienced codger like Oodles would be a shoo-in.

Oodles was reluctant. But with Madge's encouragement, they checked into The Applecart hotel to see where it went.

It turned out Bill Watley had inside information because the council works supervisor was his brother-in-law.

Larry George *interviewed* Oodles in the back bar of the hotel the next morning. Oodles paid for the two ciders but it was worth it because he was hired on the spot.

Oodles was promoted into the top job when Larry retired eight months later. His boss was Mayor James Northan.

Oodles and Madge immersed themselves into the community until most people didn't realise they had once come from somewhere else. Madge became active with the local lawn bowls club, and Oodles befriended some blokes he used to go fly-fishing with, the main ones being Sergeant Randolph 'Birty' Birtwistle and hairdresser Guy 'Snipper' McDonnell, who became his best mate. But now they had all gone.

The bench had become a spiritual home for the three remaining old men.

Everyone knew why James had always revered it.

Wish-Wash had slept on it so many times it was a wonder he hadn't left an imprint.

Oodles had painted it many times. Back in his days working on the council works gang, not many weeks went by when that bench didn't get a coat of green paint.

At first, this had thrown Oodles because he thought more urgent jobs needed to be done.

"Don't you want me to fix the population signs at either side of town?" Oodles had asked Larry after just a week on the job.

"What's wrong with them?"

"One says 3003 people, the other says 3004."

"Is that all? I think the Mayor would be happier if you gave the bench another coat of paint."

Oodles rarely got to the outskirts of town nowadays but he had no reason to think the boundary signs had been changed. But this bench he was defacing had.

It had been relocated to this end of town to make space for the huge statue of Colonel Northan in the town centre.

It was rumoured the council wanted to remove it completely. The only thing stopping them was the fear of a community outcry.

So they were happy for the bench to become a public eyesore and sway public opinion.

If old people insisted they needed a bench to sit on, the one in the town cemetery had been strategically placed between the Catholic and Church of England sections.

TWELVE
THE FIGHT

WISH-WASH AND OODLES had stood alone at the edge of the empty grave with their backs to the wind.

Wish-Wash looked around, wondering where everyone was. "I think you've come to the wrong funeral again, cobber." He started laughing like a donkey doing scales, until it turned into a coughing fit.

Oodles pinched the bridge of his nose and whispered. "Show some respect, why don't you! What if someone hears?"

"No chance of that." Wish-Wash used the back of his hand to wipe the tears from his eyes and he cleared his throat. "We're the only ones here!"

This wasn't strictly true. James was sitting on the bench not far away. He was dressed in a brown robe that made him look like the Grim Reaper, which was ironic because he always said he would never be seen dead in the Catholic cemetery. Oodles doubted he was listening to anything but his beloved Beethoven under his hoodie.

Wish-Wash had left the top two buttons of his Hawaiian shirt undone as if he were proud of the tuft of grey chest hair that poked through. His pea-green trousers matched the green carpet around the grave and were held up with yellow braces that nearly matched the colour of the nicotine stains on his hands. He could have at least have shaved.

"I don't know why you made us leave the service before it was over?" Wish-Wash said.

"Will you give it a rest?" Oodles looked around when he heard rising chatter.

He was relieved to see groups of people were coming over the rise. "You'd be the first to complain if dust blew in our eyes because we had to stand on the other side of the grave. Being here early means we've got a front-row view to see Birty off right."

As people gathered behind them, Wish-Wash said loudly, "I didn't even know they buried anyone on New Year's Eve."

Oodles flashed a searing stare. "Will you keep your voice down? Birty couldn't help dying in the holidays."

"Life goes on," Wish-Wash said. "I've heard the town already has a replacement person lined up."

Oodles rolled his eyes. "You can't replace a bloke of Birty's calibre just like that!"

"Not like for like, no. As far as I know this new bloke isn't a cop. But I heard he's taking over at the Tasmanian Tiger Museum."

"Why would they bother getting a new bloke in after the last fiasco?"

"You know why? Local heritage is why."

Oodles looked around when he heard the crackling of gravel as a vehicle pulled up to the side of the grave.

As the pallbearers slid the coffin out of the back, a chorus of sobbing and nose-blowing started.

But Oodles's eyes were on the old priest who had also alighted from the hearse and was now hobbling slowly towards them bent over his walking stick. That figured. If Father O'Boring hadn't hitched a lift, he'd probably have had to stop on the walk over and lie down.

As the pallbearers lowered the casket into the grave, Oodles felt a jab to the ribs.

"I reckon you'll be next."

"Are you sledging me now? Here?" Oodles spluttered. "I think we'd better move to the back, old cock."

Oodles started making a path through the crowd, which was five or six mourners deep now.

From their new vantage point, all Oodles could see was the tops of people's heads, hair flying and hats bobbing in the wind, and glimpses of what was happening at the gravesite. At his height, Wish-Wash probably had a better view.

Oodles pulled out a handkerchief and dabbed an eye.

"Are you crying?" Wish-Wash's voice was even louder now.

"I've got something in my eye, that's all. It's this bloody wind."

"I wish you'd make up your flamin' mind. I thought you said we were out of the wind. Perhaps you're just coming down with something fatal?"

"Will you lay off? I'm only a few years older than you!"

"But you're in much poorer health than me."

"Do you have to go on?"

"Face facts, cobber. Birty was a year younger than you but look where old age got him?" Wish-Wash nodded towards the grave. "Dead."

"Here you go again. No blinking respect! I should have been with him."

"What could you have done? Carried him out of the bush on your back?"

"I could have at least gone for help."

"Like you did with Snipper? Fat lot of good that did!" He started laughing, which resulted in more coughing and spluttering.

What happened next was pure reflex. Oodles hadn't punched anyone for three-quarters of his lifetime, back when he had earned a few extra quid boxing at Festival Hall in Melbourne. But he felled Wish-Wash with a two-punch combination.

A left-hook to the solar plexus and a right-cross to the jaw was all it took.

Wish-Wash fell backwards and he was lucky not to hit his head on 'Dobber' Leggs's tombstone.

THIRTEEN
THE OLD MEN'S TO-DIE LIST

Oodles was enjoying the sun on his face as he stretched back on the bench, closed his eyes and sucked on his pipe.

He had done his duty for another week.

But his blissful solitude was broken when he heard James and Wish-Wash returning. It was easy to tell it was them. James stomped and Wish-Wash shuffled.

When Oodles opened his eyes Wish-Wash was bouncing up and down in front of him like an overweight toddler.

"Tell him, Jimbo, tell him."

"Tell me what?" Oodles looked at James.

But Wish-Wash blurted it out before James could elaborate. "We're millionaires. Tell him, Jimbo?"

"What *are* you talking about?" Oodles said.

James rolled his eyes. "Technically only one of us is a millionaire."

"Strewth, is this about our bet?" Oodles tapped his pipe on the side of the bench and the spent tobacco tumbled to the ground.

"Correct. We've just clicked past the million-dollar mark. But only on paper."

Oodles shook his head. "I think for once you have done

your sums wrong, James. I was doing some quick calculations only the other day, and I made it no more than a hundred and forty grand — and even that's with a good rate of interest."

"I found a *better* rate of interest."

"What kind of bank pays that well?"

"Not a bank. The stock exchange."

Oodles screwed up his face. "Say that again?"

James held Oodles's gaze. "I thought it was in our best interests. I invested it in a new gold mining venture in Western Australia."

"Mining stocks!" Oodles sprang to his feet. "Without telling us?"

"I did not need to tell you."

This was true. That agreement was made around this very bench 11 years ago. Eight old men were alive then. Being all retired, they spent their days in the High Street annoying each other, jockeying for a seat on the bench and going to the cafe two times a day where they'd sit on cups of tea and play each other at backgammon with the stake of five cents a game.

"I bet I can outlive the lot of you," 'Dobber' Leggs had said. No one was going to back down on that dare, were they? It was a matter of masculine pride.

"You think so, do you?" 'Snipper' McDonnell had said. "Why don't you put your money where your mouth is? Let's say we all put $2 in the pot a week. Last man standing takes all."

That wasn't enough for James though. Oh no! "Let's make it even more interesting," he had said. "When someone dies, let's double what we put in each week."

James stood head and shoulders above the others when it came to things financial, so he was the logical pick as treasurer.

Father Ryan O'Shannessy, a.k.a. The Big O, died first, which was probably a good thing because he could never have afforded what the weekly stake had become. With the priest's death, the weekly premium went up to $4. Then 'Dobber' died and it became $8, 'Snipper' made it $16.

Oodles had been drinking with 'Snipper' the afternoon he collapsed in The Applecart. 'Snipper' was the youngest of the group and always ate and drank like he considered he was immune from death. He had still been alive when Oodles went for help. Oodles said he would be haunted by his parting words forever. "Don't let me die, mate."

Oodles went as fast as he could to the Windy Mountain hospital. It wasn't far. But Wish-Wash had been correct at Birty's funeral. A fat lot of good it did. By the time he returned with a doctor, 'Snipper' was dead.

When Terry Mason died, it made the weekly premium $32. And now, with Randolph Birtwistle in the ground, it was going to be $64 a week. That was going to be a big chunk out of Oodles's modest superannuation, and goodness knows how Wish-Wash was going to cope on his pension? It was a good thing he had been given a room for life at The Applecart, even if it wasn't much bigger than a shoebox and it was old. Oodles had paid out the mortgage on his cottage with his retirement money. James lived in a cottage in the grounds of his daughter's mansion. He had lost his fortune but his family wasn't short of a quid.

Oodles scratched his head. "But mining stocks, James? We all know how volatile they are. Remember Poseidon Nickel in 1970?"

"But I was acting on a very good tip. And look how much the shares are worth now? Nine, 10 times more than I paid for them. Imagine how much they will be worth when they actually find the gold deposits they believe are below the surface?"

"You mean they haven't actually found the flamin' gold?"

"The geophysicists are very confident."

"You and I know confidence means nothing," Oodles said. "The bottom could fall out next week? Tomorrow? Today?"

Wish-Wash's millionaire's smile had disappeared. "You mean we could lose the lot." He clicked his fingers. "Like that?"

"Too right," Oodles said.

"You didn't tell me that, Jimbo?" Wish-Wash said.

"I didn't tell you because it's not likely to happen. For goodness sake, Clarence is exaggerating."

"But it's not impossible? That we could lose the lot?"

James just looked annoyed.

Oodles put his pipe back into the top pocket of his bib overalls.

"I say get on the phone right now and cash them in," Wish-Wash said. "Get out while we're on top, split the million three ways."

James shook his head. "It's my considered advice we should all hold our nerve."

"Hang on," Oodles said. "I agree with Wish-Wash."

"Quitting is not what we agreed," the Mayor said. "Last man standing, remember?"

"Nobody told me it was going to become this expensive though," Wish-Wash said. "How much do you think they give to a former town drunk?"

"Wish-Wash has a point, James," Oodles said. "If you won't split the money now, at least cash in those shares and put the proceeds in the bank."

"I can't do that either," the Mayor said. "You'd need a majority vote to overrule the treasurer."

Oodles raised his voice. "Can't you count? It's two of us against you. Wish-Wash and I already *have* a majority."

"I guess that's another thing I didn't tell you." The Mayor's voice became much faster and much, much softer.

Even more blood drained from Wish-Wash's face. "What are you saying, Jimbo?"

"Irecruitedanothermember."

Oodles stared at him. "Say again?"

"I signed up another member," he said. "Six years ago."

"You did what!" Wish-Wash said. "I thought there was just three of us left. Who is it?"

"Give me some credit. This chap is much older than all of us so I thought it was a very good bet."

Wish-Wash closed his eyes and slowly shook his head from side to side. "I don't care how old he is. If one of you blokes goes next I've got to find $128 a week. And now, with this other bloke, I will be looking at $256! Where am I going to find that kind of money?"

"You'd have to withdraw from the group," James said. "We'd understand. Wouldn't we, Clarence? I think we could even bend the rules and give you your stake back. How much do you reckon you've put in over the years? $5000? $6000? Don't worry. I would work it out for you."

Oodles was livid James was now trying to make him a party to this. "Nobody ever gave you consent to sign anyone else up. This was between us, the blokes who were here."

"But his chap was already long in the tooth when he joined. I thought it was money for jam."

"Gawdsake. Who is it?"

"He asked to remain anonymous until such time as he dies or claims the money."

Oodles jabbed his index finger on James's chest. "I couldn't care less what he wants. We want his name, don't we Wish-Wash?"

"He swore me to secrecy."

"That just won't do because we need to speak to him. The sooner we can vote on this, the better."

"You'll be wasting your time. I think I'm a pretty good judge of character and this is a man who has stuck by his beliefs all of his life."

"Are you scared we might talk him around, make the vote 3-1?"

"I promised to protect his identity."

"But none of us foresaw this situation. Isn't it fair he has a vote?"

"Maybe. But I still can't betray the confidence of a man of God."

"A man of God?"

"Not my God. Your God."

"My God?" Oodles said. Then the penny dropped. "Gawdsake! Not Father O'Boring?"

James Northan wrung his hands together. "You didn't hear it from me."

"I'll be sure to tell him that when we go talk to him," Oodles said.

"Good grief," James said. "You don't even like him. Nor do I. He's a Catholic. I can't see the point in meeting him again?"

"Isn't that obvious. We need to persuade him to change his mind, withdraw his stake."

Wish-Wash scowled. "Do you want me to come along, too, cobber? To heavy him?"

Oodles shook his head. "No, I think this requires a more subtle approach, but feel free to vent your spleen at James."

FOURTEEN
MEET THE PROFESSOR

WHEN PADDY WALKED into the cafe, the middle-aged waitress looked like she had seen a ghost.

He hesitated in the doorway. "Something wrong?"

"Sorry, love, I thought you were someone else at first."

"Let me guess? Someone called Moose?" He heaved a big sigh. "You're not the first person in this town to mistake me for him. The last old fella wanted to hit me."

"You've met Sir Cedric then?" She breathed in a sharp gulp of air then blew a stream of smoker's breath his way. "For once, I can't blame him for getting aggro. No one wants that trouble-maker Moose back in this town."

The waitress had the kind of blonde hair that probably came out of a bottle. She had a husky voice, which sounded like the result of smoking too many cigarettes and eating too much gravel.

She pointed to one of the two tables. "Sit yourself down. It's just dawned on me who you really are."

Paddy frowned as he scraped a chair back across the tiled floor. How could she possibly know who he was?

"I just passed three old men having a heated argument,"

he said. "Should I go break it up before it escalates and one of them gets hurt?"

The waitress blew a raspberry. "I wouldn't worry about them silly, old blokes. They'll probably be in for a pot of tea later, happy as Larry. You stay where you are. What can I get you, Professor?"

He choked midway through a breath, and spluttered. Had she just called him Professor?

He ploughed on, hoping he had misheard it. "I could kill for a doppio?"

"A what?"

"A doppio . . . a double-shot espresso?"

"Sorry, love, we don't stretch to those here."

"What do you have then? Lattes? Cappuccinos?"

She held her pencil against her ordering pad. "We have tea, and we have coffee."

"Is that it? What kind of coffee?"

"Instant."

"You're kidding me?"

"Or tea bags."

He sighed again "Coffee then, I suppose." He had endured 16 years of institutional instant coffee, one more cup wasn't going to kill him. "Can I look at your menu?"

The woman looked puzzled. "We only do the one type of breakfast, love. Two pork sausages, two fried eggs, two rashers of bacon, baked beans and two pieces of toast."

"Hash browns, too?"

As she shook her head, the three men he had seen came in. The smell of old men and stale tobacco came in with them.

————

"How do?" Oodles said as he pulled back a chair from the next table and nodded. James flashed a politician's smile and Wish-Wash just gave a thumbs-up sign.

"Hiya," the big man replied in an Irish accent. He was dressed in a white shirt and blue waistcoat and wore his long hair tied back in a ponytail. He looked like Moose, all right, but he clearly wasn't Moose.

He gave the Wind Tunnel Cafe a different look, not seen since Moose.

The place had hardly changed in 45 years. Outside, the stucco was painted lemon with light-blue trim around the doors and windows. Inside was the reverse. The walls inside were painted blue and the beams and window frames were lemon. None of the recent owners had changed the colour scheme and none of them had been able to figure out how to get more than two tables into this space.

"You'd be the new bloke in town?" Oodles said. "I saw you from the church on Sunday. Are you all right after that nasty fall?

The lookalike's face turned crimson. "You saw that?"

"We all did. Daisy Rowbottom mistook you for Moose Routley."

Not another one! "How come I didn't see you?"

"The light? The trees? Who knows? We were all waiting for the doors to open."

The stranger stood up, stepped towards the old men's table and threw out his hand. "Paddy. Paddy O'Brien."

Oodles stood up and his hand was engulfed. "Clarrie Noodle."

Wish-Wash leaned across the table and extended his hand. "Bert Whish-Willson. Wish-Wash. Glad to meet you."

James did not offer his hand. He did not even give his name. All he said was, "You're Irish!" And then he removed his hearing aids, got up and walked closer to the window so his back was to everybody as he peered into the street.

"Don't mind him. Jimbo's got an aversion to anyone who's not from the finest English stock, but ignore the pigheaded idiot," Wish-Wash said. "So you're the new manager of the museum?"

"I am. But how did you know?"

"Pretty hard to keep a secret in this town."

"So I'm finding out. Not that it matters. I'm not staying for long."

"How come?"

Paddy shrugged. "I'm sure this is a very noice place, but I don't think it's roight for me. Soon as I can make a phone call . . ."

The waitress reappeared, and put the coffee cup down on Paddy's now-vacant table.

"I hope these gentlemen aren't annoying you, Professor," she said. "Breakfast won't be long. My hubby is just making it."

Then she addressed the old men. "The usual?"

Oodles nodded. "And a bowl of water for Howard. James hitched him to a post outside."

Wendy disappeared into the kitchen and Paddy returned to his chair.

Oodles leaned towards him. "You didn't tell us you were a professor, old son."

Paddy squeezed his mug like he was trying to strangle it. "Hmm."

"Seen much of the place yet? Apart from the thumb prints in the fence outside the pub."

Paddy frowned. "Thumb prints?"

"Yeah, that sandstone wall was built by convicts, as were a lot of buildings in this town. They liked to leave their marks."

"I didn't notice any thumb prints, but the fall probably looked worse than it was. I slipped in some dog shite on the footpath."

"Yes, I saw James walking Howard just ahead of you."

"James?"

Oodles pointed to the Mayor.

He didn't have time to explain further because right then Paddy's food arrived. It was swimming in fat. Obviously, no one had warned him about Gordo's food. But the Irishman tucked into it as if he had not eaten a good meal in days.

When he was finished, he tossed back his coffee with the look of someone just wanting to get it over and done with.

He banged the empty mug on the table, dug into his pocket and counted out some gold coins on to the table.

"I have to go, boys. I've got important business to do." He rose and looked at his watch. "I'll be talking to you again. If I'm still here."

As soon as he went out the door, Wish-Wash got up, walked over to James and shouted in his ear: "DID YOU HEAR THAT, JIMBO? HE'S A PROFESSOR. AT THE TASSIE TIGER MUSEUM. AND HE THINKS WE'RE STILL BOYS."

The Mayor just turned and looked at him.

———

The waitress delivered a teapot and a plate of digestive biscuits to the table and that's when it hit Oodles this was their first morning tea together without Birty. There were three teacups where there used to be four.

"Shall I be mother?" Wish-Wash didn't wait for an answer. He started pouring the tea with a trembling hand. He always spilt the tea but that never deterred him from wanting to do it.

"Why have you gone all quiet, Oodles?" Wish-Wash said.

Oodles couldn't reply. He looked down and examined his fingers, trying to disguise the fact he was all choked up. He had cut the nails so short for the funeral they still throbbed, and the tips were still red and raw from that brush he had used to clean them.

Oodles's train of thought was interrupted by the waitress clinking the crockery as she cleared the other table.

"Here, Wendy?" Wish-Wash said. "I saw your old man with Freddy and Dutchy at the pub last night. What was that all about?"

"He never tells me anything much. He did mention there was a new bloke at the museum though — so I put two and two together and realised that bloke was the professor."

———

Birty's last meal had been a good one. He had eaten Christmas dinner with his son, daughter-in-law and three grandkids.

His plate was heaped with turkey, roast potatoes, the sweetest pumpkin he said he had ever tasted, and peas and swede smothered in gravy.

He had washed it down with three glasses of mineral water, which was as fizzy as his beverages got since he had given up the grog years before.

He had two servings of trifle, then excused himself from helping with the dishes because he said he was going fishing up at Bing Bong Mountain.

His son had questioned the wisdom of this, flippantly at first by saying he'd scare the trout away if they saw that party hat on his head, but then declaring more seriously that he was asking for trouble if he went up there alone.

"Don't mollycoddle me, Robert," Birty had said. "I've been up there alone lots of times, the only difference is they haven't been at Christmas. You lot get off on your holiday and don't worry. I'll be fine."

It was true he had been up there alone lots of times in the last two years, ever since Oodles had stopped going with him.

Before Oodles's wife Madge died they had fished together for 40-odd years. They had shared a tent by the riverbank more times than he could count. For years they even had a small wager going on who would catch a wily old trout they dubbed George, which had been often seen, once hooked but never landed.

After saying what turned out to be his last goodbye, Birty went home and got his fishing gear before heading up to the upper reaches, and Robert and his family drove to the coast that afternoon.

No one else had a clue of Birty's whereabouts. And it was three days before anyone realised he was missing. When the search party found him, it was too late.

FIFTEEN
HELP ARRIVES

THE PLAQUE on the awning of the yellow, stone building said it was the Court House, established in 1845.

But another sign informed him the ornate building was now the town hall.

It had only taken him a minute or so to walk here from the cafe.

He had woken up with a bruise on his ankle but he was no longer limping.

He tried the door but it was locked. It was then he saw another sign that said the building wasn't due to open for another five minutes.

So he wandered over to see what was on the other side of the tall wrought-iron fence next door.

A sign was attached to the gate. Another fecking sign! It indicated he was standing outside the Colonel Richard Northan Memorial Rose Garden. Him again!

At his height, Paddy had no trouble looking over the fence. A splash of colourful, fragrant rose bushes were in full bloom amid the green lawns in the shade of some big oak trees.

He heard the town hall door click open, and sauntered back over.

The girl at the counter was very helpful and said the services would be reconnected later that day. He also asked her if she knew who he needed to speak to about the faulty streetlight and she told him he was already in the right place. Leave it with her.

He went shopping next. The little supermarket had most of the essentials he needed: bread, milk, tea bags, a brand of instant coffee that was superior to the brand the cafe served, two pieces of steak wrapped in plastic, sunscreen, toiletries, even rubber gloves and garbage bags. The shop had run out of phone cards but they'd be getting some in later in the week.

When Paddy arrived back at the museum he flicked on the light switch instinctively and dropped the shopping bag in shock when the lights flickered into life.

The extra illumination highlighted the grubbiness of the foyer — peeling paint and lots of cobwebs. Not to mention the soiled sheets balled up on the floor. Paddy realised he'd have to go back for more cleaning products, and at least one new light globe to replace one that had blown. He'd need sugar soap for the walls, a couple of buckets, sponges, window cleaner, furniture polish and some light-blue paint. He picked up the bread and gloves and placed them back in the bag. He was about to go upstairs when he heard knocking.

He turned and saw through the dirty glass one of the fellas he had met in the cafe – the larger, bearded old man.

Paddy put down the plastic shopping bag by the side of the door, and opened it.

"Hiya, can I help?"

"I was hoping I could help you, Professor." The man brushed past in a whiff of cheap deodorant and stale tobacco. "Remember me? Wish-Wash."

"Wish . . . ?" Paddy struggled to catch it, as he closed the door and turned around.

". . . Wash." The old man had stopped and turned around to face him. "Say it quickly. Wish-Wash. Bit like tick-tock or click-clack. It's what everyone calls me. We thought you might want a hand."

Paddy turned back towards the door, wondering if he had locked the other old men out.

"Oh, Oodles isn't coming today," Wish-Wash said.

Paddy reeled around again. "What about that other fella?"

"Jimbo?" Wish-Wash looked like he wanted to spit. "He won't be coming at all. We didn't even ask the deaf dickhead if he wanted to help you. It would just be a waste of time."

Paddy threw up his hands. "Look, I don't want you to think I'm not grateful. But as soon as I can make a phone call, I'm planning on going back to Sydney. Better still, Dublin."

"You can't do that," Wish-Wash said. "As soon as I saw you, I knew you were the bloke who would get this place back on track."

Wish-Wash started rolling up his sleeves as he looked around the foyer. "Typical. Billy Gumboots left this place in a right old state."

"You knew him?"

"I could of told them that lazy bludger would never make a go of this place."

"I can't afford to pay you." Paddy hoped that would deter the old man right away.

"Don't you worry about that, Professor. I'm happy to work for nothing. You might say I've got a vested interest in this place. Now tell me what I can do?"

———

Paddy set Wish-Wash up with a bucket filled with soapy

water and a sponge. "If you start cleaning these walls, I'll just go to the shops and pick up some more cleaning stuff."

"You trust me enough to leave me here alone! You've just met me, Professor!"

"There's not much to nick, aside from that fella's things upstairs." He cleared his throat. "You don't have to call me professor, either. Paddy will do."

Wish-Wash's face dropped. "I was brought up to respect my elders."

"Shouldn't I be saying that? I think you have the age thing well and truly covered."

"Well, I ain't never talked to a real professor before. We used to call one of the blokes who drank in The Applecart Professor Pisspot. But he wasn't a proper professor. He had just invested a lot of time and research into being a pisspot."

He paused for breath, then said, "So no one cleared Billy's stuff out for you?"

Paddy scratched his head. "You should see upstairs. Clothes, linen, shaving gear—"

"Shaving gear?" Wish-Wash said.

"An electric razor."

"Why would Billy Gumboots have had a razor when he had a beard? If you can call it that! It was about the same length as mine is now. But he tied the end together with a band of coloured beads."

"Maybe he was about to shave it off?"

"I doubt that very much. I think he was very pleased it finally looked like a beard. For a long time, he looked like he was growing pubic hairs on his face."

"So what do you think killed him?"

Wish-Wash tut-tutted. "Clearly it wasn't hard work."

"I was told he was only about my age?"

Wish-Wash scratched his scalp and gazed into space. "Let's see. Billy was 16 when Moose Routley joined the footy club in 1993. That would make Billy mid-to-late 30s now, if he was still alive."

"That's what the Asian girl in the takeaway shop thought."

"You met one of Jimbo's adopted grand-daughters then?" Wish-Wash laughed. "Jimbo's dislike of Asians goes even deeper than his hatred for Irish people and Catholics. You should have heard him when his daughter and her hubby went to South Korea and came back with twin girls! *'I' am not having gooks in my house!'* It's even worse now they're 18 and can dye their hair and paint their fingernails."

SIXTEEN
BACK AT THE SCENE OF TRIUMPH

WHEN PADDY WENT OUT SHOPPING, Wish-Wash had the best intentions of starting work. But after kneeling down and squeezing his sponge in the bucket, he felt knackered.

He staggered to his feet and looked around, and that's when a feeling of nostalgia washed over him.

The last time he had been in this foyer was about five years ago, and it smelled of new pine and freshly glued carpet then. Now it was just musty and dusty.

Wish-Wash was sure the dirty grey carpet had been bright blue on the night of the gala opening.

The consortium that had built the museum had thrown the place open for free entry that first night, and the foyer had been full of inquisitive locals.

Waiters dressed in tuxedos passed around glasses of champagne and tasty morsels on biscuits, which they brought in on silver trays.

A string quartet was providing the kind of background music that had rarely serenaded Windy Mountain before — except, perhaps, at the Northan mansion.

Two of the musicians were Jimbo's young adopted grand-daughters, back when both of them had jet black hair tied in pigtails. Vicki was playing the violin and Velda was plucking away at a double bass that was bigger than she was.

"Ladies and gentleman, may I have your attention," Dr Someone-or-Other had announced from a lectern at the back of the room. "I'd like to introduce you all to our guest of honour, Bert Whish-Willson."

Wish-Wash, who was wearing a collar and tie he had bought from the Slutz Plains opportunity shop, already felt uncomfortable but now he felt embarrassed, too. He already knew most of the people in the crowd. And he knew half of them wouldn't have given him the time of day.

"You probably know the part Mr Whish-Willson played in the establishment of this museum. So I won't go into details — except to say he is suitably represented in our gallery which you will soon be able to see."

He cut a tape which cordoned the crowd off from a door that said IN.

And the people flooded in.

Wish-Wash was glad no one was here now to see his misty eyes.

That opening night was the last time he had been in this place. Now look at it!

It had started to go downhill three years ago when it was sold and the new owners later hired that dropkick Billy Gumboots to run it.

Everyone knew the new owners couldn't care less about the Tasmanian Tiger.

Biggs and Sons specialised in wind farms. They owned and operated them all over eastern Australia. When this property had been offered for sale as part of a parcel of land around Tasmania, they snapped it up.

Word was they couldn't wait to tear the place down and use the land to erect some of those big wind turbines.

Wish-Wash wasn't surprised when Biggs and Sons

bumped the entry price up to $6.50. They didn't actually want the museum to succeed, did they?

What puzzled Wish-Wash was the arrival of this Irish professor.

Had there been a change of heart?

Bugger it. Wish-Wash threw his sponge into the bucket and headed into the gallery to see if anything had changed there.

He went in through the IN door. Just as he recalled, the gallery was U-shaped and it led visitors around to another door that deposited them back in the foyer.

On the way, they passed all the exhibits.

The tent was still there.

Dozens of photographs were pinned to the walls, some showing hunters with their prized Tasmanian Tiger skins hanging from lines, others showing the tiger in the wild.

Wish-Wash pressed the button on one display and it brought up a grainy black and white video of the last-known tiger pacing up and down in its enclosure in the Hobart zoo.

In a glass box was a stuffed model of a Thylacine, which stared back with glassy eyes.

One glass cabinet was empty and Wish-Wash stopped to read the label on the outside of the case.

"This is a model of a Tasmanian Tiger hunter," it said.

Wish-Wash looked again to make sure there wasn't something small down near the bottom of the case. But it was definitely empty.

Wish-Wash chuckled to himself. What a con? He was glad he hadn't had to pay $6.50 to see bugger-all.

Dozens of newspaper clippings were arranged along the walls. Mostly they were reports of sightings, news of study projects and the like.

Wish-Wash squinted at every one he came to, until he found the one that had put him in the spotlight.

It was the front page of *The Pick of the Crop*, July 12, 1967. Wish-Wash read every word again.

He headed back into the foyer, fully intending to go back to his bucket.

But the spiral staircase caught his eye and then it seemed to summon him.

Before he knew it, he was standing at the bottom looking up.

He had never been up there but he had to admit he was curious.

Especially about the mirror on the ceiling.

Paddy hadn't mentioned it.

But he wasn't to know you couldn't keep a thing like a mirror on the ceiling a secret in a town like Windy Mountain!

One little quick look wouldn't hurt, would it? He had never seen a mirror on the ceiling before. And what Paddy didn't know wouldn't hurt him.

So up he went. Clang, clang, clang.

He wandered into the bedroom. Sure enough, there was the mirror above the bed.

Next to the bed were two suitcases. One was lying on the floor open, and full of clothes and things, but the other one was on its side closed. The room was a mess. The floor looked like a tip and the walls were lined with tacky photos.

Wish-Wash was on his way back down the hall towards the staircase when curiosity got the better of him again.

The door to his right was ajar, and he stepped inside.

The kitchen sink was stacked with dirty dishes.

It was only when he recoiled around in disgust, he found himself facing the wall of books.

Well, I'll be!

Wish-Wash had never even seen Billy reading a book.

He stepped forward and pulled a book off the shelf and examined it.

Wow. It was Ray Bradbury's *Fahrenheit 451*. He flicked over the cover and saw it was a first edition, published in 1953. It was signed by the science fiction master himself.

Wish-Wash looked along the shelves and realised they were all sci-fi books. H. G. Wells. Isaac Asimov. Arthur C. Clarke, Scott Orson Card. John Wyndham. Frank Herbert. Even Douglas Adams. All the greats were there. He pulled out *The Day Of The Triffids* and flicked over the cover. It was another first edition.

Billy went up in his estimation and Wish-Wash found himself in some kind of time and space bubble.

He snapped out of his trance when Professor O'Brien burst into the room.

"Jaaaaaysus, man!" Paddy was puffing and his nostrils were flaring. "What the feck do you think you are doing?"

SEVENTEEN
'YOU DIDN'T HAVE TO SWEAR AT ME'

WHEN PADDY ARRIVED BACK, he had expected to see Wish-Wash where he had left him. But he saw no evidence a sponge had been used on the wall.

Paddy put the bags and blue bucket down on the front counter.

He called: "Wish-Wash?" He half-expected him to emerge from the jacks, doing up his belt. But when he heard no reply, he went into the gallery. He wasn't there either.

That just left one place to check.

Paddy's heart started pounding as he pictured the suitcases by the bed, with potential to blow his cover. He had a raft of documents that supported his new identity but he remembered now the tags on the cases still bore his actual name.

He bounded up the stairs, two or three steps at a time.

Wish-Wash looked so startled when he burst in.

———

For the next 30 minutes, the loudest things in the foyer were

Wish-Wash's trousers and shirt, and the sound of sponges swirling as the two men scrubbed the wall.

Paddy hated the silence. The longer it went on, the more the tension built and the more guilty he felt for having shouted at the old fella.

Paddy finally cracked. "Look, I'm sorry, OK?"

"I didn't mean no harm." Wish-Wash thrust out his bottom lip. "You didn't have to swear at me?"

"What you've got to understand about me is I swear at everyone. I don't mean anything by it."

"I didn't think you'd mind me having a look around and when I saw all those books . . . well, who would of thought? Billy a sci-fi reader!"

"So, it wasn't well known he read a lot of books?"

"I thought I was the only bloke in this town who liked sci-fi books. Do you have any idea what a collection like that is worth?"

"Do you want them?"

"I couldn't afford them."

"I wouldn't want money. Think of it as payment for your work."

"No, I couldn't."

"Why not?"

"It wouldn't feel right — not after all the things I've said about Billy Gumboots. People would think I was a flamin' hypocrite."

"Who am I going to tell? I told you. I'm not even planning on sticking around."

"Doesn't matter. I'd know. Billy's just the kind of no-good bloke who'd come back as a ghost so he could haunt me."

Paddy laughed. "You don't believe in ghosts, do you?"

"No, but some folks do." Wish-Wash looked around and lowered his voice. "They reckon the ghost of Colonel Northan walks around here cracking his whip."

"Oh, him?" Paddy puffed out his cheeks. "He must have

been a big deal around here, judging by the important things named after him. Big fella, too, judging by that sculpture."

"Don't believe it for a moment, Professor. Colonel Northan was only 5 foot 2. So tell me how come he's nearly seven foot tall now he's been cast in bronze?"

He didn't wait for an answer. "I'll tell you how. That sculpture was commissioned by his great, great, great grandson when he was mayor. The same bloke who was with us in the cafe!"

Wish-Wash threw his sponge into his bucket and sighed. "Must be time for a cuppa?" He looked around the room. "Where's your teapot?"

Paddy shrugged. "I saw one upstairs."

"Want me to go up and fetch it?"

"Nooooo." Paddy threw down his own sponge and started striding towards the stairs before Wish-Wash could turn around. "I'll go."

He found the teapot on the bench in the kitchen. But when he lifted it, he could feel it wasn't empty. He lifted the lid, expecting to see tea bags floating around. He just didn't expect them to be covered with wisps of white mould. It took him 10 minutes to clean the teapot in the lukewarm water that came out of the tap.

It was when he turned around with the teapot in his hand that he saw the phone extension on the bench top.

Hmm, had the line been connected yet?

He put the teapot down and picked up the receiver.

He had a dial tone!

What luck!

He dialled the mobile number he knew off by heart.

Joh answered, but he didn't seem impressed.

"I told you not to call this number," he said. "It might be bugged."

"This is an emergency."

"The word on the street is they've put a price on your head. They've hired a hitman to find you."

"Can't I take my chances in Sydney? You wouldn't believe how awful it is here."

"I don't care. Your situation has become even more dangerous. You need to suck it up because you're in the safest place you can be right now. Don't call me, I'll call you." Then Joh hung up.

———

When he returned back downstairs, Paddy laid the tray on a table in the corner.

"Sorry, it took some time to find everything."

Wish-Wash pulled up a plastic chair and sat down. The tray carried two mugs, an electric kettle, the aluminium teapot, a packet of teabags, a small bag of sugar and some milk. Wish-Wash surveyed it and he screwed up his face.

"Something wrong?"

"I normally have a bickie to dunk in the tea."

Paddy sighed. "If I had known, I'd have bought some at the shop."

"Tomorrow then. Oodles will be expecting them."

"I really don't think I need either of you."

"Nonsense. Many hands make light work."

Paddy headed towards the men's bathroom to fill the jug. When he returned, he plugged in the jug and sat down on a chair on the other side of the table.

As it rose to the boil, Wish-Wash raised his voice to compete. "Look, I know you said you don't expect to be here for long and you don't want us wasting our time helping you, but it's no trouble, Professor. I'm sure you'll change your mind when I've filled you in some more."

Paddy shook his head slowly, as he poured steaming water into the teapot.

"I haven't got many pleasures left at my age." Wish-Wash's lip quivered, but he suddenly brightened up. "Want me to pour the tea when it's drawn?"

After a period of awkward silence, Paddy watched the old man pour. Two little rivers flowed down the sides of the mugs, ran across the table and dripped on to the dirty carpet.

Wish-Wash didn't seem to notice the spillage, though, as he stirred three teaspoons of sugar into his tea, and then plunged the wet spoon back into the bag of sugar. "So do you want me to fill you in, Professor?"

He didn't wait for an answer.

The land the museum was built on, he said, used to be an apple orchard, which was planted by Colonel Northan.

"That bugger is credited in the history books for founding Windy Mountain but it's well known the Irish convicts under his command did all the hard yakka. Since then, if your name isn't Northan, it's nearly impossible to get a look-in on the job as mayor of the town. And good luck to you, Professor. If you're Irish, people like Jimbo Northan expect you to be attached to a ball and chain."

Wish-Wash broke into a grin. "A lot of people were ecstatic when Jimbo had his mental breakdown. We can thank Moose Routley for pushing him over the edge."

"Really? Moose Routley? I got the impression everyone hates that fella?"

"They do, and they don't. It was a case of who they liked least. Moose and his mates squatted illegally in a farmhouse along Blackstump Road in the early 1990s and not everyone agreed with the methods he employed trying to hunt the Tasmanian Tiger, but he got brownie points for leading the local footy team to a premiership in 1994. That's where things came to a head, the presentation ceremony. Jimbo had pushed him and pushed him until he just snapped. Jimbo was never the same after that. He maintains his wife left him after he got into financial difficulty. But I reckon he had started annoying her long before that, and she seized on the current turmoil as a good excuse to run away with a merchant banker."

Paddy's eyes became wider.

"He had to sell off the orchard to pay off his debts, but it didn't save his job. He was forced to stand down as mayor. Normally another member of the Northan family would have got the big job, but Jimbo only had one kid and she was too young to succeed him then, so a bloke called Peter Rowbottom became the new mayor. It was only when Maddie turned 18, she regained the family chains of office." He sighed. "Voters never learn."

Wish-Wash reached into his pocket and brought out a pouch of tobacco and some papers.

Paddy watched as he picked out the tobacco he needed, and rolled it in to a paper he then licked and sealed. It looked like he had the ritual down to a fine art.

"Mind if I go out the back to smoke this fag? Won't be long, Professor."

What could Paddy say? *Sure, but I'll have to dock your pay?*

Instead, all he said was: "OK, but don't go leaving your matches around."

Six tea breaks and six smoko breaks later, Paddy sent Wish-Wash home at 6pm. They hadn't done much work but Paddy was confident he could now win at a quiz night on local history.

Wish-Wash rolled down his sleeves. "Oodles and me will put in a big day tomorrow."

Paddy rolled his eyes. "For feck's sake! Weren't you listening? I really, really don't need any more fecking help."

The old man's eyes started to well up.

"Wha'?" Paddy said. "What's wrong now?"

"I can't believe you're swearing at me again."

"Was I? I'm sorry."

"You can't blame me for trying to change your mind," Wish-Wash said. "But I can tell you, Oodles won't be impressed with your language either."

EIGHTEEN
CRASH, BANG

After Wish-Wash had left, Paddy got to work upstairs.

He filled four big garbage bags in the bedroom alone. Aside from what was scattered around the floor, clothing had been stuffed into every drawer and cupboard. Gaudy shirts, cheesecloth trousers, odd socks, jocks of many colours and animal skin patterns, sandshoes and rubber thongs.

The bathroom was just as messy.

He threw the half-used tubes of toothpaste into the garbage bag. The cake of soap with the strands of hair went the same way. But he paused when he came to the sleek, shiny red electric razor hanging from a wall bracket. He had no use for it but surely he could find a home for it.

He went into the sitting room.

When it came to personal things like ornaments, CDs and DVDs, Paddy's pace slowed right down as he weighed each item up before either tossing it into the bag or deciding to keep it.

Then he reached the bookshelf, and came to a complete halt.

There were no books in his house when he was growing

up. None of his pals had many books in their houses in Dublin either. And nobody seemed worse for it.

But he had come to have some respect for books and it didn't feel right just to turf all that knowledge out. He doubted they were as valuable as Wish-Wash said but perhaps the old man would change his mind and take them. So he left them all.

His attention was caught by the clock on the wall. He could have sworn when he had glanced at it this morning the young woman pictured on the clock face had been wearing a yellow bikini. Now she was topless and the top half of her bikini bottoms had disappeared. Then it dawned on him. She was losing a stitch of clothing with every tick of the clock. It was 9pm now, by midnight she'd be naked!

Paddy stretched to his tippy toes and took the clock from its nail high up the wall, then tossed it into the garbage bag.

He surveyed the room. Anything else?

Oh, yes, all those dirty dishes on the sink.

Had the slob never cleaned up after himself?

Paddy binned most of it.

There was an awful lot. Big plates, little plates, bowls and cups, knives, forks, and spoons of assorted sizes and stages of mould. They crashed and smashed and rattled as they were thrown into the bag.

He only spared what he thought he would possibly need. A few cups, assorted plates, and a glass biscuit jar that contained one biscuit, which he took out with glee but nearly broke a tooth on when he tried to bite into it.

He was stuffed. He couldn't face going back down to work.

He'd have an early night. He'd put his own things away in the morning before Wish-Wash and his pal arrived.

The streetlight no longer flashed. So it had been fixed? Halle-fecking-lujah!

NINETEEN
FRIGHT IN THE NIGHT

SOME HOURS LATER, Paddy was awakened by someone sneaking up the stairs.

At first he thought it was part of a dream. But when he realised the creaking on the stairs was real, he opened his eyes wide. Really wide! Had the hitman found him? Already?

The footsteps on the stairs became louder as the intruder neared the top.

Paddy slid slowly out of bed and grabbed the first weapon that came to hand. He tip-toed behind the open door, and, heart pounding, raised the broom like a bat.

All he could see through the crack were shafts of light bouncing off the walls, which told him the intruder had a flashlight. He watched a dark figure turn into the hall. Feck! He was carrying a knife.

Paddy took a step backwards so he'd have room to swing at the intruder's head.

But the footsteps stopped just short of the door.

Another door creaked open and shut, and the hallway turned dark.

Paddy was puzzled as he stood there in the dark.

Why had the hitman gone into the bathroom?

Perhaps he had a nervous tummy?

He seized the moment to mount a surprise attack of his own. Was there a better time to beat the shite out of him than when his pants were down?

Paddy crept into the hallway where a sliver of flashlight showed under the bathroom door. He slowly turned the doorknob. Then he flung open the door and charged into the room, shrieking and waving the broom.

But the burglar wasn't sitting on the bog, after all. He was standing near the wash basin, and ducked when the broom whooshed past him. The beam of the flashlight flew around the room as the silhouette staggered backwards.

Paddy swished and missed again. The man shouted. "For God's sake, I'm a friend of Billy's."

Paddy reached for the light switch, and flicked it on.

The knife was actually a screwdriver with a yellow handle.

"You're kidding me!" The intruder was short, podgy, nearly bald and dressed in a dark grey suit with an open-neck shirt. "Nobody told me the power was back on." He switched off his flashlight. "You do know you're naked?"

The Irishman put the broom down against a wall and reached for the towel, which he tied around himself. "Never mind me. What do you think you're doing creeping around here in the middle of the night?"

"It's barely past midnight. I should ask you the same thing about you trying to kill me."

"I'm the manager."

"The manager? Nobody told me Billy had been replaced! Do I look like a burglar to you?"

He had a point. The only thing that looked rough about him was the few days of stubble on his face.

"Billy's dead!"

"I know. I buried him."

Paddy lowered his voice to a surprised whisper. "You're the undertaker?"

He nodded. "Dave Jenkins. And you are?"

"Paddy O'Brien."

"Billy said I could store some stuff here."

"What kind of stuff?"

Dave nodded towards the bracket next to the sink. "This razor for one thing."

"That's yours?"

"Yes. I have to conduct a funeral on Saturday. I know that's a few days away, but I'll have to meet family members first." He rubbed his chin. "And an undertaker can't look like he's been sleeping on a park bench."

"I see your problem," Paddy said. "But couldn't you have knocked instead of sneaking around with a flashlight?"

"I didn't know you were here. You must have arrived while I was out of town. I was going to have a whole week off but my assistant rang and said Betsy Smith had passed and could I come back early?"

"So what's the screwdriver for?" Paddy said.

"To unscrew the razor's bracket from the wall. Did you think . . .?" Dave put the flashlight down on the side of the sink. "If I had known the power was connected now, I would have brought an electric tool."

"Consider yourself lucky to still have your head on your shoulders." Paddy held out a palm. "You can take your razor with you but first I want my key back."

Dave reached into his pocket and pulled out the key, which he pressed down hard into Paddy's outstretched hand.

He then unscrewed the bracket quickly, brushed past the Irishman and headed for the stairs.

Paddy watched him go down towards the front door. "Next time, knock, OK?" he shouted from the landing.

It took Paddy ages to get back to sleep. So he wasn't happy when rapping on the front door woke him again.

For feck's sake, what did the undertaker want this time?

Bang-bang, bang-bang.

The room was dark. But when Paddy glanced at his luminous watch, he was surprised to see he had actually been back in bed for at least four hours. Perhaps it wasn't Dave at all? Perhaps Wish-Wash had come early with that other old fella? Yes, that made sense. Ol' ones liked rising early, didn't they?

Bang-bang, bang-bang.

"Hang on, I'm coming," Paddy shouted as he slipped into his trousers.

Bang-bang, bang-bang.

"For feck's sake," he said under his breath before shouting. "WILL YOU STOP THAT KNOCKING? I'M COMING."

As he stomped down the stairs in bare feet, buttoning his shirt as he went, he could see only one person outside the glass door, and he was poorly illuminated by the low-watt sensor light outside.

He appeared to be taller than the undertaker but thinner than Wish-Wash.

Paddy opened up and got two surprises.

Henk Van Gogh was standing there, smirking, and a bitter wind rushed in from the darkness. The weather had changed dramatically.

Paddy scowled back at the Dutchman just as coldly. "You said you'd be back on Wednesday, not five o'fecking-clock in the fecking morning a day early."

"I was just in the area and thought you'd want to know the news as soon as possible. How was I to know you'd get out of the wrong side of the fugging bed!"

Paddy did up the last of his shirt buttons. "You'd better come in out of the cold. This better be good though."

He stepped back to let the Dutchman pass by. "We started the clean-up but we weren't expecting you until tomorrow."

"This couldn't wait." Then he frowned. "What do you mean *we*?"

"One of the locals is helping me." Paddy motioned for Van Gogh to sit down at the table where the cups still were.

The Dutchman peeled off his coat, hung it over the back of a red plastic chair, and sat down. "I hope you didn't offer to pay him? You'll get no money from us for that."

"I realise that. Wish-Wash probably has got nothing better to do with his time."

"Wish-Wash!"

"You know him?"

"Not personally. But I know he used to be the town drunk."

Paddy pointed to the teapot. "He only drank tea here yesterday."

"I bet he still tells lies. He claimed to have seen a Tasmanian Tiger in the main street. That's how come they built this . . . this," he searched for the right word, "shrine — based on that one lie."

"How'd'ya know it was a lie?"

"If that old man is coming here, he's up to fugging something."

"This place obviously means a lot to him. The poor ol' fella wouldn't have many years left."

"Good. It'll be more oxygen for the rest of us. Anyway, he's wasting his time. I wanted you to be the first to know we have decided to close this museum."

The blood drained from Paddy's face. "Closing it?" What came out of his mouth next surprised even him. "You can't close it."

"We'll give you two weeks' notice at your present pay rate, of course."

"What pay rate would that be?"

"You did agree to work for free."

Paddy surprised himself further when he said, "What if I start making money?"

Van Gogh smirked. "If Billy Gumboots couldn't make it a going concern in two years, what makes you think you could do it in a few weeks?"

"But what if I could?"

Van Gogh shook his head. "I'm afraid planning permission has come through from the local council. In four weeks' time, this building is marked for demolition. We're planning to build a dozen wind turbines on this site."

"So that gives me four weeks to try to turn things around?"

Van Gogh locked eyes with him. After a moment of silence, he sighed. "Tell you what, I'll go out on a limb and give you two weeks to make it work. But I have to tell you something else. Due to rising costs, you're going to have to put the admission price up."

"What rising costs?"

"Who do you think pays for the electricity, rates and water for this place? And it's never earned us a fugging cent."

"Have you thought, perhaps, about *lowering* the price to get more people through?"

"Don't be ridiculous."

"So? How much do we need to charge customers now?"

"$19."

"Jaysus!" Paddy rolled his eyes. "How exactly do you think people will come at that?"

"That's not my problem," Van Gogh said. "How many days do you think you'll need before you can open the museum?"

Paddy tugged at his beard as he looked around. "Hard to say. Four or five days?"

"Let's make it three days then."

"You can't be serious?"

"I'm trying my best to meet you halfway."

"But three days to prepare? I'm not sure it can be done. Look at this place?"

"You'd best get to work then. I'm counting today as day one. I want this place open on Friday, 9am sharp." He handed Paddy a card.

"What's this?" Paddy looked down.

"You have seen a business card before? You can call me anytime on that number if you change your mind, and come to the inevitable realisation it's all much too hard."

———

Once upon a time, things wouldn't have ended so well for the Dutchman.

Paddy would have dragged him upstairs, dangled him from a window and seen if *he* enjoyed being woken up so abruptly. But, instead, he forced himself to smile as he opened the front door for him.

Sprinkles of sleet hit his face as more of the outdoors came in.

"Typical fickle Tasmanian weather!" Van Gogh stood buttoning his coat before he went outside. "Good luck with getting tourists out in this climate — hot one day, cold the next."

He hesitated for a second then said, "I don't suppose you've seen a mannequin of a Tasmanian Tiger hunter around the place?"

"A what?"

"A model of a hunter that used to be on display in the

gallery. Perhaps it's been stored away in a cupboard and you came across it while you were cleaning?"

Paddy shook his head. "Is that the thing that used to be in that glass cabinet? What's so special about it?"

"I just noticed it was missing, that's all."

Van Gogh walked past him and into the rain. Paddy could see his car out in the yellowy gravel car park.

"Mind how you go, Mr Van Gogh. Don't want you slipping over in a puddle."

But I hope you do, you prick, and break your fecking neck.

———

Van Gogh heard the door slam behind him. He wondered if he had done the right thing even letting the imposter stay on.

Mr Biggs had put him in an awkward situation by hiring the Irishman in the first place. Van Gogh had had a bad feeling about the application, but you didn't argue with the boss if you cared about your longevity.

Now he had met the phoney professor, however, he was certain he was an undercover cop. But to turf him out so quickly might have aroused even more suspicion.

He unlocked his car. It would be good to get out of this cold. But he'd feel even better as soon as Paddy went, so the bulldozers could destroy any evidence left on the premises.

———

Paddy couldn't see the point of going back up to bed. He wouldn't sleep.

He had stood up to bullies before but never a corporate bully. But Van Gogh had picked the wrong fella!

He threw the business card on to the reception desk and stormed upstairs.

He went into the kitchen and grabbed the biscuit jar from the bench.

He turned it upside down and shook the remaining crumbs out on to the kitchen bench. Then he took the jar downstairs and slammed it down on to the front reception counter with such force it's a wonder it didn't shatter.

Next he walked to the other side of the foyer, formed a fist and punched the wall as hard as he could.

It hurt like hell.

And he cried out: "Feckkkkkkkkkkkkkkkkkkkkkk."

TWENTY
MORE CRABBY VISITORS

WISH-WASH AND OODLES shared the cover of a colourful, tattered umbrella as they scurried towards the museum dodging puddles about 8am.

They were mostly dry by the time they had reached the portico over the front door.

Wish-Wash collapsed the brolly and shook it. "I reckon we must have look like a crab out of water just now."

Oodles shook his head. "Unlikely. Crabs have 10 legs, old mate. We can only manage four between us. And we didn't exactly escape being out of water either." He used his handkerchief to wipe droplets from his face. "Where on earth did you find a bright red umbrella with moth holes, anyway?"

"It was the pick of the bunch for sale at the Slutz Plains op shop." Wish-Wash swept a bead of water off the end of his nose with his hand. "There was one without holes but it was black. Boring as bat shit!"

The glass door in front of them was all steamed up, so they couldn't see much, apart from a shape moving around inside.

Wish-Wash was about to knock, but changed his mind and

turned around. "You still haven't told me what happened at the meeting with Father O'Boring and Jimbo?"

"You're not going to like it." Oodles coughed nervously. "Besides, I thought we were talking about carcinology."

Wish-Wash frowned. "Why would we be talking about cancer?"

Oodles slapped his thigh. "I knew you wouldn't know that! Carcinology is the scientific study of crustaceans."

Wish-Wash frowned again. "I would have guessed that to be crabology."

"That's why they never ask you to be on a team at the quiz nights at the pub."

Wish-Wash stuck out his bottom lip. "If they had questions about sci-fi, you flamin' know I'd be the first one they picked. Mind you, I just found out yesterday Billy Gumboots was a closet fan, too. He might have also made the A team."

"Your Billy?"

Wish-Wash growled. "You're not going to start on that again! So are you going to tell me about the meeting yesterday, or what?"

"I'll tell you everything once we get out of this rain, when we get the chance to be alone."

Wish-Wash turned around and knocked.

"Are you sure the professor is expecting me, too?" Oodles said.

"Just don't go upsetting him. I made that mistake, and I've never heard such swearing."

———

Paddy had seen the shadows at the door. He could hear the old men talking for ages but he only caught small snatches of their conversation.

Eventually, someone knocked and he opened the door.

Wish-Wash stepped inside. "You remember Oodles?" He

bent down to prop his brolly against the glass panel adjoining the door, then headed straight to the table.

Oodles followed him and sat down, too. Both of them had wet hair.

"I thought you'd have the kettle on, Professor," Wish-Wash said. "We're parched."

Wish-Wash was wearing an orange shirt held up with the same lurid braces he had worn yesterday. The other old man was wearing grey overalls.

Paddy threw down his sponge and walked over to the table.

"Tea for me," Wish-Wash said as he came into his peripheral vision. "As hot as it comes."

Then he spotted the jar over on the reception desk and his face lit up. "You did get some biscuits?"

Paddy shook his head as he picked up the kettle from the table. "Nothing to eat in that jar but coins. I've turned it into a swear jar. I've put $9 in already this morning. At this rate, I'll be going broke before this place does."

Paddy took the kettle into the toilets.

When he disappeared, Wish-Wash and Oodles looked at each other.

"What's he on about, old mate?"

Wish-Wash shrugged. "Beats me."

Paddy re-emerged before they even had the chance to broach the subject of the meeting with Father O'Boring again.

"You'd be pleased to know I've changed my mind." Paddy plugged in the kettle, pulled up a third chair and sat down. He fixed his eyes on Wish-Wash. "I know I told you yesterday I didn't expect to hang around, but I've decided to stay."

Wish-Wash beamed. "That is good news. Eh, Oodles?" He looked up at Paddy.

That's when he caught sight of the dried blood on the

Irishman's knuckles. "Strewth! What did you do to yourself, Professor?"

Paddy held up his hand and rotated it. "Oh this? Cleaning injury. I've had worse."

"It looks like you hit a brick wall," Wish-Wash said.

Paddy glanced over at the offending brickwork. "I kinda did."

Oodles winced. "What made you angry enough to punch the wall?"

"You ever met Henk Van Gogh?"

"Dutchy?" Wish-Wash's eyes widened. "We see him in town every now and then, don't we Oodles? But we steer clear of him because by all accounts he's a bad bugger."

"You won't get any argument from me about that line of thought." Paddy held out his palm. "That'll be a dollar, by the way."

Wish-Wash tilted his head slightly and scowled. "Me? What for?"

"If I've decided to try to stop swearing, you fellas can show a little support."

"*Bugger* ain't swearing. It's not like I called him a bastard."

Paddy held out his other hand, too. "That'll be $2 now."

"What's come over you? You were happy to swear your flamin' head off yesterday."

"Yeah, well, that Dutchman was here earlier this morning." Paddy walked over to the swear jar and pulled his last two gold coins from his pocket. "That *fecking gobshite* has given me two weeks to make this place start turning a profit. If not, he says they're closing it."

"That stinks, old son," Oodles said.

"He says we have to open by Friday," Paddy said.

"By *this* Friday?" Oodles looked around him and tutted. "Is it even going to be possible to clean up this place in three days?"

"I suspect that was part of his plan to make sure I fail,"

Paddy said. "He said they already have planning permission to pull down the place and build some wind turbines on the site."

Wish-Wash pinched the bridge of his nose. "That was the flamin' rumour going around when they bought the place. The rotten rotters."

"And that's not all. I've been told to raise the admission cost."

Wish-Wash's face had become red. "Blooming heck. Admission is already $6.50!"

"They want it to be $19 now," Paddy said.

"Nineteen bucks!" The whistle of the kettle masked whatever Oodles said next, and saved him a gold coin.

TWENTY-ONE
SPLITTING UP

WISH-WASH TOOK a noisy slurp of his tea and looked around the foyer before swallowing. "I'll say this, Professor, you must have worked like crazy in here this morning. What's say, we split up? One of us can stay here to finish off and two of us can get cracking on cleaning up the gallery."

"Good idea." Paddy rose and scooped up his bucket. "Come with me, Oodles, and Wish-Wash can finish off in here."

Oodles looked at Wish-Wash and shrugged.

"Grab that empty bucket in the corner, Oodles," Paddy said as he headed towards the door.

Oodles picked up the red bucket and followed him through the IN door, which swung shut behind them.

Inside the gallery, rain pounded on the ceiling-to-floor windows.

Paddy used the side of his hand to squeakily wipe away condensation. The trees that appeared in the porthole were bending in the wind. Low cloud had shrouded the bushland in the background.

"It sure is a wild ol' day," Paddy said.

Oodles craned his neck to look out. "I doubt this will stop for a while, Professor."

Paddy sighed. "Van Gogh reckons Wish-Wash made up a story he saw a Tasmanian Toiger."

"What would he know! He comes from the blinking city." Oodles pointed towards the fogged-up window. "All kinds of wild things live at the foothills of Bing Bong Mountain, and some of them are bound to stumble upon the town. Wallabies, possums, native cats, Tasmanian devils, snakes —"

"Snakes!" Paddy's eyes widened.

"Well, not so much stumble but I've seen tiger snakes slithering along the High Street more than once." Oodles raked his hand over his stubbled chin, which made a rasping noise. "I used to see them every time I went trout fishing, too. Most of the time you only see them twisting away. But once in a while you'll meet an aggressive one who'd arc up."

"What do you do?"

Oodles averted his eyes. "It's not an issue any more because I've retired from fishing." The old man blew out a whistle of air. "I'm too damn old to be traipsing around the bush now. Have you ever been fly-fishing, Professor?"

Paddy shook his head.

"You ought to try it while you're here. It's good for the soul. Imagine if you could walk into a landscape painting and become as much part of the picture as the birds and the trees and the fish. No phones, no TV, no interruptions. Bliss."

"So you never saw a Tasmanian Toiger out there?"

"No. If there was one out there, I reckon Moose Routley would have found it years ago."

"Wish-Wash told me about how he was a Tasmanian Tiger hunter."

"Did he tell you how Moose kicked the winning goal in the 1994 grand final, too? People have a love-hate opinion of the man."

"I'm beginning to get that, too."

"Back to your first question, Wish-Wash is the only bloke I know who says he actually saw a Tasmanian Tiger around here."

Paddy scratched his head. "We should get to work. Are you OK with washing windows?"

"As long as it's on this side. I'm still drying out."

Oodles nodded towards a stepladder leaning against one of the display cabinets. "Got any window-cleaning detergent?"

"I'll go fetch it from upstairs. You're all right working at heights?"

"I spent half my working life up ladders, Professor. I lost count of the amount of bird shit I had to clean off Colonel Richard Northan's blinking bronze head."

Paddy glared at him, and Oodles realised what he had just said. He dug into his pocket and pulled out a $1 coin he handed to the big man. He looked at the stepladder. "Didn't want that money rattling around in my pocket up there, anyway." He sighed. "You get the detergent, and I'll get myself set up here."

———

Wish-Wash nearly spat out a mouthful of tea when Paddy appeared. As soon as the others had disappeared, he had gone back to the table for a rest, all the time willing Oodles to come out alone to fetch something.

"The teapot wasn't quite empty," he spluttered. "I didn't want it to go to waste."

"That's understandable." Paddy turned a plastic chair around and sat on it backwards. His voice dropped to almost a whisper. "I've been told you saw a Tasmanian Toiger here in Windy Mountain?"

Wish-Wash puffed out his chest. "It didn't take you long to read about that in the gallery?"

"Read about it?" Paddy looked confused. "No, Henk Van Gogh told me and Oodles just confirmed it."

Paddy locked on to Wish-Wash's eyes. "Van Gogh said you used to be the town drunk?"

"What if I was?" Wish-Wash raised his voice. "That doesn't make me dishonest. All it means is I once had a drinking problem. I don't now."

Paddy raised his open palms above the back of the red chair. "All I'm trying to work out is why he dislikes you so much."

"That's flamin' obvious. The last thing he needs is for the only fellow ever to see a Tasmanian Tiger in this town to appear on the scene and remind everyone why his plan to tear this place down isn't such a good idea. He probably knows I've swung public opinion around in the past and I might do it again."

"When was that?"

"I saw the Tiger in the High Street in 1967. I would have had proof, too, if Doggie Dougall hadn't shot it."

"Someone *shot* it?" Paddy gasped.

"He took the carcass to the tip for incineration before anyone could examine it."

Paddy's eyes widened. "Why?"

Wish-Wash shrugged. "You'd have to ask Doggie that because I haven't spoken to him for nearly 50 years. I know what I saw though. That's why I feel some responsibility for this museum. It probably never would have been built if it hadn't been for me. Mind you, it took them long enough and I've never been given any of the profits."

"Did they by any chance give you the key to the front door?"

"Why would they?" Wish-Wash said. "Until yesterday, I hadn't set foot in this place for five years. Do you think Oodles and me would have stood out in the rain knocking if I had a key?"

"OK, tell me what were you looking for upstairs then? Van Gogh mentioned a model of a Tasmanian Toiger hunter. Were you looking for that perhaps?"

"What's so special about that?"

The Professor shrugged. "No idea. I'm just trying to piece a jigsaw together. Do you know a fella called Dave Jenkins?"

"Dave?"

"You do know him?"

"Everyone knows Dave. It pays to be nice to the local undertaker. Not for me personally, mind you, but old blokes like Oodles and Jimbo would be fools to get him offside."

"But why would the local undertaker have a key to this museum? He frightened the shite out of me when he came here last night. When I confronted him, he said he had a key Billy Gumboots had given him. He said Billy had let him keep stuff here."

"That doesn't make any sense. How could Billy give him permission when he's dead? What kind of stuff?"

"All he took was that electric razor. But when Van Gogh started banging on about a missing model I started wondering what he really came for."

———

Wish-Wash was glad when the Professor went upstairs to get the window cleaner for Oodles, thus ending his interrogation.

He was even happier when he came downstairs and noticed a patch of blue outside the window.

"I'm famished," Paddy said. "Do you think Oodles would mind if I duck out for breakfast and take advantage of this break in the weather?"

"Of course he won't," Wish-Wash said. "We don't want you wasting away."

Paddy handed the bottle to Wish-Wash. "Thanks. Can you give this to Oodles? Do you need anything from the shop?"

"Have you forgotten already? We need chocolate digestives."

"Of course. And what type of biscuits does Oodles eat?"

"Don't worry about him. At his age, even fresh air gives him indigestion."

When Paddy left, Wish-Wash went through the IN door and found Oodles at the top of the stepladder. He was using a small broom to brush some cobwebs from the top of the window frame, and he looked down with a startled look. "What have you done with the Professor?"

"I forgot to tell you: he doesn't like being called that."

"Now you tell me? Where is he?"

"He's gone to the Wind Tunnel Cafe to get some breakfast."

"I've never known someone to eat Gordo Bennett's breakfast two days in a row."

Wish-Wash held up the bottle of blue liquid. "He said to give you this."

Oodles shook his head. "Hang on to it, I'm coming down."

When Oodles reached the ground and turned around, Wish-Wash said, "Finally, we get a chance to talk."

Oodles screwed up his face. "You're not going to like hearing this though." He sighed. "Father O'Boring said he likes his chances of outliving the rest of us."

Wish-Wash squeezed his eyes shut. "Did you point out he's 92?"

"Yes, but it didn't seem to matter to him."

"He couldn't have long, could he?" Wish-Wash opened his eyes again. "I still don't know how the doddery old fool managed not to topple over into Birty's grave on Saturday. Did you tell him he could get a nice payout right now and have time left to spend it?"

"He said he doesn't want to sell the shares now. He'd prefer to win *all* the money and *leave it to the poor*."

"Christ Almighty!" Wish-Wash said. "What does he think I am?"

"I tried that line, too. He said you at least had a regular roof over your head these days."

"What did Jimbo say?"

Oodles tut-tutted. "I should have known James would shirk his responsibilities. He kept refusing to come to the meeting, saying it would be a waste of his *valuable* time. So it looks like we're back to where we were before — willing each other to die first."

"I never thought that of you. Not really. I *was* sledging at the funeral. But it was all meant in good humour."

"So you're not going to try to push me off this ladder when I climb back up?"

"Why would I do that to a mate? I'm only sorry you didn't hit me harder. I deserved it."

Oodles put his arm up around Wish-Wash's shoulder. "I should have saved up my anger for James. It's been building up inside me for years. That's a good reason for helping the Irishman. To get up James's nose."

Wish-Wash laughed. "Yeah, that'll work! Did you see the way he looked at Paddy in the cafe? Like he was lower than a snake's armpits, and that's even lower than me? When he finds out we're helping him . . . "

"But now I have another good reason," Oodles said. "Van Gogh is doing a real mongrel thing to the Professor."

"You reckon Jimbo is involved, too?"

Oodles shook his head. "I can't see how he can be? Mind you, Maddie must be party to the plans to rezone this place."

"What's the Professor going to do?"

Oodles thought about it. "I think we should introduce him to Gus Foot. If anyone knows what Paddy needs to do, Gus will know."

TWENTY-TWO
FATHER O'BORING

GOD HAD BEEN LOOKING out for Father John O'Rourke for a long, long time.

Born into poverty in western County Cork in 1924, he considered it a miracle he had survived malnutrition and any number of childhood diseases. Diseases wiped out entire families in those days. Each disease brought its own brand of pain — in limbs, in guts, in heads — and most of them resulted in death in the very young and the very old.

John O'Rourke was 17 when he chose to leave Ireland in search of a better life in Australia.

His parents waved goodbye to him when the two-funnelled motor-ship pulled away from the dock at Cobh.

Another ship had left from the same port a few years earlier with much more fanfare. Bound for New York, the Titanic was fast and heralded as unsinkable. Fat lot of good all those streamers did though. The unthinkable happened to the unsinkable. The Titanic ran into an iceberg on April 15, 1912.

Here's where it got confusing. Cobh was called Queenstown by the British overlords back when it farewelled the Titanic. But before that, it was called Cove — which was probably the same departure point one of John's ancestors had left from. Great-great uncle Donal had been one of the many convicts shipped to Van Diemen's Land, never to see Ireland again.

John leaned against the rail on the deck of the two-funnelled motor-ship, and wiped back tears because he suspected he'd never see his mam and da again either.

John shared a cabin way below deck with 17 other third-class single men.

During the long voyage he began the habit of a lifetime: the nocturnal stroll. He'd roll out of his hammock around midnight, put on some clothes and climb the rope ladder to get some air and stretch his legs on the main deck.

It was during one such excursion, the ship hit rocks off the coast of Java.

John jumped into the oily water. He could see little in the dark but he could hear the screaming as he swam as far away as possible from the ship. When he touched something solid, he wondered if it was land. But it turned out to be one of the wooden lifeboats. When no one reached down to help him, he clambered into the boat on his own and saw no one else was there. He turned when he heard a sucking noise. All he saw was the silhouette of the ship against the moon sliding bow-first into the ocean.

He could see no land, and no other lifeboats.

He drifted for three days, during which time he made a promise.

"If ye spare me, God, I will devote the rest of my life to ye."

When he was rescued, and told he was the only survivor of 633 passengers, he vowed to make good on his pledge.

When he arrived in Sydney, he bypassed the taverns near the wharf and sought out a seminary. He emerged seven years later as a priest, and was sent to Tasmania where he worked at several parishes around the state before spending his twilight years at St Benedict's at Windy Mountain, and his post-twilight years in the nursing home at the edge of the town.

James Northan had known nothing of this background when he had approached him with his proposal. How could he? Nobody knew. Father O'Rourke hadn't even told his closest confidantes the story, so why would he ever tell those Church of England lot across the road?

He hadn't even told Daisy Rowbottom, yet he had shared forbidden things with her.

He had first noticed her when he was a regular staff member at St Benedict's. But he had been strong then. Resolute. Incorruptible.

His resolve began to weaken the day they met at the school fete years later.

Although by then she had retired from the position of head nurse of Windy Mountain Hospital, she was a spring chicken next to him and she oozed sex appeal as she weighed the jar in her hands at the guess-how-many-jellybeans stall.

Who would have thought she'd be spot on with her guess? But it wasn't a mere guess, was it? It was a God-given gift, honed with years of practice weighing babies at the hospital, that allowed her to give her answer of 822 jellybeans.

Her prize had been the whole jar.

When she saw him standing by, she offered the open jar to him. "Take a handful, Father."

"Oh, ye mustn't tempt me. Black jellybeans are my biggest weakness."

"Go on," she said. "You know you want to."

"Ye are so clever, Daisy. Was dat just a lucky guess?"

"Certainly not, Father. A better test would have been to get people to guess how many different colours there were in the jar."

He said no one would ever be able to guess that.

It's quite possible she misinterpreted that as flirting because before he knew it they *were* flirting. He reached the point of no return when he told her it was about time she called him John, because although he was still a priest he was mostly off duty these days.

But she didn't give up her jellybean secrets easily.

It was way later in the night she whispered in his ear in bed. "One hundred and fifty-six white ones, the 105 aniseed-flavoured black ones you've eaten, 107 red ones I've eaten, 144 orange ones, 108 green ones, 98 yellow ones and 104 purple ones."

Father O'Rourke wasn't ashamed of what he had done. Who would have believed the story of the 91-year-old virgin, anyway?

But people would talk if they suspected. That's why he and Daisy usually met under the cover of darkness, usually starting with a brisk walk and a few jellybeans before getting down to rumpy-pumpy.

And that's how they happened to be in the High Street the night the large stranger had arrived. They were just two long shadows strolling down the street.

"That was Moose Routley, I'd know him anywhere," Daisy had said when they got far enough away they couldn't be heard.

TWENTY-THREE
THE COW ON THE WALL
WEDNESDAY MORNING

THE FRAMED PHOTOGRAPH of the cow on the wall was what puzzled Paddy the most.

His eyes fell on it as he looked around the investment adviser's office tucked above Roses Supermarket.

The Irishman was sitting with Oodles and Wish-Wash behind a big, blackwood desk.

The black leather ergonomic chair on the other side was empty. Gus Foot's secretary had apologised. He wasn't normally late. Would they mind waiting?

Oodles saw Paddy studying the photo and offered an explanation. "That is how Gus got his first big break."

Paddy looked around at him. "He made his fortune from a *cow*?"

"Not exactly, but he raised enough from her milk to get a stake together to invest in a dot.com company in the mid-90s. He sold his shares just before the bubble burst and made a nice pot of money. People reckon Gus doesn't even need to work any more, but he probably has a sentimental attachment to the place downstairs."

Paddy's frown lines deepened.

Oodles elbowed the other old man, whose head was

bowed and had started breathing heavily like he was on the verge of sleep. "It wasn't always a supermarket, was it Wish-Wash?"

Wish-Wash sat up, startled. "What did you do that for, cobber?"

"You were nodding off."

"I wasn't. I was just resting my eyes."

"What were we talking about, then?"

"Gus?"

"I rest my case. I was actually filling Paddy in on the history of Roses Supermarket." He turned back to the Irishman. "When Gus came to town in the early 1990s downstairs was the venue for the Windy Mountain Dancing Academy."

"A dancing school? Here? Really?" Paddy's eyes widened.

"No, not really. It was actually a front for a brothel. But if you ever want to see James go off his tree, try ribbing him about it. He secretly owned the building but he didn't have a clue what his frontman, Tiger Kowalski, was really doing with it."

"Or so he says." Wish-Wash pulled at a stray yellow cotton on his shirt. "He was only the flamin' mayor at the time. Don't tell me he didn't know?"

Oodles shook his head. "Whether James was party to it is beside the point. For the purposes of this story, all Paddy needs to know is Foetus and his gang stopped there."

Paddy squinted. "Who's Foetus?"

"Sorry. Gus Foot. Foetus is what his motorcyclist mates called him."

"He rides a motorbike?"

"He rode a motorcycle the day he and his mates came to town," Wish-Wash said. "By the time Foetus emerged, his gang had done a bunk and stolen his Suzuki."

Oodles butted back in. "Seeing as he couldn't actually go anywhere, he joined a squat up on Blackstump Road with Moose Routley."

Paddy ran his fingers through his hair and said, "I'm not sure this is such a good i—"

He didn't finish the sentence because a middle-aged man with a shiny forehead and a ponytail entered the room, and everyone stood up.

"Oodles, Wish-Wash long time no see." The man shook their hands. "Sorry, I'm late. Trouble with the Beemer."

He extended his hand to Paddy. "And you must be the new bloke at the museum?"

He had a firm grip. He wasn't as big as Paddy, but he was big enough, and his paisley tie resting on his protruding stomach highlighted his advantage in girth.

"I'm worried I might be wasting your time," Paddy said.

Gus gestured like a traffic cop making a stop signal. "Nonsense. No such thing."

"I can't afford to pay you."

"Now, don't you worry about that. Oodles, Wish-Wash and I go back a long way. Always happy to help old friends. Besides, when they told me about your beard . . . " He swept his hand in a semi-circle motion. "Let's sit down, shall we? And you can fill me in, Professor."

Wish-Wash scowled. "The Professor don't actually like being called professor."

Paddy nodded.

"He just likes Paddy," Wish-Wash said.

For the next half an hour, Paddy found it hard to get a word in edgeways as the old men explained the situation. He found it hard to think straight, what with them talking over the top of each other and him wondering how his beard could possibly be of relevance.

Gus Foot listened and nodded his head, occasionally picking up the motorcycle-shape paperweight from his desk and pouring it from one large hand into the other.

When the old men seemed to have nothing left to say, he said, "I think what you need to come up with, Paddy, is an advantage. You need something that sets your museum above all the other Tasmanian Tiger museums in this state. You need to find something they haven't got, but you have and people will be clamouring to pay $19 to see."

"I can't think what, short of an actual Tasmanian toiger," Paddy said.

Oodles's expression changed from concerned to joyous. "Foetus, you're brilliant. You've given me an idea."

"Have I?"

"I think Wish-Wash and I need to go some place and nut a few things out." They both stood up.

"I'll come, too," Paddy said, getting to his feet.

"Nooooo," Oodles said as hand shaking began. "This is Secret Old Blokes' business. Besides, you have an appointment across the road with Katy McDonnell."

"Who's Katy O'Donnell?"

"McDonnell," Wish-Wash said. "She's the hairdresser."

"Why do I need a hairdresser?"

Gus looked at Oodles, then at Wish-Wash. "I thought you said he knew what my fee was?"

———

As they descended the stairs, Oodles said, "We didn't know how to tell you. You didn't seem all that keen to see Gus in the first place. If you had known what the fee was I reckon you would have pulled out for sure."

"But I've had this beard for years!"

"It'll grow back, won't it?" Oodles chuckled. "A small price to pay for the good idea, I reckon."

Wish-Wash was first to the bottom and he opened the door. Three steps down and they were on the footpath.

Oodles pointed to the hairdresser's shop on the other side of the High Street.

"Katy is Snipper McDonnell's girl. She'll be expecting you."

Quick as a shot, Wish-Wash said: "Whatever you do, don't tell her Oodles let her father die."

Oodles glared at Wish-Wash. "That's not funny, old cock."

Paddy stepped between them. "Knock it off. Is someone going to explain why I have to have my beard shaved off?"

"You should be glad, old son," Oodles said. "My grey whiskers and Wish-Wash's fluff don't cut the mustard any more but your facial fungus will be famous in the US soon."

"Wha' are you talking about?"

"We'll explain later. Right now we have to talk about seeing a man about a dog."

He waved a finger at Wish-Wash. "C'mon. And I'm warning you. Keep your smart-arse comments to yourself."

TWENTY-FOUR
SHORT BACK AND SIDES

KATY MCDONNELL WAS WEARING a lemon-coloured summer dress when she greeted Paddy at the door, ushered him to a chair and wrapped a gown around him.

"Relax." She started snipping away at his beard. "It's not like I haven't done this a thousand times before. You're just my first professor."

Paddy drew away from the scissors. "Not you too! What makes you think I'm a professor?"

"Easy. Gus made the appointment in the name of Professor Paddy O'Brien."

She used her free hand to reposition his head. Her light touch felt nice and he could smell her perfume.

He sank back into the chair. "I still don't know what I'm doing here."

"Beard removal, ponytail removal and general hair tidy up," she said matter-of-factly as if she had memorised some kind of shopping list.

"Whoa! No one said anything about my ponytail!"

She walked over to the counter and checked the book lying there. "Yep, Gus has paid for that, too."

Paddy looked sideways and saw an Asian girl with spiked

purple hair snipping off the beard of a fella perhaps in his mid-20s. She looked familiar. It had to be Velda's twin sister!

Katy resumed snipping. Paddy surveyed her in the mirror as she cut off clumps of his beard with the scissors.

She was tall, slender, with tied-back auburn hair, green eyes, mid 30s, and with no wedding ring.

More of Paddy's whiskers dropped to the floor.

"What's in this for Gus?" Paddy said.

"Don't know. Don't care. Head back please. I've got to go as close as I can.

Paddy could see in the mirror she was zeroing in on his beloved ponytail.

"I don't get many of these," she said. "The only other fellow I know with a ponytail is Gus himself — and he won't let me near it."

"Probably compensating for the lack of hair on the front of his head?" Paddy said.

Katy laughed. "I wouldn't say that too loudly. You do know he used to be a bikie, don't you?"

A large clump of hair fell in the mirror.

"That was the last connection with my schooldays."

Katy's hand pressed on his head. "I'm surprised the school even allowed boys to have ponytails."

"They didn't." Paddy grinned. "It annoyed the shite out of them."

Katy continued snipping with the scissors, all over his head, then started up the electric razor and cleaned up the stubble around his neck.

He broke the silence. "That's noice."

"Nice? That Gus wants the hair off your head, too?"

"No, I mean it feels like a noice haircut. Incredible, too, that you were able to do it without putting a bowl on my head."

Katy laughed and placed a hand mirror at the back of his neck so he could see what kind of job she had done.

"You reckon this one makes me look thin or fat?"

She giggled, and he liked the sound of her laugh. "I get it. It's one of them trick mirrors that makes it look like my pony-tail isn't there any more."

"I'm afraid not. This mirror doesn't lie."

Paddy smiled at her reflection in the main mirror. "When's your break?"

"Why?"

"I want to buy you a coffee to tank you for the shave and haircut."

"I only drink tea. Besides, you don't have to thank me. I told you: Gus pays me."

"But I want to. No harm in a cuppa?"

"That depends where it comes from? You do know this town only has one cafe?"

"It's a date then?"

"Whoa! A date? You've just met me!"

"I didn't mean it like that. Not a *date* date."

Katy bit her lip. "Sorry," she said. "I'm sure you're a nice guy, but, no, I can't."

———

After Paddy had gone, Katy swept up the hair and packaged it into plastic bags.

She actually knew exactly what Gus did with those whiskers.

She wondered what Paddy's red beard would be marketed as in the United States. The Yanks couldn't believe Ned Kelly's beard was still growing, could they?

TWENTY-FIVE
FAME BECKONS AGAIN

WISH-WASH COULD TELL by the way Oodles packed tobacco into the bowl of his pipe he was deep in thought.

He hadn't said a word since they had left the Professor. Now they were sitting on the bench in silence. Oodles couldn't still be angry at him, could he? It was just a joke, for Christ's sake.

Oodles struck a match, held it to his pipe, and sucked it into life. Only when he blew out his first stream of smoke, did he finally speak. "Do you reckon James would lend us his dog?"

"Have you lost your marbles, cobber? What would we want with that little mutt anyway?"

"Gus said we need to find an advantage."

"I think I know what you're thinking. But we'd never get away with painting stripes on Howard. People would twig he's too small to be a proper Tasmanian Tiger."

"Gawdsake." Oodles sucked on his pipe once more and mumbled, "Give me some credit. That'd be fraud."

He puffed his cheeks and blew out a series of smoke rings. "But do you think anyone would know if a scat came from a small dog or a larger Tasmanian Tiger."

"What's a scat?"

Oodles looked at him oddly. "What do you think it is?"

Wish-Wash thought about it, then screwed up his face as it dawned on him. "You must be flamin' joking! Who'd pay good money to see a piece of dog shit?"

"You're right. But what if they didn't know it came from a dog? What if they thought it came from a Tasmanian Tiger? And what if they thought it came from around here? And what if it was fresh? Meaning there could be a real live Thylacine in this neck of the woods? Wouldn't that be the kind of advantage Gus said we needed?"

"Wouldn't that be fraudulent, too?"

"Not if we didn't actually watch Howard. I wouldn't want to watch, would you?"

"Of course not."

"There you go. If we happened to come by a scat . . ."

"That we reasonably assumed had come from Jimbo's dog?"

"Yeah, but we couldn't be absolutely sure. And neither could anyone else peering at it through a glass cabinet. We wouldn't even have to lie. All we'd say was it might be a Tasmanian Tiger scat or it might not be. *Judge for yourself, folks.* You'd be famous again."

"Me?"

"Of course you. It's gonna make a way better story if the same man who saw a Tasmanian Tiger in the High Street all those years ago is the same bloke who finds the scat this time. Don't you want the Professor to succeed?"

"Course I do. But I'm not so sure about this."

"Remember how the journos hung on your every word last time. Some people round here doubted you but no one could prove you wrong. It was your word against theirs. And when you think of it, Doggie Dougall might have done you a favour."

Wish-Wash puffed out his chest. "You really think that?"

Then his mouth dropped again. "The way I see it, he could of proved I was right and had a share of the reward. I did see one, honest."

"Who am I to doubt you? If anyone's going to see a Tasmanian Tiger walking along the High Street at three o'clock in the morning, it's gonna be a bloke who's just been roused awake from his kip in the bus shelter."

"I was already awake. No amount of pages from the local rag could keep me warm that night."

"I imagine it was worth it. You had much more than your 15 minutes of fame."

The memory filled Wish-Wash with warmth. "I did, didn't I?"

"And you can have it again. All you have to say is: *Wow, look what I found in the High Street?* Paddy would put it on display and, bingo, there's his advantage."

TWENTY-SIX
SEEING A MAN ABOUT A DOG

WHEN OODLES first came to Windy Mountain, he had never seen so many dogs in one place. Townsfolk had to be careful walking on the High Street if they didn't want to slip in something nasty.

It rarely happened these days.

Once in a while James did miss a bit. But credit where credit's due. If Howard as much as farted, the super trooper was usually on hand with his pooper-scooper.

Oodles remained amazed how James had ever got a by-law through council forbidding normal citizens to own dogs. But he did. Now only the present or a past mayor was legally allowed to keep a canine.

The new law had allowed people to keep their dogs until they died. Oodles had benefited from that small mercy. He had owned a Great Dane called Raj.

But Howard was now the only dog left in town, and Oodles and Wish-Wash were on the way to borrow him.

"What if he says no?" Wish-Wash said as they walked.

"We're not going to tell him the *real* reason we want to borrow him, old mate."

"Aren't we?"

"Of course not. We'll just tell James we feel so bad about what's happened we'll try to make it up to him by taking Howard for walks."

"And you reckon that'll work, do you?"

"We won't know until we try."

"We'd probably have a better chance if we had ever offered to take him for a walk previously."

They reached the mayor's flash estate and Oodles opened the white picket gate.

James must have been peering out of a window because when Oodles and Wish-Wash went up the steps he was standing at the front door of his unit like a guard dog — though with more sneer than snarl.

"You chaps have a cheek coming here after what you said to me," he barked.

"We were only trying to make you see sense about the shares," Oodles said.

James stood blocking the doorway.

"It's OK, we don't want to come in," Oodles said. "We've actually come to make it up to you. How would you like it if we started taking Howard for walks?"

James bared his teeth. "You know you have to be a mayor or a former mayor even to walk a dog in this town. That is the law."

"We're just trying to offer you an olive branch," Oodles said. "No one would see us — we'd walk him in the dark. And we'd clean up after him, I promise."

"Sorry, I cannot possibly sanction that. Even more so when it is the likes of you two degenerates."

"Degenerates?" Wish-Wash said. "That's a bit flamin' harsh."

James pointed a shaking hand at Oodles. "When Clarence had a dog, it left the biggest droppings in town up and down the High Street. And do not tell me he has changed? You know what he is doing to the bench in the High Street. You said it yourself. He's a vandal!"

He turned his finger on Wish-Wash. "And you? We all know how you used to live!"

———

"So what do we do now?" Wish-Wash said as they trudged despondently back towards the bench.

"Buggered if I know," Oodles said. "But we have to come up with something though. We can't leave the Professor in the lurch."

It was starting to rain lightly again and neither man had an umbrella.

"Stop for a sec, please, cobber." Wish-Wash pulled a striped handkerchief from his pocket and tied knots in the corners before placing it on his head.

"Gawdsake! Do you realise how dicky that looks?" Oodles said.

"I don't care how it looks as long as it keeps me dry."

"And that will keep you dry, will it?"

"Drier than you."

When they reached the bench again, the rain had stopped but the wood was glistening with wetness. Little puddles of water had settled between the patches of flaking paint, and some of the notches had become mini-swimming pools.

Oodles reached into his pocket and produced a crisp, white hanky, which he carefully unfolded before wiping down a portion of the bench.

Wish-Wash watched him sit down, then pulled a face as he sat down on the wet end and the water began seeping through. "If only we could get our hands on another legal dog?"

"What did you just say?" Oodles looked at Wish-Wash and broke into a grin. You'd think the theory of relativity had just been relayed to him. "I don't know where it comes from, but sometimes you have these streaks of brilliance."

Wish-Wash scratched his knotted-handkerchief hat. "Do I?"

TWENTY-SEVEN
SEEING A MAN ABOUT ANOTHER DOG

"Where are we going?" Wish-Wash said as he struggled to keep up.

Oodles kept striding on, but turned his head. "We're going to see a man about a dog."

"I thought we had already done that, and the answer was no."

"This is another man, another dog." Oodles stopped and let Wish-Wash catch up. "Strewth, it was your idea!"

"So you keep saying, cobber. But I think you need to explain it to me."

"Two words: Peter. Rowbottom."

"You're joking, aren't you?" Wish-Wash pulled back the sodden fabric at the back of his pants. "'Bumface' is flamin' cat crazy; he doesn't even have a dog."

"But he's entitled to own one as a former mayor." Oodles looked at him oddly.

Wish-Wash realised Oodles was zeroing in at the top of his head, and remembered he was still wearing the hanky on his head.

"I know what you're thinking, cobber. Yes, the rain has stopped but those clouds still look threatening."

"It's not that. It's just that I used to have a hanky just like it. Blue and white stripes, frayed at the edges."

"What happened to it?"

"I threw it out. Katy insisted on taking away a whole garbage bag of old clothes."

"She didn't take them to the Slutz Plains Op-Shop, did she?"

Oodles shrugged.

Wish-Wash yanked it off his head, stuffed it in his pocket and started walking, trying to put the thought out of his mind. It was one thing buying second-hand clothes, it was quite another matter when you knew where they had been.

He thought instead about Peter Rowbottom and James Northan. Everyone knew they had never got on.

James was born with a silver spoon in his heterosexual mouth and thought he had a divine right to become mayor, which he managed to do for nearly 30 years.

But Rowbottom rose through rough and tumble union ranks, door knocked for state Labor politicians, got himself elected on to school boards and on to the show committee, and built his profile up until the day he was voted on to the council as the first openly gay man to gain office in the municipality's history.

In just his second term, he was elected Deputy Mayor, a position he held for the next 10 years, much to James's chagrin.

When James proposed the banning of non-mayoral dogs from Windy Mountain he probably didn't expect much resistance from his deputy.

But James was livid when Rowbottom opposed the motion on behalf of his dog-loving constituents. How dare that mincing feline-lover stand in the way of civic progress!

Rowbottom said he had never heard anything so utterly ridiculous as the proposed by-law.

"You would soon change your tune if you knew one day you could be among the chosen few," James had hit back.

"Me? With a dog? You must be joking."

Heaven knows how the motion passed! But it did.

Rowbottom, of course, did become mayor. After James had his breakdown, he was the right person, at the right place, at the right time. He was the first mayor of Windy Mountain not called Northan.

———

When they crossed the road and walked along the footpath alongside Doggie Dougall's house, Wish-Wash screwed up his face.

"Gawdsake," Oodles said "Doggie's probably not even home."

Wish-Wash nodded towards a petite dark-haired woman, who was pegging out washing on the rotary hoist in the yard.

"Looks like he's got himself one of those young Asian brides," Wish-Wash said.

"What makes you think that?"

"He's just the type, isn't he? I've never seen her before, have you? Who else would she be? At his house? At his washing line. Hanging out his Y-fronts."

"You do know if the wind changes, your face will stay like that?"

When they reached Peter Rowbottom's place, the front gate was open.

"That's careless," Oodles said, as he went ahead towards the front door.

"Not really. I wouldn't waste my energy either," Wish-Wash said. "Even if Bumface bothered shutting the gate, all those cats of his would just jump over it go to stalk native birds in someone else's garden. That's what cats do. As well as sleep and make people sneeze."

Oodles pressed the doorbell and turned. "Just let me do the talking, old cock. Look, I know you don't get on with cats and vice-versa. All I want you to do is to sit quietly and nod from time to time."

When Rowbottom opened the door, he looked them up and down like he was metaphorically arching his back at the same time.

"Can we come in?" Oodles said.

"I suppose. I was just about to cook a soufflé. Do you want something to eat?"

"No thanks, this won't take long, Pete," Oodles said.

They were ushered into the living room.

Rowbottom sat down and motioned for his visitors to do the same. "Just move Tiddles out of the way, Clarrie. He's only pretending to be asleep in order to make you feel guilty about moving him."

"How do you know he's thinking that?" Wish-Wash said as he sat down opposite. "He's a flamin' cat." He pointed with one hand. "He's probably got an IQ similar to that red cushion there." He pulled out the soggy hanky with his other hand and blew his nose like a trumpet.

Rowbottom glared at him.

Oodles cut in. "What Wish-Wash means . . ."

"Is that you really need a dog," Wish-Wash said, putting the hanky back in his pocket.

Now Oodles glared at Wish-Wash.

"A dog is the last thing I need." Rowbottom glanced down at Tiddles, who had jumped from Oodles's chair into his lap. "Remember what this town used to be like? You couldn't walk down the street without getting something disgusting on your shoe."

"But you opposed the dog ban?" Oodles said.

"Yes, but mainly to stick up for the underdog." Rowbottom laughed at his pun. "And to annoy James Northan."

"You succeeded with that." Oodles laughed, too. "But don't you want to annoy him even more?"

"By getting a dog? You must be joking. What would I do with a dog? I'm retired."

"You'd have lots of time to walk it, then." The comment came from Wish-Wash and this time he was caught in a crossfire of glares.

"What Wish-Wash means is: you wouldn't have to walk it at all. We'd take care of that, wouldn't we, Wish-Wash?" Oodles turned and winked at the other old man.

"Now you mention it, I suppose we would," Wish-Wash said. "And we'd pick up its poo."

"Really?" Rowbottom look stunned. "You'd do that?"

"Of course," Oodles said. "You wouldn't even have to feed it. We'd do that."

"And we'd kennel it," Wish-Wash said. "Not me personally," he added quickly. "The pub has a no-pets rule. But it could be kept at Oodles's and the Professor's place."

"The Professor?"

"Professor Paddy O'Brien, the new bloke running the Tasmanian Tiger Museum," Oodles said. "He's Irish, which is another thing James doesn't like. So you'd really be twisting the knife."

"I would, wouldn't I?" Rowbottom gazed into space and a smile came to his face. "So this Irishman wants a dog, eh?"

"He doesn't know anything about this," Oodles said. "I have no idea if he wants one, but he sure needs a dog."

"Why?"

"You don't really need to know that," Oodles said. "All you need to know is you'd be annoying James."

"I don't know." Rowbottom bit at a fingernail. "I'm not sure it'd be legal for me to own a dog, which actually lives somewhere else."

"No one would have to know what its living arrangements were," Oodles said.

"Surely this Irishman would," Rowbottom said.

"Let me worry about that, Pete." Oodles picked at the armrest. "All we need from you is your consent. Let us take care of the details."

"I don't know. I'm 77 and I've got through my whole life without a dog. What would my cats say?"

Wish-Wash planted his face in a palm. "You really have lost it, Bumface! First we have thinking cats, now we have talking cats? Christ Almighty!"

Oodles rolled his eyes.

Rowbottom stiffened and woke Tiddles, who promptly jumped down. "Did you gentlemen come here just to insult me?" Rowbottom said. "Don't think I don't know what people say about me? Just because I like cats."

Oodles could tell by Rowbottom's change of tone the cause was now lost, and braced himself for what came next.

"You can just find yourselves another ex-mayor," Rowbottom said.

TWENTY-EIGHT
BIRTH OF A PLAN C

PADDY PUT down his paintbrush when Oodles and Wish-Wash came into the foyer, and ran a hand over his smooth chin.

"Who's this new bloke?" Oodles said to Wish-Wash, who was trailing behind again. Then he turned back to Paddy. "What did you think of Gus?"

"I think I lost my ponytail for no good reason."

"Don't be so quick to judge," Oodles said. "I wouldn't say it was a complete waste of time. At the very least, Gus has made you look quite respectable. But he's also given Wish-Wash and me an idea."

"Only an idea, not an actual plan? I can't stop thinking how that oily Dutchman is going to get the last laugh." Paddy kicked at the wall with his right foot. "I don't even know why I'm bothering to waste my time doing this work."

Oodles scowled. "What did that achieve? First your hand, now you have paint on the end of your shoe and a spot on the wall you'll need to paint again. I told you: Wish-Wash and I have an idea, we just have to figure out how to get it done."

"Easy for you to say. You've got nothing to lose."

Wish-Wash's face reddened. "You're probably the flamin'

one with the *least* to lose, Professor. Oodles and I don't get to leave here when it all looks too hard to manage."

Paddy raised his palms. "Sorry. I was out of line. It's just it's been such an awful day. First Gus. Then I have to give up my beard and ponytail, and nobody will tell me why. Then I ask the hairdresser out and she knocks me back."

Oodles blew out his cheeks. "I knew there was something I should have told you."

"What?"

Oodles shot him a look that could have snap-frozen hot chillies. "You'd be well advised to give that young lady a wide berth."

"Why? She's lovely."

"Underneath she's a simmering mess, old son." Oodles said. "She went out with Roger Riley for years. But he died in a hunting accident five years ago, a week before their wedding was scheduled."

Oodles's eyes kept burning into Paddy. "I don't know how Katy manages to keep up such a brave face?" he said. "Anyone else would struggle to carry on." He finally blinked and broke into a smile. "But, look at you, she's given you a bonza haircut." He turned to Wish-Wash and raised his eyebrows.

Wish-Wash took the cue. "Jimbo might like you better clean-shaven like this."

"You think?"

Wish-Wash shrugged. "Probably not, come to think of it. Your Irish accent is the big problem. If that dog of his started talking one day and it had a lilt, I reckon he'd have it locked up as an illegal immigrant."

Oodles's eyes widened as he looked at Wish-Wash. "What did you say, Einstein? Gawd, I've never felt like kissing you before!"

TWENTY-NINE
A FIST FULL OF DOLLARS
THURSDAY

OODLES usually only backed his pale blue ute out of his garage far enough to wash it with the hose and buff it until it was as shiny as the day he bought it in 1995.

But today, dressed in his best overalls, he backed it all the way past the gate, turned towards town, and drove it down the hill with a grind of gears and a puff of smoke.

A minute later he stopped outside The Applecart and tooted his horn.

He jumped when Wish-Wash immediately opened the door. "Gawdsake, are you trying to give me a heart attack now?"

"It's not my fault you didn't see me waiting, cobber. You did say to be out here by eight o'clock." Wish-Wash slammed the door shut.

Oodles shook his head as he watched Wish-Wash buckle up. The big oaf was dressed in a thick yellow jumper and was wearing lime green gumboots. He was clutching his folded-up red umbrella.

"Are you expecting bad weather?" Oodles turned the ignition key and pulled on to the road. All ahead was blue sky.

"I still don't know where we're going, do I? Or why?"

"I just didn't want you to blab it to everyone at the pub last night. But I can tell you now. We're driving to the pound in Launceston to buy Paddy a dog."

"To Launceston? All that way with you driving! Do you want to get us both killed?"

Oodles shook his head. "You know I'm a very careful driver."

"I know nothing of the sort. What I do know is you lost those demerit points for speeding."

Oodles held up four fingers on his left hand, as he steered with his right. "Strewth! That was four years ago. Count them! I've got the points back now."

"How do I know you haven't lost more?"

"Unlike you, I don't lie."

"I resent that."

"Granted, you don't tell the whoppers you used to tell. But you've never really been able to put the brakes on your imagination, have you?"

"You just worry about putting your own brakes on. I'm still trying to process how we can even buy Paddy a flamin' dog. How can we do that when Jimbo said no and Bumface said no? We'd be breaking the law!"

"We'll have to keep our dog hidden, that's all. If you hadn't put your big foot into it, I reckon I nearly had Peter Rowbottom." Oodles took his left hand off the steering wheel again and held up his outstretched forefinger and thumb. "I was this close."

Oodles shook his head again as the car built up speed. He reached into his pocket and pulled out a roll of notes tightened with a rubber band, which he handed to Wish-Wash.

"What's this?"

"What's it look like?"

Wish-Wash gasped when he peeled off the rubber band. "I didn't even know they made $100 notes?"

"Dogs aren't free these days, old mate, so this is the rainy day I've been saving for. I would have chipped a bit more but bugger if I can remember where I hid the rest of it."

"Well, don't go ask me to contribute. You know I don't have any savings."

"Don't worry about it. You came up with the idea."

"Did I?" Wish-Wash scratched his head. "When?"

"When you got talking about illegal immigrants yesterday."

Cleared land turned to bush on both sides of the road as the car headed towards Launceston.

"Irish convicts weren't the only group the English brought to Van Diemen's Land," Oodles said. "The First Fleet had dogs aboard and so did virtually every convict ship thereafter."

Wish-Wash shook his head. "Is there no limit to the mindless trivia bouncing around your head?"

"All we're doing is just following a great British tradition of bringing illegal immigrants to the town. The only difference is that in our case our illegal immigrant will be a dog."

The old men fell into silence.

Oodles broke that silence about halfway into the hour-long drive.

"Strewth! Where did you think we were going? Antarctica?"

"No idea. If I had known we were intending to break the law though, I probably wouldn't have come at all."

"It's not like you've never broken the law before!"

"You can't count all my drunk and disorderly charges. They went with the job."

More silence. More bushland whizzed by.

On the outskirts of Launceston, Wish-Wash piped up again. "You do realise we don't really know anything about the young bloke we're putting our necks on the line for."

"Sure we do. He's trying to save the museum that is so important to you."

"But what do we really know about him? I've never heard someone swear so much."

"You've got to give him credit for trying really hard to break that habit. The least you can do is support me in supporting him."

"You have a hide saying that! Remember who went to the museum first to lend a hand?"

"That doesn't mean you have a monopoly on liking the young bloke. Unlike you, I never had a son."

Wish-Wash bow his head and pinched an eyebrow. "Please don't start on about that again?"

THIRTY
SPEAK OF THE DEVILS

WHEN PADDY WALKED into the Wind Tunnel Cafe about 4pm Wendy took one look at him, put two fingers to her mouth and filled the tiny room with a wolf whistle.

"So you've let Katy have her way with you already, Professor?" The other two customers roared with laughter, and Paddy's face burned.

He sat down at the other table, which looked like it had just been vacated. Two empty cups with spoons and saucers sat either side of a teapot dressed up in a green tea cosy, and someone had left a puddle of tea on the table surface.

Paddy looked up when a bell tinkled and a familiar face walked through the door.

Jaysus, it was only Katy McDonnell!

He just hoped she hadn't heard Wendy.

He stood up, sidestepped around to the other side of the table and pulled out a chair. "We meet again, Katy. Can I buy you a coffee?"

Katy was wearing an orange cotton dress, and had her hair tied back. "I don't drink coffee, remember? But you can buy me a tea in a takeaway cup if you like."

Wendy stepped towards them holding an empty tray. "Sorry love, we're all out of takeaway cups. So you'll have to sit down if you still want a cuppa." She started clearing the table and loading everything on to the tray. "I'll just fetch a cloth."

Just as Paddy was thinking what a sensitive soul Wendy must be under that rough exterior, she winked at him and said loudly, "I'll also fetch a pot of tea. Shall I bring out some romantic candles, too?"

Then she backed her way through the swinging doors into the kitchen.

Katy sat down and sighed heavily. "She's always doing this to me."

Paddy put on his sombre face. "I'm very sorry for your loss."

Katy looked at him, puzzled. "My loss?"

"Oodles told me how your fiancé died in a hunting accident? I understand perfectly how the memory is still raw, even after all these years."

"He told you that? And you believed him!" Katy rolled her eyes. "Between Wendy wanting to marry me off and Oodles wanting to always protect me . . . " She sighed again. "Oodles thinks it's his job now my father's gone to vet potential suitors?"

Paddy lifted his head. "He made it up?" He frowned. "Why would he do that?"

Katy shrugged. "I think he was a chivalrous knight in a past life. He'd lock me up in a chastity belt in a tower if he could. The thing is I already live in a tower, if you can call a flat above the salon a tower."

She sighed. "My big worry right now is what people will say when they hear we're sharing this table?"

Paddy looked over to the other two customers, who were engaged in conversation at the other table. That left Wendy as the only other witness.

"Only three people have seen us," he whispered.

"You don't know how the rumour mill works in this town. Have you ever seen how fast a bushfire moves?"

Paddy shook his head. He couldn't care less about what people said. It was what Oodles had said that was foremost on his mind.

Wendy came back with a tray carrying a teapot, two cups, saucers, spoons and a cloth.

"I didn't mean to embarrass you, Professor. When I asked if you had let Katy have her way with you, I was talking about you becoming a bushranger. Your missing beard is a dead giveaway, isn't it? I wouldn't want you to think, love, I'd been peeping through the mirror above your bed?"

Paddy felt more heat rise to his face.

"No need to feel embarrassed, love." Wendy looked down at the dirty surface, figuring out the best way to tackle it. As she wiped, she said, "We know it wasn't you who put the mirror up. But you can't keep a thing like that a secret in a town this small. Can you Katy?"

Wendy stood back and examined the table, which was glistening with only a thin veneer of wetness now. "Daisy Rowbottom just left with that old priest, Father O'Boring. He came in first and ordered a pot of tea, then she arrived a few minutes later and sat down opposite him and asked for another cup. Between them, they made a right old mess. Old people!"

Paddy looked up at the blackboard on the wall. All it said was, TODAY'S SPECIAL: PIE. ASK.

So Paddy enquired. "What kind of pie is on the menu today?"

Wendy looked at the sign and sighed. "My lazy lump of a hubby was supposed to change that a good two years ago."

"So no pies?" Paddy said.

"Not unless you want to cook them yourself."

"You don't do anything sweet?"

Wendy put her hands on her hips and smiled. "Feel free to lick the table before it dries. I've never seen someone try to put so much sugar in his cup than that old priest. No wonder it overflowed."

Wendy disappeared back into the kitchen.

"What makes her think I've become a bushranger?" Paddy whispered.

"Oh, that? It's a bit of an in-joke." Katy sighed. "Wendy's sense of humour can take some getting used to."

Paddy had been cleaning and painting like a crazy man since 7am and this was his first break for the day. "You haven't seen Oodles or Wish-Wash today, I suppose?"

"Come to think of it, no," Katy said. "Normally they're almost permanent fixtures on that bench. If they're not there, you'll generally find them drinking tea and dunking biscuits here in cafe."

"They didn't turn up to help me today."

She sounded surprised. "Helping you with what?"

"Getting the museum ready to open tomorrow morning."

She blew out her cheeks. "Tomorrow? What's the big rush?"

"The area manager is giving me two weeks to make a go of the place, otherwise he's closing it down."

"Wow, that's tough."

"Yeah. I could have done with the extra sets of hands today."

Katy looked up at a man coming through the door. "Speak of the devils," she said. Oodles led Wish-Wash in.

Oodles looked taken aback to see Katy and Paddy together but after a moment of hesitation he doffed an invisible hat. "Thought we'd find you here, Paddy, because the museum was all locked up."

Wish-Wash looked happier than his yellow jumper. "Wanna come and see the surprise we have for you in the back of Oodles's ute?" he said.

Both Paddy and Katy rose from their seats but Oodles motioned for Katy to sit back down. "Just Paddy, sorry sweetie. Secret men's business."

THIRTY-ONE
A LONG WAY FROM DUNMANWAY
THE BIG DAY ARRIVES

THE UNKEMPT IRISHMAN was straddling a high stool behind the counter at five minutes past nine waiting for the first customer.

Oodles and Wish-Wash were standing on the other side of the foyer. Paddy had requested the old men's presence in order to make the grand reopening look busy.

Oodles was wearing his best overalls again and Wish-Wash was dressed in a body shirt that hugged the contours of his stomach and was very nearly the same shade of green as his trousers.

But Paddy knew he wasn't looking his best. His bloodshot eyes matched his red shirt-sleeved shirt that was only partly tucked in. He had tossed and turned all night wondering why Oodles had thought it necessary to lie about Katy. So he had been short-changed on sleep. He had now straightened the name tag he had pinned on upside-down but he felt a bit wobbly perched on that stool.

When the door was pushed open, he looked over to the old men in surprise and they looked more surprised than him.

———

"What's he doing here?" Wish-Wash whispered when Father O'Boring hobbled to the counter on his walking stick.

Oodles was puzzled, too. "Perhaps he's changed his mind about the bet."

A few minutes later, Daisy Rowbottom arrived.

Oodles whispered to Wish-Wash: "What's *she* doing here?"

———

"Oh, hello Father," Daisy said when she saw Father O'Rourke leaning on the counter deep in conversation with Paddy.

The priest turned and gave her a big smile. "Morning to ye, Miss Rowbottom. I didn't know ye were interested in Tasmanian Toigers?" He nodded towards Paddy. "Have ye met the Professor?"

She examined his face to make sure the man behind the counter really wasn't Moose Routley, then leaned across to shake hands. "Welcome to our town. Professor."

"Call me Paddy."

"I'm Daisy Rowbottom." She nodded towards a vase on the counter. "Nice roses."

"My man Wish-Wash thought they'd give the place a noice welcoming feel."

She looked around and saw Wish-Wash and Oodles on the other side of the room, and tapped the priest on the top of his left arm, which made him look, too.

She smiled. "Wish-Wash hasn't changed his ways then."

Paddy smiled back. "We used to have a swear jar where that vase is on the counter. It's gone, so I guess he thinks I have kicked the habit."

"So, where are you from, Paddy?" Daisy asked.

"Dublin."

"Oh, like Father O'Rourke?"

Father O'Rourke looked at her, perplexed. "I tought ye would have known I'm actually from County Cork, Daisy. I come from Dunmanway, a little town west of the city of Cork. Cork isn't that far from Dublin but it's half a world away, it is." He winked across the counter. "I'm amazed Paddy can even understand me."

Paddy shook his head. "Your accent isn't the thickest I've heard out of Cork."

"It's kind of you to say tat. Some folk around here aren't so forgiving," Father O'Rourke said. "Dat's always a surprise to me, given I've been here so long."

"How long exactly?"

Father O'Rourke laughed. "Some of the cheeky buggers around here tink I came here as a convict. But transportation to Tasmania ended in 1853 and God's truth is I've only been in this state for 68 years."

Paddy gasped.

"And dat's how long I've been copping it about my accent," the priest said. "So ye don't know how glad I am to have another Irishman in town to share the burden and talk craic with."

Father O'Rourke's accent grew thicker as he spoke.

"Do you get home much?" Paddy asked.

Father O'Rourke shook his head. "No point. I don't know anyone there any more. I did go to France on holiday a couple of years ago, but dat's as near as I got."

"Parlez vous francais?"

"Oh, a few words — not dat they understand me there either."

"Your jacket looks like Irish tweed?"

"Oh dis?" The old priest pinched at the fabric. "It's not mine. It's one of the tings ye come to get used to living in a nursing home. Ye send yer stuff away for dry-cleaning, ye get someone else's clothes back."

Father O'Rourke turned back to Daisy. "Care to tour the museum with me?"

"Why not?" She opened her purse to find her $19.

————

Oodles and Wish-Wash watched the priest and the former nurse walk towards the gallery door. The visitors acknowledged the old men with a nod before disappearing.

"I'll be buggered," Oodles said as he watched the door wobble to a stop. "It's obvious now Father O'Boring didn't come here to talk to us."

"He wouldn't have had a choice if the two of us had bailed him up," Wish-Wash said with a raised voice.

"That's not going to happen now, is it?" Oodles kept staring at the door. "Did you see the way he was looking at Daisy? Strewth, their eyes were virtually holding hands."

Wish-Wash pointed to the door but nothing came out of his gaping mouth.

"I'll eat my hat if either of them are much interested in the Tasmanian Tiger," Oodles said.

Wish-Wash found voice again. "Y-y-you really think he's having his way with Daisy Rowbottom? At his age? Don't you micks have rules against that?"

Paddy walked over to them. "What are you two fellas going on about?"

"Nothing," Wish-Wash said. "We were just giving them a few minutes before we follow them in." He nodded towards the door. "What'd'ya reckon, Oodles? Now?"

Oodles nodded, and they went through.

As they entered the other room, Wish-Wash heard Father O'Boring say, "See, I tol' you it wasn't Moose."

———

Father O'Boring and Daisy stopped at the glass box where the model of the Tasmanian Tiger hunter used to be.

Daisy read the hand-written sign out loud. *"This might be a Tasmanian Tiger scat. It was found right here in Windy Mountain by an anonymous local dignitary."*

They studied the strange exhibit like it was a precious gem.

Wish-Wash smiled with satisfaction as he watched them.

He and Oodles and the Professor had been up to the early hours of the morning urging the dog to produce the goods.

An Irish wolfhound had been on offer at the pound in Launceston but Oodles had decided it was much too big, so they settled on a mongrel which was nearer the size of Howard and would thus give them better cover.

They also bought a bag of raw kangaroo mince. Well, Oodles paid for it but Wish-Wash said he could get his hands on a nest-egg of his own after all, and once he did he'd reimburse him for his half.

They stopped on the drive home to collect bits of fur and feathers in the bush.

When they got back to the museum, they realised they didn't have any dog bowls.

But Paddy found a couple of old mixing bowls in the cupboard under the sink, which he placed near the light pole behind the museum.

The dog sniffed suspiciously at the offering but once he started eating he gobbled with gusto.

The men sat on two decrepit garden chairs and one upturned pot, and waited.

And waited.

And waited.

Whoever heard of a dog with constipation?

But two hours later, the dog was unmoved.

Oodles guessed the bits of fur and feathers they had mixed in with the mince were the clogging culprits, but they agreed these were essential ingredients if they wanted a convincing end product.

The men tried massage.

They put lentil soup into a bowl.

At this point, Wish-Wash said he had to go out.

He returned about an hour later carrying a vase full of roses.

"I thought they'd brighten up the foyer. I'll just take them in." He looked down at the dog. "Any luck?"

"Not yet," Oodles said.

"Where'd you even get flowers from at this time of night, anyway? "Paddy said.

Wish-Wash clasped the vase in one hand and tapped his nose with the other. "That's for me to know, Professor, and for you to find out."

He went inside.

He was in there for a long time but finally returned rubbing his hands. "Still no luck?"

As the clock ticked towards midnight, in desperation they tried making potty-like noises but the only result was that three grown men made themselves look silly.

What finally worked was the simple act of giving the dog a name.

After much debate, they settled on Gough — named after Labor Party stalwart Gough Whitlam, not because they were particular devotees of the left-wing colossus who reshaped Australian culture, but because they knew James certainly wouldn't have been.

The wait had given the old men ample time to tell Paddy about the town's strict dog policy, and emphasise why it was so important to keep Gough out of the public eye.

But the delay also gave Wish-Wash time to get cold feet. He decided there was enough about him in the museum already and he didn't want to go on record as being the discoverer of the scat. He agreed to be known on the sign as an anonymous local dignitary instead.

THIRTY-TWO
THE RUSH BEGINS

"WHY DON'T you fellas call it a day?" Paddy suggested to Oodles and Wish-Wash around lunchtime.

"Are you sure?" Wish-Wash said. "If we leave now the museum will be really empty."

Paddy pointed to the dirty tea cups on the table. "I'll be too busy washing them up to notice we haven't actually got customers."

The old men had consumed a number of pots of tea.

The bright start with Father O'Boring's and Daisy's entrance had ended with Father O'Boring's and Daisy's exit.

Wish-Wash was actually happy to see them leave.

He had seen Father O'Boring giggling over the write-up about him in *The Pick of the Crop*. Rude bugger. The decrepit, old priest knew damn-well he was standing nearby.

"If you're sure, Paddy?" Oodles said.

The Irishman waved his both his hands towards the door in a shooing motion. "Go get some lunch, stretch your legs. Tanks for your support today."

They walked across the road to the bench. Oodles sat down first and the structure leaned a bit towards him. Wish-Wash balanced it when he sat down.

The big man looked left and right, as if he expected to see a surprise. "Is this it?"

"Is this what?" Oodles reached into the top pocket of his overalls for his pipe.

"Is this how far we're going? I think Paddy had somewhere further in mind."

"I'm dying for a smoke. Aren't you?"

"I suppose I am." Wish-Wash dug out his pouch and rollies from his pocket.

———

When a minibus pulled up across the road, Oodles and Wish-Wash felt like they were exhibits in a zoo.

The way the passengers peered excitedly from the bus window, you'd think they had never seen two old blokes sitting on a bench having a smoke before.

"I'll be buggered," Oodles said. "Paddy has got some customers."

"Do you think the Professor would want us to come back?" Wish-Wash said.

"What for? With all of them, the museum will look busy all on its own."

They watched them file into the museum.

All Asians.

Wish-Wash did the arithmetic.

Eleven people. $209. Plus Father O'Boring and Daisy Rowbottom. That took the day's takings to $247.

Not a bad first day, after all.

They finished their smokes and headed off to the Wind Tunnel Cafe to spread the news.

THIRTY-THREE
OLDEN GLOVES
DAY TWO

PADDY COULDN'T HELP but grin when he opened the door for Oodles and Wish-Wash just before 8am.

Before he had the chance to explain why he was so happy, Wish-Wash handed him a bunch of yellow roses. "We saw them from the bench across the road," the old man said.

Paddy told them to come in. "Which visitors did you see?"

"The minibus. Don't tell me there were more?"

"Six more people." Paddy took up his spot behind the counter so he could keep an eye on the door. While he was talking, he tipped the old red roses into the bin and replaced them with the yellow ones.

"What are you doing?" Wish-Wash said. "You would have got a few more days out of them."

"But we've only got one vase."

"Why didn't you say? I can borrow one from next door. I don't even know why a pub has such things."

Paddy shrugged and returned the conversation to the six extra visitors. "They were locals who said they had heard good things about the place from that priest. Apparently, he was really taken by the Toiger scat."

Oodles smiled. "Told you that would be a winner."

"I'm not sure how I'll ever be able to tank you fellas."

"No need," Wish-Wash said. "It's the dog you need to thank. Where is Gough, anyway?"

"I put him in the big shed out the back," Paddy said. "He's out of earshot there."

Oodles grimaced. "You can't lock a dog up in the dark, old cock. Tell you what: I've got an old kennel somewhere in my shed. I'll dig it out this afternoon."

Paddy was distracted by what he saw over Oodles's shoulder.

Two men were at the door and they were carrying cricket bats. Oodles turned, too, and looked skyward when he saw them.

Paddy stepped towards the gate in the counter. "I'll go and see they want."

Oodles put up his palm to stop him. "No, I'll go. I'm pretty sure they want to talk to me."

———

"Hello Oodles." The greeting came with a whiff of beer breath. "Didn't I tell you to expect me and Gordo to come calling again!"

"Gawdsake!" Oodles's heart started to race again. "Are you trying to intimidate me with those bats?"

"Intimidate you?" Freddy twiddled the bat handle. "You don't get off as lightly as being intimidated. Not after what you and Wish-Wash did what you did at the funeral?"

"You two are nothing but blinkin' thugs."

"Be nice. We just want a friendly chat with you."

Oodles stepped outside and slammed the door behind him. "Why do you need those bats? Are you planning to bash me first, then Wish-Wash gets his turn?"

"Wish-Wash?" Freddy smiled. "Everyone knows *he* hasn't got any money?"

"I told you. I'm not expecting a brass razoo from Birty's will. He would have left anything he had to his son and grandkids."

"Maybe? But maybe not? In any case, you must already have a few bob, Oodles? Did Madge have a life insurance policy?"

"You're just a nasty so-and-so, Freddy."

"Ooh, I've hit a nerve." Freddy exchanged glances with Gordo and laughed.

"You've got another thing coming if you think I'm going to let you extort me," Oodles said.

"I guess we'll soon find out," Freddy said. "Amazing what people will say when they want the pain to stop, eh Gordo?" He eyeballed Oodles again. "Old blokes like you always have money stashed under their mattress."

"You're wasting your time if that's what you think."

"It's hard to ignore the evidence to the contrary, old man. Nice house, nice car, you're often digging into your pocket at the cafe. Do you ever let Wish-Wash pay?"

Freddy grabbed the top of Oodles's left arm and Gordo grabbed the right. "Let's go somewhere a bit more private for a little chinwag, shall we?"

They frogmarched the old man to the back of the building where they heard a yelp coming from the shed.

Gordo cocked an ear. "What's that noise?" he said.

Before Oodles could answer, Paddy appeared around the corner.

"Look who's here?" Freddy said. "The cavalry! Aren't you going to introduce us to your brave friend, Oodles? Is this the big Irish git everyone is talking about?"

———

When Paddy had seen Oodles being forcibly escorted towards the back of the house, he had followed.

"I run this museum, fella," he said.

Freddy swished his cricket bat, making a whistling sound in the air. "Why don't you just bugger off, Seamus, pretend you didn't see any of this."

"My name's not Shamus, and you're the ones who need to go."

Gough barked again, his yap echoing from the shed.

Freddy tutted. "Have you got a dog in there? Naughty, naughty. You do know it's against the law here?"

"You must be hearing things, fella."

"You don't mind if I take a look then?" Freddy started moving towards the door but Paddy blocked his path.

"This is private property."

"Oh, very brave," Freddy said. "Looks like you want some of what Oodles is going to get? Eh, Gordo?"

The other man laughed. He looked familiar but Paddy couldn't place him. He was not as tall as Paddy, but he looked much heavier — especially around the middle.

"So you have some more fellas coming?" Paddy said.

Freddy frowned.

"Well, I can't see you two feckwits being able to handle this on your own."

Freddy's smile turned into a snarl. "Oh, very cocky. You should have left while you had a chance. You and this old bloke against us two? In case you haven't noticed we're the ones with the cricket bats."

Paddy scratched his head. "You know, I think you're roight. We need to even up the odds a bit."

Freddy smirked.

"If you let Oodles go, it'll be two of you against one of me. Give you more of a chance, like."

Oodles's face reddened. "I'm not going anywhere, Paddy. I used to do some boxing, you know?"

"Did you hear that, Gordo?" Freddy said. "He used to do some boxing? Olden gloves, do you think?"

That's the last thing he said for a while because when Paddy lurched forward and hit him with an uppercut, Freddy toppled backwards.

Before Gordo could even raise his bat, Paddy was upon him and hit him on the side of the jaw. The fat man sank to his knees, a steady stream of blood dribbling from his mouth as he bowed towards the ground, his bum crack showing. Then he spat out some bits of teeth. "You bastard," he said.

Freddy staggered to his feet and shaped up.

"Are you fecking kidding me?" Paddy unleashed another flurry of punches which put Freddy back on his backside.

He must have tried to break his fall with an arm because there was an audible crack.

Paddy picked up one of the bats on the ground and twiddled it in his right hand, feeling its weight, before gripping it with both hands like a cricketer about to face up.

Oodles stepped in front of him. "Don't do it, old son. You'll end up in jail."

"Jail? Is that all?" Paddy looked at him in disbelief. "They had the morgue in mind for you."

"Don't lower yourself to their level," Oodles said.

Paddy threw the bat down on to the ground. It bounced between the groaning men.

"This happens to be your lucky day, tanks to Oodles. But if I ever hear you've even raised a finger against this ol' fella, I'll be fecking coming after you — alone."

THIRTY-FOUR
THE SCAT THAT GOT THE CREAM

PADDY HAD SENT OODLES HOME. He was clearly shaken up but Wish-Wash guessed the main reason he had agreed to go was to get away from intense questioning from the Irishman.

Wish-Wash was being evasive on Oodles's behalf now. It was like a ping-pong match. Paddy fired questions over the counter and Wish-Wash returned a cryptic answer from the other side.

Their contest was interrupted by the sound of spitting gravel, and they looked towards the window.

A blue BMW sports car was reversing into a parking spot.

Wish-Wash assumed it was Gus Foot paying a visit. But then he scratched his head. "My mind's playing tricks on me. I thought Gus's sports car was red."

When a woman they had never seen before got out of the driver's side, it solved one puzzle but threw up another question.

What did she want?

Paddy and Wish-Wash looked at each other.

She didn't look like a customer.

She was wearing high heels, a green, pleated skirt and a blue blazer, and was heading for the door.

She came in, and crossed the deserted foyer towards the counter.

"I don't believe it. Looks like I beat the bus here." She extended a hand. "Sally Hopkins, tour manager."

She was about 40, and she had a handbag slung over her left shoulder.

"There was no room for me on the bus," she said. "By the time I walked to my car I thought I'd be at least 20 minutes behind them. Amazingly, no. Perhaps they took a different route here because I definitely didn't pass the coach."

She put the handbag on the counter, opened it, and peered inside. "They'll be thirty-seven of us," she said, her head bowed.

Paddy gasped. "A whole tour bus! How did you know we were even here? We haven't even advertised."

She glanced up. "Word of mouth. We had a small tour stop here yesterday. Koreans, self-drive. They were supposed to drive on up to Slutz Plains to visit the timber museum, but got mixed up. Good thing for you they did, as it turns out, because they came away raving about the place. They were especially taken with the Tasmanian Tiger scat. You're the only Tasmanian Tiger museum I know offering that kind of exhibit."

Paddy forced a smile. "I'm glad they liked it."

"So, what's the entry fee for all of us?" she said.

Paddy started tallying it up on a notepad but became embarrassed by the size of the figure he came up with. "Hmm, let's make it $500 even."

"Deal, Mr . . .?"

"O'Brien. Paddy O'Brien."

"*Professor* O'Brien." This came from Wish-Wash, who was gawking over the tour guide's shoulder.

"Professor?" She looked around at the man in the Hawaiian shirt and smiled. "Oh splendid, that nod to academia will give this place real gravitas."

She turned again and peered back into her cavernous handbag. "My husband says he doesn't know how I find anything in here. But, look, there it is."

She pulled out a cheque book. She dipped into the bag again and came out with a pen.

As she began to write, a bus pulled up outside and the passengers disembarked and headed towards the door.

Mrs Hopkins handed the cheque to Paddy. He counted out 37 green tickets and she disappeared through the IN door with the group.

The foyer was left empty, except for Wish-Wash at the other side of the counter.

"Did that really just happen?" Paddy said.

"Unless we're both having the same dream," Wish-Wash said.

THIRTY-FIVE
DOBBER

Wish-Wash watched Paddy opening cupboards below the counter and shaking his head.

"What are you looking for?"

"The swear jar. It must be here somewhere."

Wish-Wash blew out his cheeks. "I thought you said you liked the flowers on the counter now."

"I do. The blossoms really brighten up the place. It's just that I feel obliged to put a few coins in the jar. I did some swearing outside earlier."

"I never heard a thing."

"But Oodles did, and those two thugs did."

"Those two rotten wasters probably had too much ringing in their ears to have heard any bad language," Wish-Wash said. "And do you really think Oodles cares what you said? You saved him from a beating."

Paddy kept opening cupboards, only to see either other stuff or empty spaces. "You were the one who told me to clean up my act."

"That was different."

Paddy walked through the gate in the counter, and strode

urgently to the other side of the room, where he opened another cupboard.

"You're wasting your flamin' time," Wish-Wash said. "I threw the swear jar out."

Paddy turned around with his hands on his hips. "But it had money inside!"

"How do you think I paid for the kangaroo mince?" Wish-Wash said. "I didn't just scrape it up from the middle of the road, you know? I had to buy it from the butcher."

"You bought it back from Launceston! I thought you said Oodles paid for it."

"He did, but I reimbursed him."

"But why did you toss the jar? It was perfectly good."

"It was only ever flamin' perfect when it had biscuits in it. Anyway, I didn't think you'd need it now you're not swearing any more. How was I to know Freddy and Gordo would come around and you'd suffer a relapse?"

Paddy walked back to the counter. "Got you! How come you know them by name when Oodles says he's never seen them before?"

Wish-Wash clenched his eyes shut. "I'm no dobber, but I suppose they deserve it." He took a noisy intake of air, then opened his eyes. "Oodles knows them both, all right. He was just afraid you might go after them if you knew their names, and make things worse for him."

"Is he roight to be afraid?"

"I was glad to see them get what had been coming to them for a long time." Wish-Wash smiled. "Gordo will probably keep a low profile in the kitchen from now on."

Paddy frowned as he tilted his head.

"He's the fat, blond one who cooks the breakfasts at the Wind Tunnel Cafe. Wendy's hubby?"

"Really? He's cooked my bacon and eggs? Remind me to refrain from cooked food from now on — in case he does something to it."

"Like what?"

"Just trust me, OK?" He stared into the distance. "And who's the other fella?"

"He's a petty criminal named Freddy Cuthbert. Oodles reckons he was probably just going to put the frighteners on him. You never can tell just how far these kind of blokes will go though. Lucky you were around."

"What did they want?"

"Money."

"Does Oodles have money?"

"He has more than I have, but not enough to satisfy those two scumbags."

THIRTY-SIX
BUT WAIT, THERE'S MORE

HALF AN HOUR after she went in, Sally Hopkins emerged from the OUT door and approached the counter again.

"I'm very impressed with your museum, Professor O'Brien." She looked around the foyer. "But where's your cafe?"

"We haven't got one. Is that a problem?"

"Hmm, perhaps not this early in the day. But our experience is people start craving for morning tea after spending any length of time looking in a museum."

"The Wind Tunnel Cafe is along the street," Paddy said.

"That's promising."

"It's only small, though, and I've just found out the cook might be out of action."

"Would you agree to set up a couple of urns in this foyer? Serve decent tea and coffee?"

"I suppose that's possible . . . " Paddy's voice trailed off as he thought about the cost of such a set-up.

She read his mind. "What if we promise to bring three buses a day?"

"You can do that?"

"We can during the high point of the tourist season," Mrs

Hopkins said. "In this industry, though, you really have to make hay while the sun shines. Demand will start falling off in February, and by winter we'll only have one or two buses running for a whole week, so it's advisable to open seven days a week while the going is good."

Paddy exchanged glances with Wish-Wash.

Mrs Hopkins took the pen out of her top blazer pocket, and produced the cheque book from her handbag again.

Paddy craned his neck to see what she was writing on her side of the bench. Had she forgotten she had already paid him?

When she handed it over, his eyes bulged. It was for another $1000.

"That's advance payment for two more buses today. That OK?"

"Of course," Paddy said. "But-but-but what about the refreshments? We can't possibly make it happen that soon."

Mrs Hopkins produced a business card from her bag, put it on the counter, and started to write on the back. "Ring Sam and mention my name. He supplies us with all our catering equipment."

She handed Paddy the card and he examined it and flipped it over.

On one side was the phone number she had written.

On the other side was her name and title in fancy type, and the company's logo.

"I didn't know managing directors ever got to leave the office?" Paddy said.

"I normally don't." Mrs Hopkins said. "But we had a guide who didn't turn up for work today."

THIRTY-SEVEN
ANYTIME, RIGHT?

IT WAS ONLY when he had sent Wish-Wash home for the day and was going through the cash register that Paddy gave Oodles another thought. He wished the old man had been there to see what a raging success the star exhibit had become.

Paddy counted out $1675 — two big cheques, some banknotes and a few coins.

This was going to make that smarmy Van Gogh eat his words. "Does that scat in the glass cabinet look like something produced in 1936, you Dutch twat?" *Billy Gumboots couldn't make it a going concern in two years. What makes you think you could in a few weeks?* Paddy held up one of the cheques. *Well, suck on this!*

He looked at his watch. Nah, it was too early to ring Van Gogh and tell him the good news.

It wasn't too early for the other call he needed to make though. He rang Katy to get her advice, and arranged to meet her the next day.

But the call to Van Gogh could wait.

He'd clean up first.

Paddy started straightening chairs, wiping down every surface, cleaning the bathrooms, and mopping the floors.

It had been a long day, but what a day!

What made the whole thing even sweeter was the dog shite was housed in the same cabinet that had once featured the model of the Tasmanian Tiger hunter, which Van Gogh obviously was so pissed off about losing.

He must remember to tell Van Gogh that!

———

Paddy finished cleaning at nearly midnight. The work had taken five hours, six if you counted the break he took to cook himself a steak and make a salad, then eat it, and wash up.

He wondered how he was going to be able to keep up this pace.

He could see the sense in trading for seven days a week. But Oodles and Wish-Wash at their age couldn't be expected to help keep the place clean and help with the tea and coffee.

Paddy looked at his watch again.

With any luck the gobshite Dutchman would be sound asleep by now. Wasn't it nice of him to leave his card and tell Paddy he could call *anytime*?

Paddy walked over to the land line.

THIRTY-EIGHT
ANOTHER STRANGER IN THE NIGHT

PADDY OPENED HIS EYES. Someone else was coming up the spiral stairs in the dark again!

How long had he been asleep?

Jaysus! Bad enough a burglar might have jimmied the cash register and stolen the day's takings. Now he was coming up to see if anything else was worth nicking!

Paddy rolled out of bed, and grabbed the broom. He now wished he had taken possession of one of the hefty cricket bats. His heart raced, and adrenalin pumped through his body as he tip-toed across the room and hid behind the door again.

Perhaps it wasn't a robber? Maybe one of the thugs was back, hoping to catch him when he was more vulnerable. Or, worse, perhaps the hitman had tracked him down?

The footsteps became louder as the intruder neared the top.

He wasn't creeping; he was stomping like he owned the place.

The sound of footfalls getting louder told him the intruder was now walking up the hall.

Paddy stepped to the edge of the door and raised the broom.

But when a thin, gangly silhouette strode confidently into the room, Paddy decided to watch what he did.

He didn't expect what happened next.

The string-bean figure walked over to the bed, sat down on the edge, kicked off his shoes, removed his shirt, stripped down to his undies and slipped between the sheets.

What was going on?

Paddy reached out and flicked on the light switch.

The man sat bolt upright and yelled. "Moose? You're here already? You frightened the shit out of me!

Paddy stepped over to the bed and raised the broom again. "I'm sick of people thinking I'm that fella Moose. You've got two seconds to tell me who *you* are and why you got into my bed?"

The man relaxed back on to his elbows. "Ah, I can see now you're not Moose. But you're wrong about this being your bed." He twiddled the coloured beads that tied up the end of his beard. "I'm the manager here. Billy Gumboots."

Paddy lowered the broom and gasped. "But I was told you were dead! I replaced you."

Billy shook his head slowly. "They sure didn't muck around, did they?"

"You were *buried* months ago!"

Billy laughed — like a donkey doing scales. "Oh, it wasn't me in that coffin!"

"You faked your own death?"

"I had to." *Hee-haw, hee-haw, hee-haw.* "It was either that, or suffer the real thing."

"How come?"

Billy eyed him suspiciously. "For all I know you could be one of them."

"One of who?"

"The bad guys," Billy said.

"I don't even know what you are talking about."

"Best to keep it that way."

"You can't stay here," Paddy said.

"But I have to," Billy said. "At least until Friday."

"What happens then?"

"I thought everyone knew that?" Billy climbed out of the bed. He had a ring through his left nipple and a big silver, earring drooping from his right ear.

Billy picked up his yellow, striped trousers from the floor and slipped one leg into them, then the other. "I've come back for the 1994 premiership reunion. No one thought to send me an invitation but I reckon they'll be glad to see me, seeing as the winning goal came off my boot."

"I was told your man Moose kicked the winning goal?"

"Technically, that's true," Billy said.

"Either he did or he didn't?"

"It's complicated."

"You're not the first fella to think I was Moose, by the way."

"I wasn't fooled for long though," Billy said. "I ought to have known straight away when you turned on the lights that you didn't have a beard. But the biggest clue was that thing." He pointed, and Paddy realised he was still naked. He reached down, picked up his undies off the floor and put them on.

"I've shared enough showers with Moose to know you definitely aren't him," Billy said. "Christ Almighty, I don't even know why you needed a broom when you have a weapon like that?"

Billy glanced upwards. "Still got the mirror then. Putting it to good use?"

"None of your business."

Billy scanned the room. "I see that streetlight is no longer flickering. But what happened to my posters?"

Paddy shook his head and walked over to a drawer to get

some more clothes. When he turned around, he said, "I would have thought you would have shaved off that beard to give yourself the best chance of not being recognised?"

Billy raised an eyebrow. "If you didn't know who I was, how come you even knew I had a beard?"

"Wish-Wash told me all about it."

"Dad actually noticed something about me that wasn't negative!"

Paddy gasped again. "Wish-Wash never said anything about being your father."

Billy shook his head. "That'd be right. Dave said Dad didn't even come to my funeral. He denied paternity when I was born and he's still in denial. But I'm sure you see the similarities." He turned sideways. "See, same nose. Same style of beard." He kicked up a heel. "See, same big clodhoppers. We both played for the Windy Mountain Tigers in our time with the same number on our backs, too. Number 13."

THIRTY-NINE
THE DAY HE MET HIS FATHER

BILLY GUMBOOTS GREW up as Billy Kretocek, the illegitimate son of a Polish immigrant.

He took to football at an early age.

He had extraordinarily big feet as a child, and the wide-spread verdict was he was like a puppy with big paws who would grow into a whopper.

The worse he got at maths and English at primary school, and the more the other kids taunted him for being different, the more he concentrated on becoming the best footballer he could be.

He became pretty good, too, but he didn't fill out as much as people expected. If only he had been a half a head taller or half a yard quicker, he might have pursued a career as a professional player for a team in the big league. Instead, he turned up at the Windy Mountain Football Club in 1992 and offered his services.

It was a long way from the big time but he had heard the players could expect to return to their lockers after games and find little payments in their shoes, so it was at least semi-professional.

He found a mentor in one of the older players — a tough, nuggety Scotsman named Wee Jimmy McMartin.

But his biggest fan was his mum.

Marta had been so proud when he got his first senior game later that year.

His mother had always juggled three or four cleaning jobs to make ends meet. But the struggle never stopped her from shepherding him towards his dream.

Marta, in the absence of a father, had given him his first kicking lessons in the backyard.

Marta had driven him to games at other schools.

Marta had washed his dirty footy gear for all those years.

And it was Marta who had presented him with new shiny-red football boots on the eve of his first game with Windy Mountain.

"Mamma, you can't afford these."

"Don't you worry about that, darling booy. I've been putting money aside. So throw your other tatty pair of boots away."

Marta was among the meagre crowd for his first game.

Windy Mountain had not won the premiership in 97 years of trying, and none of the locals were expecting anything different that year.

But that didn't stop Marta from turning out fully decked out in the club's colours, and cheering loudly every time her boy touched the ball.

Windy Mountain lost the first game, and the second one. But they won the third match and coach Tiger Kowalski cracked a barrel of beer in the change rooms straight after the game so the players could celebrate.

Billy was still too young to drink but he was thrilled when he found a purple $5 note tucked inside his shoes. It was a big step up from the couple of $1 coins he had found there after the first couple of games.

That's how the season progressed — more losses than

wins, but the team at least showed some promise and attracted a few more fans.

One regular visitor to the ground, however, wasn't even a supporter.

He was the former town drunk and he'd often be found napping beneath some sheets of newspaper in one of the coaches boxes on the boundary when the players arrived for training.

It often fell to Billy, as the youngest of the group, to move him on.

"Get out of here you old soak," was what he said the very first time.

Wee Jimmy overheard it, and later admonished him.

"You sh'dt speak to your father like that, laddie. "

His father? That was news to Billy. His mother had never even told him who his father was but never in a million years did he suspect it was Wish-Wash.

FORTY
THE DOG HOUSE ARRIVES

After finally getting back to sleep, Paddy was awakened again. The room was still dark but someone was rapping on the front door.

He looked at his watch.

For feck's sake.

Billy was sleeping downstairs, so why couldn't he answer it?

Rap, rap, rap.

Paddy rolled out of bed again but this time he pulled on his jeans and shirt.

Rap, rap, rap.

"I'm coming, hold your horses!"

Rap, rap, rap.

As he tramped down the stairs he could see someone's feet through the door every time he circled around.

He also looked down on Billy Gumboots, who was sitting up on his beanbag.

"I didn't want to answer it," Billy said in answer to Paddy's glare when he reached the bottom. "I don't want anyone to know I'm here — especially the bad guys."

"Jaysus!" Paddy said. "If you had moved nearer to the door you could see through the glass who it was?"

"Oh great! And he'd be able to see me, too!"

Paddy could now see exactly who was at the door.

"It's only Oodles," he said to Billy. "I expect you'd know he's hardly one of the bad guys! What he wants at this hour is another matter."

Billy wasn't waiting around to find out. As he started closing the broom cupboard behind him, he said, "He mustn't know I'm here."

Paddy opened the front door and rubbed his eyes. "Oodles, it's five in the morning!"

"I thought it was best to come early so I could avoid Doggie Dougall."

Paddy looked at him blankly.

"I didn't want Doggie to catch me bringing the kennel here. It'd be a bit of a red flag."

"Who is Doggie Dougall and why would he care?"

"I thought you knew? He's the town's dog catcher."

"Why does Windy Mountain have a dog catcher when it's only got one legal dog?"

Oodles started unbuttoning his coat. "Long story."

Paddy blocked his path and stuck his head out the door. He looked left, then right. "So where is the kennel then?"

Oodles pointed to the ute at the kerb. "I'm glad I dug it out of my garage. I had forgotten it's where I had hidden some of my money."

"Haven't you heard of a bank?"

"So are you going to invite me in or what? I could do with a hot cuppa."

"It's, um, too early."

"I think we need to talk."

"Can't this wait?"

"It's about what you did yesterday. I feel I owe you big time."

Paddy held out an outstretched palm. "Nonsense. I was just helping out a friend. Anyway, it looked like you were capable of taking care of the business yourself. I just got in first."

Oodles exhaled noisily. "Don't kid a kidder."

"Wish-Wash told me their names."

"That'd be right! Big mouth!" Oodles started buttoning up his coat again.

"I'm glad he did. Now I know to keep up my guard at the Wind Tunnel Cafe. Last thing I want is that fella messing with my food in the kitchen."

"I wouldn't worry. That's probably beyond the scope of Gordo's limited imagination. That bloke needs someone to put ideas in his head."

"And the other one?"

"Freddy's as mad as a meat-axe. I'm just glad I found my money. It's now in a place he'd never find it. But less about me. What is it *you* want so I can repay my debt of gratitude?"

"Don't be silly," Paddy said. "You got the dog, I'd say we're even?"

"No, I insist that I repay my debt. Besides, Wish-Wash contributed to the dog, too. I don't know where he got so many flamin' one-dollar coins from." He tried to look past Paddy. "Are you sure I can't come in?"

"I'm sure." Paddy lowered his voice. "I've got company, see."

"You sly devil, you. You've only been here a matter of days!" Then he squeezed his eyes shut. "Please tell me it's not Katy?"

"Of course it's not Katy. What do you think I am?" Paddy had to think quickly. "If you really must know, it's a fella."

Oodles's eyes nearly popped out.

"Not like that. Jaysus! If you must know, it's my cousin . . . " He searched for a name and came up with: "Nigel."

"Why didn't you say that in the first place?"

"It's, er, awkward."

"Awkward?"

"Well, um, nobody must know he's here."

"Is he hiding from the law?"

"Yes, that's it." Paddy was glad Oodles was helping him invent his story. "He's overstayed his visa. If the authorities catch up with him, they'll probably put him behind bars. So that's why I need you to keep this a secret."

"Mum's the word." Oodles zipped his thumb and forefinger across his lips.

"Tanks for that. And tanks for the kennel. Can you put it around the back? I'll see you at eight o'clock?"

"Have you forgotten it's Sunday?"

Paddy smacked his forehead. "Of course! You weren't here yesterday when we made the decision to open today. I hope you don't mind. I'll explain when you return."

Paddy started to close the door but Oodles thrust his foot out to stop it.

"Hang on, old son. I can't possibly be here at eight. I've got to go to mass."

"Mass?" Paddy widened the gap. "I never thought of you as a church-going fella."

"Is that a problem?" Oodles withdrew his foot.

"Not at all. It's fine. Really. Wish-Wash said he'd be here to give me a hand early. We'll be seeing you later in the morning?"

"Suppose so," Oodles said. "But why have you decided to o—"

Too late. Paddy had closed the door and Oodles found himself looking at his own reflection.

FORTY-ONE
THE REAL MOTIVE REVEALED

BILLY LOOKED at the tatty armchair and sofa. "You're joking, aren't you?"

"You're the one who said you wanted to stay out of sight. The way I see it, I'm doing you a favour letting you hide in my sitting room."

"I'll go stir crazy sitting in this little room all day with the restrictions you've placed on me." He counted on his fingers. "I'm not allowed to move around. I can't turn the TV on because someone might hear it. I can't even flush the frigging dunny."

Paddy pretended to play a violin, then sat down on the sofa.

Billy sat down on the chair, or, at least, fell into it. "Why did you even have to go and tell Oodles I was here?"

"I did no such thing. I said you were my cousin."

"Like he'll believe that!" Billy wriggled himself up into a more upright position.

"What else could I do? He wanted to come in."

"Now he might want to meet your cousin?"

"I swore him to secrecy."

"Still, he might insist. And he knows what I look like."

Paddy pinched the bridge of his nose. "Relax the cacks, will you? I'm the only one who comes up here so no one will even know you're here if you stay quiet. But you do need to level with me if you want me to keep you in hiding."

"You think I have a death wish?"

Paddy pointed towards the window. "Would you prefer to take your chances out there?"

Billy's voice dropped to a whisper. "What do you know about the owners of this place?"

"Enough to know your name is mud with Henk Van Gogh."

"The Dutchman is still around? I would have thought Mr Biggs might have dealt with him by now?" Billy drew a hand across his throat and made a gurgling noise.

"Really?" Paddy said. "That makes me feel better about the thoughts I had about him."

"Are you just saying that to make me think we're on the same side? How do I really know I can trust you?"

"I'd say you haven't got a lot of choice," Paddy said. "I've already discovered you faked your own death. But if it makes you feel better, I really don't know anything."

"And you're not an undercover cop?"

"Do I look like a guard?" Paddy shifted in his seat. "All I'm trying to do is arm myself with enough knowledge to steer clear of trouble."

"In that case, if I were you I'd get the hell as far away from Biggs and Sons as possible. Ireland might not be far enough. These guys are into some heavy shit."

"Are you just trying to get your bed back?" Paddy said.

"Are you sure you're not with them?"

"I don't even know who *them* are? I'd say you've taken vagueness to a new level."

"OK, but don't say I didn't warn you this museum is just a front."

Paddy tilted his head. "A front for what?"

"Are you sure you want to know?"

"Now you're really testing my patience, you know that?"

Billy closed his eyes for a moment. When he opened them, he said: "Don't say I didn't warn you? They're into people smuggling."

"Jaysus! I thought they were actually into building wind farms, and were only interested in the land here."

Billy lowered his voice further. "That's just a ruse, a rumour *they* spread to cover their tracks. Their real game is to smuggle Tasmanians to the mainland."

"People do that?"

"Too right," Billy said. "Tasmania's economic prospects have never been too flash and people will do anything for a better life. I overheard Van Gogh talking to Mr Biggs on the phone. He said he had hidden the captain's diary in the museum where no one would think to look."

"Let me guess? You found it!"

"It wasn't hard once I knew it was around here somewhere. I found it in a pocket of a mannequin of a Tasmanian Tiger hunter we had on display. It makes for interesting reading. I bet the cops would love to have it."

He looked Paddy in the eye. "You sure you're not a cop? I bet Van Gogh thinks you're a cop. He suspects anyone who's tall of being a cop. He even thought I was a cop at the end. Me! The diary contains details of crossings, names, where they came from, where they went to. The map inside shows where they make landfall in Victoria."

"So that's why Van Gogh was so keen to find the dummy? Where have you hidden it?"

Billy waved a finger. "Oh no. You really think I'm going to tell you that? It's my insurance policy! All I'll say is it's somewhere no one would ever think to look for it."

"Who else knows you faked your death?"

"Just Dave. I couldn't have done it without his help. It's hard to know who to trust though. These guys are serial blackmailers. They plant spy cameras all over the place on the off-chance they might catch someone doing something wrong. If that person turns out to be a cop, a judge or even a librarian who could be useful, they consider they've hit the jackpot."

Paddy rose from his chair. "Look, we'll talk some more later. I have to get downstairs now because we're expecting a heap of customers."

Billy's surprise showed on his face. "How did we suddenly get customers?"

Paddy stopped at the door and turned around. "We have a new star exhibit. A scat."

"A what?"

"A piece of shite that came from a Tasmanian toiger. Recently."

"Recently!" Billy laughed. *Hee-haw, see-haw.* "I'd like to see that?"

"Oh, you can," Paddy said. "If you have $19, I'll show you later when everyone is gone."

"You know I haven't got 19 bucks!" Billy's whisper exploded in volume. "Unless you have life insurance, they don't actually pay dead people."

"How did you afford food, shelter while you were in hiding?"

"My mamma came to my rescue. She was in a right old state when she came home from my funeral. But when she found me on the doorstep alive, I've never seen her happier." He mimicked her: "My boy, my darling boy, you are all not died."

"You shouldn't make fun of your mammy like that."

"I'm just telling you what she said. Anyway, I reckon I could have laid low there and enjoyed her baking as long as I wanted, which is funny because I always had the impression she didn't really like me once I grew up."

"And you had no life insurance?"

"Even worse, I come home to the museum and find out you've not only taken my job, you've thrown out all my worldly possessions."

"Not all of them." Paddy pointed to the bookshelf.

"Do I look like I read books?"

"But . . . "

"Oh, I get it? You thought it was my book collection. Sorry to disappoint you, but it's not."

"If they're not your books . . . " Paddy said, ". . . whose are they?"

"Dave's. Lucky you didn't turf them out, eh? That collection is worth a fortune."

"Dave the undertaker?"

"He's the only Dave I know of around here."

"And . . . and . . . he keeps the books here? Why?"

Billy got up, stepped over to the book case and scanned the middle shelf for a particular tome. He handed it to the Irishman. "What would people think if they saw this one on Dave's bookshelf at his premises?"

Paddy looked down at the motley green hardback in his hands. The book was called *The Body Snatchers* by Jack Finney.

"They'd be barking up the wrong tree," Billy said. "That book has nothing to do with undertakers."

"I thought you said you didn't read books?"

"I saw the movie, which was based on the book, didn't I? Only they called it *Invasion of the Body Snatchers*. It's about aliens from outer space taking over earthlings. Nothing for Dave to worry about, but you know what people are like?"

"So you let him store them here?" Paddy replaced the book.

"Yeah, them and his electric razor. Which reminds me, I didn't see that in the bathroom?"

"He took it the other night," Paddy said. It was falling into place now. "So it was you who gave him a key? He frightened me half to death when he came up the stairs in the middle of the night, just like you did."

Billy laughed. "Dave did that, too?" *Hee-haw, hee-haw.*

Billy wiped the tears from his cheek with a hand. "Did you know this place is haunted? I've heard Colonel Northan makes a terrible racket up here when he's watching TV in the middle of the day."

"Is that so?" Paddy put his hands on his hips. "If you so much as touch that TV set and make a noise, two ghosts will be walking around this place. Since your mammy has been to your funeral once already, I wonder if she'd bother again?"

FORTY-TWO
THE BEGINNING OF THE END

BILLY SLOUCHED BACK on the couch and wondered if Moose was out of prison by now. You could never tell with a bad bloke like that. He might have done something else wrong and be back inside again.

He sure hoped this wasn't the case though and he'd be there on Friday.

If so, Billy hoped to upstage him for a change.

Billy could trace the end of his own sporting career back to the day Moose joined the Windy Mountain Football Club early in the 1993.

People had laughed when he came for the tryout.

Fair dinkum, he just looked like an extra-large hippy with that ponytail swinging down the back of his neck. He ran on to the oval in bare feet, which had the other players sniggering.

Twenty minutes later, none of them were laughing though. He could kick, he could run, and his dead-eye handballs were like bullets.

Coach Tiger Kowalski summoned Moose from the track. After talking to him for a few minutes, he called Billy over, too.

"Billy, meet Moose," Tiger said. The two of them shook hands. "Billy, I want you to lend Moose your boots."

"But coach! I've only got one pair of boots."

Tiger growled at him. "You're always thinking about yourself, not what's good for the team!"

That's how the deal was done. Some deal though!

With Moose spearheading the team, the Windy Mountain Tigers stacked up win after win, and the fickle crowds started growing.

Billy warmed the bench in most games. The selectors thought he lacked mobility in his alternative footwear, a pair of old blue gumboots.

Worse, people started calling him by his new nickname.

Admittedly, it was marginally better than the moniker he had carried through his school years, but he found it embarrassing to see it in print whenever the team was listed in *The Pick of the Crop* newspaper on Friday mornings. 20th man: Billy Gumboots.

———

Moose's heroics ensured Windy Mountain went all the way to the 1993 grand final, and Billy expected to be named on the bench again.

When Moose was arrested two days before the game, Billy got his hopes up.

But those hopes were dashed when Moose was unexpectedly released from jail and seemed set to take the field.

But then came another twist.

Tiger called Billy into the clubrooms an hour before the game. He looked as unhappy as Billy had ever seen him.

"I don't understand," Billy said. "Where's Moose?"

"He's come down with hepatitis. So I'm promoting you into the team. Just don't mess up, OK?"

"Does that mean I get my footy boots back?"

Tiger shook his head. "This all happened so quickly and I have no idea where those boots are. You're used to playing in gumboots, aren't you?"

Billy played a cracker of a game until almost the end.

But no one remembered that. What they remembered were two things:

The local newspaper brought a jersey cow on to the ground during the half-time break. *The Pick of the Crop* was giving the cow away to the person who came up with the best name for her. But nobody noticed her drop a cowpat in the forward pocket.

Billy had a shot at goal just before the final siren. Had he got it, Windy Mountain would have won the match. Most other players would have slipped in the cowpat. But Billy kept his feet, thanks to the sure-footedness of his gumboots. His footwear, however, wasn't designed for kicking the ball. Both a blue gumboot and the ball left Billy's foot at the same time. The ball cartwheeled end-over-end but it fell just short, which meant the Tigers were one lousy yard short of the premiership.

That was the end of Billy's football career. The selectors gave him the tap on the shoulder after the loss. The shame was he no longer had proper boots to hang up because the remained in Moose's possession — which turned out to be a good thing.

The charges against Moose Routley were reinstated, and he was sent to prison. But he returned fitter than ever for the next season and picked up where he left off.

This time he took the team all the way to glory.

And then he went to prison again.

FORTY-THREE
OODLES'S WIFE

PADDY OPENED the door for Wish-Wash at 8 o'clock, and the old man thrust a vase full of pink-and-white speckled roses into his hands.

He then brushed past, and crossed the room to switch on the kettle. "Did anyone tell Oodles the museum is opening today?"

"He will be here later." Paddy looked down at his vase, wondering what to make of it. "He was at the door about 5 o'clock this morning."

Wish-Wash spun round. "Crikey, did he wet the bed?"

Paddy closed the door and strode over to the counter where he put the vase down next to the other one. "He was delivering that dog kennel."

Wish-Wash burst into laughter. "Have you ever seen such a big kennel?"

"I didn't see it at all."

"You didn't? Oodles used to own one of the biggest dogs you've ever seen." *Hee-haw, hee-haw*. He pulled out his hanky and dabbed his weeping eyes. "That kennel will seem like a cathedral to your little mongrel."

Paddy was horrified. "He didn't tell me it was that big."

Wish-Wash took two cups out of the cupboard. "Tea?"

"No tanks, I'm worried now. He never asked for my help. What if he did a hernia carrying it on his own?"

"It'd have to be a major injury to cause him to miss church!"

"I wouldn't have picked him as a fella who went to mass."

"Well, he does, the sentimental old fool. He goes on and on about the clothing choices I make from my favourite op-shop, but he dresses up every Sunday in the vintage suit he wore to his wedding all those years ago. It just keeps getting more shiny around the bum and knees." He shook his head. "The ironic thing is his wife hounded him for years to update that wrinkled suit, but he was too pig-headed to admit he had already outlived it. Now Madge is the only reason he goes to church at all."

"Oodles has a wife?" Paddy's eyes widened. "Why doesn't he bring her around?"

"Bit hard to do, Professor. She passed on nearly two years ago. She got caught in a bushfire that jumped the highway. She was driving back from a bowls tournament with her three teammates. The other ladies managed to get out of the vehicle before it was engulfed, but Madge's seatbelt got stuck."

"That's horrible." Paddy checked his watch. "Look, I want to hear the whole story later, but I have to go out now. Do you mind minding the shop?"

"You want to leave me alone *again*?" Wish-Wash said. "What if someone comes?"

"Take their money. $19 for adults, $10 for children and pensioners."

"But what if a whole lot of people arrive at once? Like a whole bus full of people?"

"Easier. The guide will write you a cheque. We're expecting three busloads through today, at $500 a bus."

Wish-Wash rubbed the side of his neck. "You'd trust me with that amount of money?"

"Why wouldn't I?"

"Nobody else ever has." Wish-Wash nodded towards the cash register. "I haven't got the foggiest idea how that thing works."

————

Wish-Wash saw Katy McDonnell walking towards the front door.

So did Paddy. "Sorry, got to go."

"But . . . " Wish-Wash was too late. Paddy had closed the door behind him.

Paddy and Katy crossed the road and headed towards town.

"What's so urgent?" she asked.

"Let's eat first. Is the Wind Tunnel Cafe open?"

"No, it's closed on Sundays."

"Probably for the best," Paddy said. "I am hungry though."

"We'll have to get some pies from Taylor's Takeaway and take them to the Colonel Richard Northan Memorial Rose Garden. We can sit at the picnic table."

"I hope it's not riddled with holes like the bench across the road from the museum."

"I'll fill you in over breakfast about what's going on there."

The takeaway shop was in sight now as they walked.

"If it's any consolation, the Wind Tunnel Cafe probably wouldn't have been open even if it had been mid-week," Katy said. "Wendy's hubby Gordo is in hospital."

"That so?" Paddy didn't know how much she knew about it but decided to test the water. "Do you know what happened to him?"

"He told Doc Jenkins the rotary clothes line spun around

and knocked some of his teeth out and broke his jaw. But no one believes that."

"Why would he lie?"

"Cooking is not the only thing Gordo does badly. He also keeps bad company and I doubt he's pegged out any washing in his life. Besides, he's not that tall."

Katy got one pie at Taylor's. Paddy got two and would have ordered more if there weren't only three left.

FORTY-FOUR
BUSHRANGERS' WHISKERS

THEY WALKED through the gate carrying their pies in white paper bags.

The picnic table was set back in the park, away from the road.

"How are you going with your old blokes?" Katy said, as she sat down.

"I don't know how I would have coped without them." Paddy noticed the denuded bushes nearby before stepping over the bench seat and sitting down, too. "Should I be worried Wish-Wash keeps bringing me roses though?"

Katy laughed as she took her pie out of its bag. "He's up to his old tricks then."

"I've left him holding the fort back at the museum."

"You're open today?" Katy looked up. Then her shock gave way to a look of astonishment. "And you left Wish-Wash on his own!"

Paddy unwrapped his pie and bit into it. When he had swallowed the mouthful, he said, "You don't think that's wise?"

"I'm not sure he's ever handled money before. What if you get customers?"

"That's the same thing he said."

"I can't believe you're even opening on a Sunday."

"That's what I needed to discuss with you. What do you do when busloads of people turn up on your doorstep?"

"Are you serious? Last I heard you were all doom and gloom, and now you're asking me about busloads of customers!"

Paddy swallowed another mouthful and wiped his mouth. "I was a bit down about it all, wasn't I? But things changed a bit tanks indirectly to your man Gus. The old guys came up with a novel idea, just like he said. That's what all that was about when they came to the cafe the other afternoon."

Katy's face turned white. "It's something dodgy, isn't it?"

"It depends what you mean by dodgy."

"I'm right, aren't I?"

"The less you know, the better."

"Even Gus Foot trusts me with his secret."

"What secret?"

"I thought you would have surely twigged when Wendy called you a bushranger."

Paddy gave her a vague look.

"Why do you think Gus wants all those whiskers? He sends them to the United States, where he passes them off as bushrangers' whiskers. He makes a pile of money from it."

"You said you didn't know what he did with them!"

"I know. Fibbing is my first line of defence. But the cat's out of the bag now. Truth is, I took over from dad when he died."

"Jaysus." Paddy ran a hand over the veneer of new growth on his face. Then he realised what he had just said. "Sorry, I didn't mean to sound insensitive. It never rains but it pours. I just heard that Oodles's wife died, too."

"Yes, about two years ago. Poor Oodles."

"Poor Oodles? Poor you! When did your da die?"

"He died a few months after Madge. But it must have been a terrible time for Oodles because him and dad were best friends."

"Oh, Katy, I'm sorry."

She bowed her head. "Dad used to cut all the beards in this town. People used to call him *Snipper the Bushranger Beard guy* but I never knew why. Even when I worked as dad's apprentice I never, ever wondered why bearded guys were always coming to the shop, and why dad packaged their whiskers into plastic bags and sent it over to Gus instead of making me sweep it up into the rubbish with all the other hair. I must have been thick, really naive."

"So how did you find out?"

"Gus approached me at dad's funeral. He wanted to know if I was OK keeping his little sideline going. I said yes, even though I didn't know what he was talking about."

"Oodles must have known. Why didn't you ask him?"

"He wasn't there."

"I thought he was your father's best pal!"

"He went to the wrong funeral by mistake. He only got to the wake at the pub later and that's when he told me what I had agreed to. I don't mind. I really don't. Aside from honouring dad's memory, it helps my bottom line."

Paddy shifted on his bench seat. "Business not good?"

"It fluctuates. Having the only hairdressing shop in the region gives me a captive market. But when the farmers have a bad season, a lot of kids in this town have to make do with bowl-on-the-head haircuts by mum, and I see a lot of women in the street with grey streaks."

"But it's OK at the moment?"

"Yes and no. I've taken a girl on to help me two days a week."

"I think I saw her when you cut my beard? Purple hair, roight? I saw her twin sister at the takeaway shop, only that one has green hair."

"Vicki has been with me for more than six months now. She's incredibly good at what she does but I can't blame our elderly lady clients being scared of her. Imagine how you'd feel if you were 75 and came in for a blue rinse? I've lost count of the old dears who have taken one look at her purple hair and her nose ring and suddenly *remembered*" — she emphasised the word by raising both hands like quote marks in the air — "they've double booked and have another appointment elsewhere."

"Old ladies do that?"

"It's not like I actually lose their business. I mean, where else would they go? But when they reschedule they are very specific about who they want to do their hair. Me. Not the *punk girl*."

"How do you feel about that?"

"I wear it. It makes it all the harder to keep work up to Vicki, but I feel I have a civic responsibility to provide work for the youth of this town."

"That's very noice of you."

"Not really. It's simple economics. What's the alternative? The town dies because young people have to go elsewhere to find work?"

"So tell me about Oodles's wife?" Paddy munched into his second pie. "Wish-Wash said she was coming home from a bowls tournament?"

"The fire started up in the high country and swept this way so fast, the rural fire brigade was caught off guard."

"Oodles didn't go?"

"God, no. As far as I know, he's never played bowls. When Madge went bowling, he usually went fly-fishing. That's how he cleared his head. It was therapy for him. But he didn't go that day because he had a cold. Just as well, too, because the fire started up that way and he might have been caught in it, too. Madge's car was incinerated when the fire crossed the highway."

Paddy gasped. "That must have been horrible. Wish-Wash said Oodles goes to mass every Sunday to fulfil some kind of promise to her."

"He sure does," Katy said. "And after every time he carves another notch into the bench opposite your place."

"It's him? Really? Why would he do that?"

Katy shrugged. "I'm not a shrink. I probably shouldn't be telling you this, but you're his pseudo employer and it might help you to understand him better. Doc Jenkins prescribed Oodles some medication for anxiety but what he really wants to do is refer him to a professional who will give him some therapy."

"Let me guess? He prefers his own version of therapy."

"You've hit the nail on the head. But he hasn't been fly-fishing since the fire either, and he used to love going bush."

"Can't he be persuaded to go?"

"People have tried. But he has always said no. He reckons he's too busy swotting up for his next pub trivia meeting."

"Really? That's another thing he hasn't mentioned. These old fellas are full of surprises. Did you know Wish-Wash reads science fiction books?"

"I did. And ask Oodles anything that happened before 1962, and he'll probably be able to answer it, as long as it featured in the Encyclopaedia Brittanica that year."

Paddy frowned.

"Quite early in their marriage, Madge bought a full set of those encyclopaedias. It took them years to pay them off and about half that time for Oodles to commit all that knowledge to memory."

FORTY-FIVE
THE NEAR MISS

THE DRIVER WAS LEANING against the front of the bus and blowing smoke rings when Paddy reached the car park of the museum.

This fella wore green shorts and white knee socks, and his enormous nose added a new meaning to middle-aged spread.

"Hiya," Paddy said, coming to a stop. "I'm the manager. You're not going in?"

"I went in quickly, but only to hand over the cheque," the driver said. "To tell you the truth, I'm happy to get away from this group of passengers for a bit. Roger must have had a premonition."

"Roger?"

"Sorry, I didn't explain that well. The bloke who's rostered on to be tour guide phoned in and said he would be late, so I'm doubling up. Just my luck to get a demanding lot though!" His broke into a whiny voice. *"Can't you turn the air-conditioning up? Can't you turn the air-conditioning down? Go faster. No, go slower. Whinge, whinge, whinge."*

He blew out another smoke ring. "Anyway, I saw the inside of the museum yesterday. I doubt it's changed any."

That's when the penny dropped for Paddy. It was necessary to change the scat over each day to keep it looking fresh. But what if repeat visitors detected a difference?

Paddy tried not to let his panic show as he got moving again. "I'd better get inside to see if I'm needed."

Wish-Wash was beaming when Paddy walked through the door.

He pointed to the cash register. "I worked it out. I collected $587 all up: a five hundred buck cheque for the tour bus, like you said, $57 cash for four more adults and $30 cash for three more kids."

"You've done a grand job." Paddy smiled when he saw Wish-Wash's tea mug on the counter next to the cash register, the two vases full of roses, and at least half a dozen rings left by spilt tea. "Heard from Oodles yet?"

Wish-Wash looked at his watch. "Soon, I guess."

"Will we see him across the road first? Katy says he's the one carving notches all over the bench."

Wish-Wash shook his head. "He does that tomorrow when the holiness has rubbed off."

"You've seen him doing it?"

"Sure have. Everyone has. He's the oldest vandal in town."

"That's a bit harsh, isn't it? Katy told me it's all to do with his wife dying?"

Wish-Wash rolled his eyes.

"And Katy says he hasn't been fly-fishing since Madge's death either? You think that's healthy?"

"It is for the flamin' fish."

"Don't you think we should try to get Oodles back up there."

Wish-Wash scoffed. "To Bing Bong Mountain? Even Birty couldn't persuade him."

"You never got into fly-fishing?"

"When I was a kid I knew my way around the bush better than navigating through some stupid school book on the geography of England. When you grow up, though, you come to realise buying your fish from the shop is a lot easier."

Paddy turned and glanced out the front window. The bus driver was lighting up another smoke. "We've had a near miss there. If that fella had decided to come in for another look, he might have noticed the scat that's there today is different to the one that was there yesterday."

FORTY-SIX
DEAD AGAIN

PADDY GESTURED TOWARDS THE STAIRS. "I've just got to go upstairs for a minute."

Wish-Wash slammed his cup down on the counter. "I was about to make myself a brew. What if another flamin' bus arrives?"

"What happened to your new-found confidence?"

"But what if—?" Paddy was already clunking up the spiral staircase, and all Wish-Wash could see were his disappearing legs.

When Paddy reached the closed door, he stopped and listened.

Nothing.

He turned the handle slowly and it creaked open wide enough for him to see in.

Billy was sprawled out on the couch lifeless.

Oh, Jaysus! Had Mr Biggs's henchmen paid a visit? How would Paddy explain finding a corpse of a man who was already supposed to be dead?

The answer came quickly.

Billy's chest was going up and down, and Paddy realised he was merely asleep.

He opened the door wider, tip-toed over and put a hand over his mouth. Billy opened his eyes and tried to talk. "MmMmFFFFMmMn."

Paddy raised a finger on his other hand, and whispered. "At the count of three, I'm going to take my hand away. But you need to be quiet. Understand?"

Billy looked up at him with terrified eyes and nodded.

"One . . . two . . . three."

Billy sat bolt upright. "What the frigging-hell do you think you are doing?"

"I told you to keep your voice down?"

"You scared me half to death!"

"I scared *you* half to death? I thought someone had topped you in my sitting room."

"I was asleep."

"I know that *now*." Paddy rolled his eyes. "How could you fall asleep in broad daylight?"

"You should try kipping on that beanbag downstairs. I hardly got a wink last night."

"What if someone downstairs had heard you snoring?"

"I don't snore."

"How do you know that?"

"Mamma would have told me." Billy paused. "Or any number of the young women who saw their reflection in the mirror above our bed." His smile turned into a frown. "I ought to sue you. That's taken years off my life."

"How else do you suggest I should have woken you?"

"Bacon and eggs is always a nice aroma to wake up to. My mother always used to bring me breakfast in on a tray."

"Go home to your mammy then."

Billy folded his arms. "She lives up in Slutz Plains."

"Is that far?"

"Excuse me for not asking permission to stay in my own flat!" Billy rubbed his eyes and scratched his stomach. "All this talk about food is making me hungry."

"Why didn't you make yourself a sandwich?" Paddy pointed to the kitchen bench where there was a loaf of bread and two cans of sardines.

Billy screwed up his face. "I'm not eating cat food! And God knows what's in that bag in the fridge! It stinks."

"It's kangaroo mince, if you must know. But you should have smelled the fridge you left me!"

"Oh, blame me, why don't you!"

Paddy brightened. "Do you like veal cordon bleu? I've found lots of microwave packs."

"Is that old freezer still out in the shed?"

"You know about that?"

"No way am I eating that muck again. Besides, those packs were way past their use-by dates when I was last here."

"Beggars can't be choosers!"

"Why can't you get me a takeaway?"

Paddy just glared.

Billy held his stare. "*I* can't go, can I? People would recognise me."

"Even if I did want to get you a takeaway — AND I DON'T — where would I buy it in this town on a Sunday?"

Billy pondered this for a moment. "What about a pie from Taylor's?"

Paddy shook his head. "Katy McDonnell and I have just eaten the last three pies in Windy Mountain."

"Katy McDonnell? Let me guess? She cut off your beard for Gus?"

Paddy nodded.

"So you did look like Moose? With your clothes on, at least! Do you reckon you can bring Katy here to cut my beard?"

"What?"

"I need the money. Please."

"I thought you wanted to be incognito."

"She's not going to tell, is she? Not with what we know about her illegal dealings."

Billy tugged at his hippy beard. "I'm skint, and these whiskers are the only things I have to sell."

Paddy slumped his shoulders. "OK, I'll talk to her."

Billy smiled. "I knew you'd come through. Are you and her—"

Paddy cut him short. "No!"

"No need to snap. I was just asking. What about fish'n'chips?"

Paddy looked at his watch. "Taylor's doesn't turn its cooker on for an hour or two. But I thought you were broke?"

"I am. But it's not my problem. If you're going to keep me cooped up here, you've got to feed me until I leave for the reunion on Friday."

"What do you think this is? A hotel?"

Billy reached into his pocket for his wallet and produced a $10 note. "OK, you win — but just this once, and only because I'm really, really hungry and don't want to waste away while I'm arguing with you. But I want the change."

Paddy stared at the blue-coloured note. "You're kidding me! You won't even get a small piece of flake with that."

"Get me ten bucks worth of chips then."

Paddy kept staring at the note. "So, you're not completely broke?"

"I will be when you spend this. In case you hadn't noticed, my earning power has taken a nosedive. It's not like I can grow a beard in a few days, like Moose. Or probably you."

Paddy waved the note away. "Keep your money, Billy. I'll get your takeaway. THIS TIME. But from tomorrow, you can make your own sardine sandwiches, OK?"

FORTY-SEVEN
ROY ORBISON

WHEN HE CLOSED the door to Billy, Paddy heard lots of people talking downstairs. The din became louder as he descended the stairs. Groups of Asian men in suits and ties were standing around jabbering in half a dozen circles in the foyer.

"Here's the boss now," he heard Wish-Wash say to a gesticulating blind man at the counter.

Boss? The old fella had never called him that before.

"I'm the manager here." Paddy extended his hand to the agitated man. "Paddy O'Brien."

"Roger Dykes, tour guide."

Paddy could see now the man wasn't actually blind; he was merely wearing dark glasses and his breath reeked of last night's booze. He was dressed in the tour company's uniform of sky-blue blazer and green trousers. Paddy heard a bus start up, and looked towards the window. The first bus was departing, leaving an empty coach in the car park.

"How can I help you, Mr Dykes?"

The red-faced tour guide looked daggers at Wish-Wash. "Your employee here won't let me take my group into your museum," he said with a shaky voice. "Do you know who these people are?"

"The boss doesn't care who they are," Wish-Wash said. "We don't care if you did come dressed as Roy Orbison. Unless you pay, you can't g—."

Paddy raised a palm to stop Wish-Wash.

"My understanding is we have already paid," Dykes shouted.

Wish-Wash returned the loudness with interest. "No one's paid me," he blurted before Paddy motioned for shush again.

"This is most embarrassing," Dykes said. "My group consists of Chinese businessmen who have come here for a convention, and are seeing some of the sights in their down-time. What must they think? I understood whoever is in charge of our first bus through each morning pays for the whole day."

Paddy looked at Wish-Wash, searching for an explanation.

The front door opened and in rushed Oodles. He was at the counter before the door had swung closed behind him.

He gasped for breath. "Did you hear?"

Paddy raised a palm. "Not now. Please. Let me sort out one crisis at a time."

Paddy turned back to Wish-Wash. "How much did you say you took from the first bus?"

"$500, like you said."

"Did I say that? It's my fault then for not explaining it. Mr Dykes is roight. The arrangement I had with Mrs Hopkins was the guide on the first bus would pay us for the whole day."

Wish-Wash slapped a hand against his forehead. "It all makes sense now." He pointed outside to where the other bus had been. "Big Nose wrote me a cheque for $1500."

Paddy glared at Wish-Wash, hoping he'd get the message it wasn't appropriate to call the driver that name in this company. "I thought you said he gave you $500?"

"Only after I gave the first cheque back to him. I told him he had given me too much."

"What did he say?"

"Nothing. He wrote me another cheque. See." Wish-Wash held it up. "I thought you'd be proud of me for picking that up."

"I am, Wish-Wash. I am. But I think we need to let Mr Dykes and his group into the museum. We can sort this out later."

He turned to the tour guide. "I'm sorry for the inconvenience."

Dykes's mouth looked like it belonged at the back end of a cat. "We couldn't even get a cup of coffee or tea. It's all very embarrassing."

"Sorry about that, too. Catering is on my to-do list. Why don't you and your group follow me?"

Paddy led him to the IN door and held it open, bowing his head to each member of the group who filed past him. Dykes brought up the rear. "Don't think I won't be complaining? You can't go calling us names like Big Nose and Roy Orbison either!"

Paddy smiled politely and closed the door. Only then did he suck in a big breath and mutter, "Tosser."

It wasn't meant for anyone's ears but the room had a bit of an echo now it was nearly empty.

Wish-Wash muttered: "I didn't know?"

"It was my fault for not taking the time to explain it," Paddy said.

Oodles pinched at an eyebrow. "Looks like I've arrived at a bad time."

"Not at all," Paddy said. "In fact, I've been wondering when you were going to get here. I wanted to talk to you."

"Me first. I heard at mass Billy Gumboots is back."

Wish-Wash scoffed. "As if! You went to his funeral, you drongo."

Oodles closed his eyes. "I know I did, but now Daisy

Rowbottom says she saw him on the High Street about midnight."

"Oh, she'd know!" Wish-Wash said. "She only swore black and blue she saw Moose Routley, and he turns out to be the Professor here!"

"Don't look at me." Paddy laughed nervously. "Until a week ago I had never even heard of Billy Gumboots. If he comes in here asking for his old job back, I'll be relying on you fellas to verify his identity."

FORTY-EIGHT
CALLING IN A FAVOUR

Oodles slouched against the counter. "So, what is it you wanted to ask me?"

Paddy was back behind the reception desk, having sent Wish-Wash on a break. The Asian group had emerged from the gallery, looking happy enough before they had filed out.

"A few things. First, I want to pick your brain."

Paddy was distracted when he saw the tour guide wearing the sunglasses standing in the car park as the bus pulled away.

He focused back on Oodles. "It occurred to me the problem with changing the scat each day is someone might notice that it's different to how it was yesterday. The passengers on the tour buses are likely to be different each day. But what I'm worried about are the drivers and the guides."

"Can't we just ban drivers and guides from going in?"

"How would that look? They'd think we had something to hide?"

Oodles stared at his feet.

"Just give it some thought," Paddy said. "Maybe one of us will think of something overnight."

"Will do," Oodles said. "What were the other things you

wanted to ask? Something to do with your cousin? I've got a tarp for the back of my ute if you want me to take him somewhere under cover."

Paddy looked at him blankly, then remembered his fib.

"Oh no, I wouldn't want you to do anything else illegal. I just need you to keep quiet about him."

"Don't worry, my lips are sealed."

"The thing that is the most urgent is Gough. I've realised I can't leave him chained up all day. I need to take him for walks after midnight."

Oodles clenched his eyes shut. "Of course. You want me and Wish-Wash to start walking him?"

"No, he's my responsibility."

Oodles shook his head. "Us old blokes don't sleep too well anyway." He looked around. "You've got enough to do around this place."

"Tanks, but I feel guilty enough already about you fellas breaking the law for me. I'm happy enough walking him myself. I was just hoping you might have a leash though?"

Oodles did a face palm. "Silly me! I saw Raj's leash hanging up in my garage. I ought to have known you'd need it. I'll drop by with it tonight."

Paddy stroked his chin and smiled.

"Was there something else?"

"I was curious as to why you don't go fishing any more?"

Oodles scowled. "I told you. I'm too darned old to go traipsing around the bush now."

"Nothing to do with your grief?"

"That's personal!"

"Wish-Wash and Katy told me about your wife dying. You never said anything?"

Oodles scowled. "Why would I?"

"I can't think how long it takes to get over something like that. Katy says you carve a notch into the bench across the road now every time you go to church."

Oodles clenched a fist. "Why can't that girl mind her own business?"

"It seems to me it's another one of those secrets the whole town knows about. People are worried about you."

"Worried? Are you worried about me?"

"Yes, I am," Paddy said. "You said you owed me a favour. Well, I'm calling it in. I want you to take me fly-fishing."

FORTY-NINE
WOOLY BUGGERS AND GREEN NYMPHS

"Something important has come up. Would you mind looking after the museum while I go out?"

"Me?" Oodles said.

"That's just what Wish-Wash said." Paddy started walking across the foyer.

"I'm no good handling money."

Paddy stopped and turned. "Jaysus, he said that, too. What is it with you old fellas? Are you going to spill your tea all over the counter, too?"

"What's so urgent you have to go out again, anyway?"

"I have to speak to Katy McDonnell."

"Again?" Oodles scowled.

"I need to discuss something important with her. I'd ask Wish-Wash to cover for me but I don't know when he's coming back."

Oodles walked around to the other side of the counter. "I don't even know how to use the t—"

Too late. Paddy was already half way out the door.

Oodles shouted. "I haven't got the first idea what to do if someone comes." But he realised he was talking to himself. The front door had closed behind Paddy. He saw the

Irishman stop briefly to talk to the tour guide in the car park, but then he started walking towards town with purpose.

Oodles heaved a sigh.

Paddy couldn't have known he had decided to resume his fly-fishing, anyway. Oodles had been worried how he was going to break the news to everyone; now he had a way out.

The truth was Birty's death had started him thinking. Once he got past the guilt of not having been there for his mate, he realised there were worse places to turn his toes up than on the banks of the upper tributaries of the Bing Bong River.

Oodles couldn't see the point any more of trying to win the lottery he had going with James, Wish-Wash and now Father O'Boring. What would he do with the money anyway? He already owned his home and his car.

If he drew his last breath up on the mountain, Wish-Wash would edge a bit closer to the jackpot, which wouldn't be a bad thing.

He'd be able to afford to move out of the pub, go shopping for clothes in places other than op shops and get himself on to a healthy diet.

Then there was yesterday. If Paddy hadn't intervened, Oodles was quite sure Freddy and Gordo would have put him in hospital at the very least. Madge would have been annoyed he had deprived himself of two good years of doing what he loved, only to end up in plaster, or, worse, inside a coffin.

When Oodles had rifled through his shed looking for the dog kennel, he had found more than just his savings; he had stumbled on his fishing rods and his box of flies. It was like opening a box of lost treasure — no gold, just lures. Wooly Buggers and Green Nymphs.

The clincher had been mass this morning. Father O'Boring might as well have been a mile away because Oodles couldn't hear a word he was mumbling. Oodles decided there and then it was probably time he resumed the quest to catch George. It would give him great pleasure to throw the tough old trout on to Birty's grave and say, "Told you I'd win?"

This, of course, had gone to the back of his mind when Daisy Rowbottom had shared her startling story outside the church after the service. She said she was certain she had seen Billy Gumboots striding along the High Street in the early hours of the morning.

"Perhaps it was his twin brother?" someone said.

"He didn't have a twin," Daisy said. "I should know. I helped deliver him."

Someone else said, "Maybe you saw his ghost."

Daisy said she didn't believe in ghosts.

"What about the ghost of Colonel Northan?"

Daisy snarled. "It was Billy Gumboots I saw, I tell you. In the High Street and very much alive."

Michael O'Grady, who had been one of the pallbearers at Billy's funeral, shook his head. "I would have noticed if the coffin had been empty."

FIFTY
STANDING HIS GROUND

OODLES LOOKED up when he heard the door open. It was Wish-Wash returning from his break.

"Where's Paddy?" Wish-Wash asked.

"He's gone out again,"

"What's that singer doing loitering around in the car park?"

"What singer?"

"Roy Orbison."

Oodles glanced out the window and twigged when he saw the man was wearing large sunglasses. "Oh him? I guess he's waiting for the next bus."

"Paddy's left you in charge, has he?"

"As if I had any choice?" Oodles said.

"Do you know how much to charge everyone, then?"

"Not at all," Oodles said. "Paddy left in an almighty hurry."

Wish-Wash became all business-like as he opened the gate in the counter.

"Feel free to take over." Oodles stood up, then he came straight out and said it. "Paddy has asked me to take him fly-fishing."

Wish-Wash sat down. "Let me guess? You said no?"

"Actually, I agreed." Oodles rounded the counter and stood on the other side.

"But —"

"But nothing. I told him I owed him for saving my skin and I meant it."

Wish-Wash looked across at him. "When are you going?"

"I thought I'd take him out on the January long weekend. The less time I have to think about it, the better."

They turned towards the window when they heard a hiss of brakes outside. It was the third bus pulling up.

Dykes greeted the passengers as they stepped down.

Wish-Wash waved a finger. "He's just the kind of joker who'd notice we had changed the scat."

"Good thing we haven't then," Oodles said. "He was only in the gallery an hour ago."

"Doesn't matter." Wish-Wash watched Dykes approach the door. "It's the principle. No way am I letting him come back in!"

FIFTY-ONE
THE TRUTH ABOUT BILLY

KATY STEPPED BACK when she opened the door to find Paddy standing there. "What are you doing here?"

"I wouldn't be here if this wasn't really important."

She sighed. "I suppose you'd better come in." She led him up the stairs to her flat above the salon.

She ushered him into a small kitchenette and pointed him towards a table with a fixed bench that wouldn't have looked out of place in a caravan. As he squeezed into the cavity over on the far side, she filled the jug and took tea bags out of an overhead cupboard.

"Do you know Billy Gumboots?" Paddy asked.

Katy turned sideways from the sink. "I did. I think I know what this is about. I've already heard on the Bush Telegraph that Daisy Rowbottom is saying she's seen him."

"Daisy is right this time. Billy faked his death."

Katy dropped the teabags into the teapot and turned again. "Come off the grass! Are you trying to tell me Dave Jenkins and the pallbearers didn't know he wasn't inside the coffin?"

The penny dropped for Paddy at that very moment. Of

course Dave knew what was in that fancy, wooden box! Billy would have had to have confided in him.

Katy raised her voice so she could be heard above the rising din of the boiling kettle. "Daisy Rowbottom obviously needs new glasses."

"I've seen him with my own eyes." Paddy shuddered as he replayed the episode in his mind. "He turned up at the museum last night and scared the life out of me. Anyway, Daisy wasn't even wearing glasses when I saw her the other day."

"Yes, I heard she toured the museum with Father O'Rourke," Katy said.

Paddy's eyes widened. "You heard about that, too?"

"What did I tell you about the rumour mill in this town? Gossip travels pretty fast up and down the aisles of the supermarket."

"Billy is probably asleep on my sofa as we speak."

Katy poured water into the teapot. "How can you be so sure it's him?"

"Oodles and Wish-Wash told me all about him. And your girl Vicki pierced his left nipple."

"She told you that? When? No, why?"

Paddy shrugged. "Her sister Velda was the one who told me."

"And you've seen this fellow's left nipple, have you?"

"Yes, he got into my bed last night." Then he realised what he had said. "Not when I was in it! Jaysus! He let himself in with a key because he assumed the place was still empty. But he has a nipple ring all right. And he knows stuff that only Billy could know."

"He *knows* stuff?" Katy gave the flicker of a smirk as she slid Paddy's mug across the table. She took the milk carton out of the fridge, placed it on the red formica table and sat down opposite him. "That doesn't sound like the guy I knew at school. You know he was Wish-Wash's illegitimate son, don't you?"

"That's more proof, then! See, that's what he told me."

"Oh, that's conclusive then. Not!" Katy sighed. "Everyone around here knew Wish-Wash was Billy's father; well, everyone except for Wish-Wash. But you only had to see them in the same room to see the similarities. Even their noses slanted the same way."

She shook her head. "So sad! Billy grew up without a dad and died without a dad. Wish-Wash didn't even go to his funeral."

"But don't you see? Wish-Wash didn't miss out. *No one* went to his funeral because Billy's death was a lie. Phony, pretend, staged." Paddy kept pressing. "But he's certainly alive and kicking. I've seen enough of Wish-Wash to know this fella is a dead ringer for him."

"Except for the nipple ring?" Katy smiled.

"Who knows what lurks beneath Wish-Wash's Hawaiian shirt? But you're right about the slant of their noses. It's like both of those snozzers were broken by the same left hook."

Katy rolled her eyes. "I'm still not buying it is him. If he really did turn up at the museum last night, how come you didn't mention him to me this morning?"

"Oh that . . . ?" Paddy's voice trailed off. "That was a secret this morning. He didn't want anyone to know."

"But he does now?"

"Only you."

"Why me?"

"He says he's skint and he wants you to shave off his beard for him. So he can make some money as a bushranger, like."

"Does he just?" Katy sighed. "The Billy I knew started growing his beard when he left school but no one else saw a single whisker on his face for at least four years. That didn't stop him making an annual trip to the salon. And each year

Dad told him to try again in 12 months' time. He was in his twenties by the time he finally got accepted."

"You said you didn't even know about the scam in those days!"

"Billy told me himself. I inherited the business, remember? I saw him a few days after Dad's funeral and again 10 months later. He died two days before his next scheduled appointment."

"Here's your chance to make good on it, then." Paddy put on his best spruiker's voice. "*Herewith are the whiskers of Australia's very own walking dead. The legend of Billy Gumboots.*"

"Very funny," Katy said. "You know Billy Gumboots isn't his real name? At school roll-call his name was Billy Kretocek. Even us younger kids used to call him Billy Cretin in the playground." She gazed into space. "That was cruel now I think of it. But to be fair he wasn't the sharpest tool in the shed."

"So you'll cut his beard?"

Katy put her hands on her hips and sighed. "I suppose so. But I'm still not convinced it's him."

"It is, believe me," Paddy said. "Oh, and I forgot to mention, Oodles has agreed to take me fly-fishing."

Katy raised her eyebrows. "He didn't? How did you get him to agree to that?"

"I have my ways." Paddy smiled. "Which reminds me? I have a favour to ask of you . . ."

FIFTY-TWO
KILLER

As Velda submerged the chip basket into the deep fryer, Paddy became conscious of someone standing next to him.

He looked sideways and saw the man was wearing green trousers, a sky-blue blazer and familiar sunglasses.

"Oh, hello again." Paddy put on his best smile. "I thought you said you were waiting for the next bus?"

Roger Dykes lifted his glasses, revealing bloodshot eyes, and he spoke in that shaky voice again. "It arrived, but your old fellow wouldn't let me come in."

Paddy frowned. "Wish-Wash?"

"He was the same old jerk as before. Big bloke. Colourful shirt with sweat-stained armpits. Only this time he had a bouncer with him. He called him *Killer*."

Paddy scratched his head. "You must have misheard. His name is Oodles."

"I know what I heard. *Killer* sounds nothing like *Oodles*," Dykes said. "Not that I really mind not being allowed in again. I've already seen the scat, and I badly needed a coffee. You reckon they sell aspirin here?"

Paddy shrugged. "Ask her." He pointed to the girl with

the green hair now leaning on the other side of the Taylor's Takeaway counter.

"Sorry, we don't," Velda said. "Coffee, I can do though. Instant. Is that all right?"

Dykes screwed up his face.

"You won't find anything else around here, mister." Her hand hovered over a stack of takeaway cups. "Yes or no?"

"Oh, OK, then." He turned to Paddy again. "I wouldn't suppose you have any headache tablets on you?"

"We might have some back at the museum. When we're done here, we'll go and see."

"Is that a good idea? I got the strong impression, I'm not welcome at the museum. Ever."

"I'm sure there has been a misunderstanding?"

Dykes shook his head, then seemed to regret it because his hand flew to his temple.

"Oodles wouldn't hurt anyone," Paddy said.

"I told you, this one was called *Killer*. The big bloke behind the desk reckoned he used to be a professional boxer, and I'm in enough strife with the company without getting into a scrap with your muscle."

"My muscle?" Paddy laughed. "The only weights Oodles lifts these days are tea cups."

"I wasn't taking any chances."

Paddy pinched his nose. "So what did Wish-Wash say exactly?"

"He said I was a disgrace to my company and he planned to report me if I didn't leave the premises."

"He said that?"

"Yeah, and he told me I didn't want to mess with *Killer*. He said I had 10 seconds to leave the premises. He said he was feeling charitable and would admit my group but I had to wait for them outside."

FIFTY-THREE
IN SEARCH OF ASPIRIN

From his spot behind the desk, Wish-Wash had a good view through the window. The last he had seen of Roy Orbison, he had been walking into town.

That was nearly 15 minutes ago and judging from the noise coming from the gallery the tour group were doing fine without him.

Wish-Wash broke the uncomfortable silence in the foyer. "That was a close one."

"Close all right," Oodles said. "I only wished you hadn't gone and called me what you called me?"

"It worked, didn't it? I thought you played the strong silent part masterfully.

"Strong and silent, be buggered! I was just too flabbergasted to talk."

"You *are* handy with your fists." Wish-Wash rubbed his jaw. "Look what you did to me?"

A noise from upstairs interrupted their conversation.

Wish-Wash tilted an ear towards the stairs. "Is that sound what I think it is?"

Oodles knew fine well it was Paddy's cousin turning the television on but he didn't know if Wish-Wash even knew about Nigel. So he played it safe. "It sounds like Paddy forgot to turn off his telly?"

"You'd better go up and turn it off," Wish-Wash said.

Oodles looked oddly at him. "Why?"

Wish-Wash stared back. "Well, I can't go. You should have heard Paddy go off the last time *I* went upstairs."

"What makes you think he'll be any more happy with me?"

"How will he even know? I'll yell out if I see him coming. While you're up there, go to the room at the end of the corridor and take a look at the mirror above his bed."

"No, that's definitely Paddy's private business," Oodles said. "Anyway, he didn't install it. *Your* Billy did."

"Here we go again!"

"I don't know why you keep denying it?"

"Because it wasn't true when he was alive. And it's still not true. That's why."

"I'm still not going up those stairs," Oodles said.

"Why not? Paddy'd probably thank you for saving him on his electricity bill." Wish-Wash added, "I don't know what he was watching up there this morning anyway? All you get on the box on Sunday mornings are church services."

"It sounds to me like someone laughing. So if it's a church it must be a different church to the one I go to." Oodles scratched the side of his head. "Anyway, let's just ignore the telly. We've got a bigger problem of our own."

"You can say that again," Wish-Wash said. "Have you worked out yet what we're going to do about our lottery?"

"I wasn't talking about that. I'm more worried right now about how we're going to explain to Paddy what happened to the tour guide."

"In light of his new concerns about the changing of the scat, I reckon Paddy will be pretty happy."

"You think so, do you?" Oodles nodded towards the window. "I guess we'll find out pretty soon."

Wish-Wash looked over Oodles's shoulder and saw Paddy and the guide walking side-by-side as they crossed the road. Paddy was carrying a white parcel and the guide was holding his head in one hand and a take-away cup in the other.

"He's got to be joking." Wish-Wash banged his fist on the counter, and the cash-register shudder probably registered on the Richter scale. "Why on earth would he want to bring him back?"

Oodles shrugged, and walked over to the door to let them in.

"Tanks." Paddy brushed past. "You must be the fella they call Killer?"

Oodles looked towards Wish-Wash. "We can explain. Well, Wish-Wash can. Can't you, big fella?"

Paddy glared at Wish-Wash. "Later, all roight? Have either of you fellas got a couple of aspirin for Mr Dykes?"

Wish-Wash stabbed an index finger at the tour guide. "If your company knew you were still as drunk as a skunk when you started work this morning . . . "

"That's enough, Wish-Wash," Paddy said. "I take it you haven't got any headache tablets?"

"No." Wish-Wash was getting a whiff now of what Paddy was carrying. "Are those fish'n'chips for us?"

"Noooo," Paddy said. "Didn't you eat during your break?"

"I did, but it was only a sanger."

"These are for . . . " he looked at the guide, ". . . Mr Dykes."

The tour guide looked at him quizzically. "All I want is an aspirin."

"Those tablets are better absorbed with food. Feel free to leave your empty coffee cup there on the counter. *Killer* is really good at cleaning up." Paddy ushered Dykes towards the spiral stairs. "Let's see what I've got in the drawers upstairs?"

FIFTY-FOUR
MY DEAF COUSIN

BILLY WAS FURIOUS. Who did this Irishman think he was? Making him take a vow of silence in his own flat?

The sitting room was directly above the gallery, and it sounded like a herd of buffalo was running around below him.

How much longer would he have to wait for his fish'n'chips?

Billy tried staring at the wall. That's when he realised his prized clock was missing. The frigging bastard! Was nothing sacred?

The only things familiar to him in this part of the room were the tatty chairs, possibly the world's smallest television, and the array of stupid books. The Irishman had to be joking if he expected him to sit quietly and read.

He had a brainwave.

The noise from downstairs would drown out the telly as long as he kept the volume down low. So he turned it on and began channel-surfing.

He should have known! The satellite channels that been once there had been replaced with fuzzy white screens. Wouldn't you have thought someone would have kept up the subscription? All that was left were three free-to-air channels but all three were showing church services.

Billy had another brainwave.

He checked the DVD drive and sure enough discovered he had left a movie disk in the slot. It was *Porky's 2*, one of his old favourites.

That's what he was laughing at when Paddy burst in.

Paddy was tailed by someone else. And it wasn't Katy. It was a bloke wearing sunglasses.

"What the hell are you doing?" Paddy winked at Billy and added quickly, "It's not as if you can actually hear the TV, Nigel."

Paddy threw the fish'n'chips on the kitchen server and turned to face the other man. "This is my cousin Nigel. You'll have to face him and talk clearly, Mr Dykes, because he's deaf and dumb, but he can read lips."

The man smiled and started gesturing with his hands.

Paddy's face turned white. "You know sign language?"

"My mother was deaf and dumb."

Oh great, Billy thought. Suddenly, he was supposed to be someone called Nigel, and he was supposed to be deaf and dumb. Only he didn't have a clue what this bloke was saying with his hands, and he didn't have a clue how Paddy would get them out of this fix.

"I'm impressed," Paddy said. "But do you speak Gaelic sign language, too?"

That stopped the man in mid-motion.

"I always thought sign language was international," he said, turning his head.

"Afraid not. Nigel comes from Dingle in County Kerry. What he was brought up on was a local sign language dialect known colloquially as Dingle-Dangle."

Paddy launched into some hand movements of his own. Billy could have sworn he saw a rude gesture in there.

The stranger looked impressed. "What are you saying?"

"Two things. The first is: does he know where any aspirin are? The second is: is he hungry?"

Billy got up and walked to a drawer in the kitchen, which he thrust open. He extracted a packet he handed to the stranger.

Then he sat down at the table and ripped apart the parcel of fish'n'chips. The contents looked as nice as they smelled.

"Didn't you want me to have some of those, too, Professor?" the man said.

"No, let's get you back downstairs." Paddy placed an arm on his shoulder and guided him to the door. "We can get some water for you from the bathroom."

The stranger pointed to the kitchen sink. "But there's water up here?"

"The stuff downstairs is better."

"Just one more thing," Paddy said with his hand on the doorknob. He lowered his voice. "No need to mention to the old fellas downstairs about Nigel being up here. They wouldn't understand his handicap. You've met them. They're noice fellas but they're a bit bigoted."

FIFTY-FIVE
BOSS

Wish-Wash was still venting his spleen when the door upstairs creaked open.

"Shush," Oodles said. "Here they come."

Paddy and Roy Orbison were soon snaking their way back down the spiral stairs.

"All roight?" Paddy said when he reached the bottom and locked gazes with the old fellas.

"Did you leave the telly on earlier, boss?" Wish-Wash said. "I think I heard it."

"That?" Paddy tilted his head. "Oh, don't worry about that? I leave it on sometimes for security. Oodles knows about it, didn't he tell you? It makes people think there's someone up there when there isn't."

He turned to the tour guide. "Follow me, Mr Dykes. We'll get you some water."

He grabbed a cup out of the cupboard near the drink's table and they disappeared into the gents.

Wish-Wash and Oodles watched them go.

"How come the Professor took *him* upstairs if privacy is so important to him," Wish-Wash said.

"Obviously, he feared for his life if he left him with us,"

Oodles said. "Relax, will you? He only took him up there for a few minutes. Now you know what you have to do to get an invite? Get a headache."

"Maybe." Wish-Wash said. "But you don't think there's something fishy going on? What happened to the fish'n'chips he took upstairs? They couldn't have eaten them that quickly?"

Oodles guessed what had happened but, since he was sworn to secrecy about the illegal cousin, suggested that perhaps Paddy was keeping the fish'n'chips for later.

He was saved from defending his theory when Paddy and the tour guide came out of the bathroom. But even as Dykes swallowed the tablets, he couldn't escape Wish-Wash's hostile glare.

"If you don't mind, I'll go lie down in the back of the bus until my lot comes out." He headed for the door with the urgency of someone escaping a building on fire.

When the door shut behind him, Paddy said, "Jaysus! We can't treat the tour guides like that?"

"What else could I do?" Wish-Wash said. "You said it yourself? We can't allow repeat visitors."

"I didn't mean we have to threaten them with violence? Ever hear of diplomacy?"

Paddy turned to Oodles. "And what were you thinking? Posing as a killer?"

"Go easy," Oodles said. "It wasn't my idea but I'll give Wish-Wash this: he was just trying to help. It wasn't his fault you weren't here, boss."

Paddy fixed him with a look of exasperation. "What is it with you both calling me boss?"

"You never seem comfortable with us calling you *Professor*," Wish-Wash said.

"What's wrong with *Paddy*?"

"I thought you'd like being called *boss*."

"*Boss* implies you are employees, and I pay you, which I

obviously can't afford to do."

"You might if these buses keep coming at $500 a pop?"

"They won't keep coming if you frighten off all the tour guides, that's for sure." Paddy ran a hand through his hair. "Anyway, I can't pay you yet. I'm hiring us some other help."

———

Oodles walked Wish-Wash home. Luckily, it was only to the pub next door because he couldn't have taken much more of Wish-Wash's laments. Strewth, he thought the big fellow was going to burst into tears any second.

"Why do you think he's gone and hired someone else?" Wish-Wash said. "Did we upset him that much?"

"I think you're overreacting, old cock. It sounded to me like it was already a done deal."

"Maybe. But I shouldn't have spoken to the Professor like that. I was out of line," Wish-Wash said.

"I wouldn't let it worry you. We all get hot under the collar sometimes. I don't think he was Mr Calm Under Pressure himself today."

"Maybe not. But I want to make it up to him. Do something special for him."

FIFTY-SIX
GIVE THAT FELLA A FEATHER DUSTER

BILLY CREPT DOWN THE STAIRCASE, going from vantage point to vantage point so he could scan the foyer below.

"Trust me, no one else is in the building," Paddy said as he bounded ahead.

Billy was still looking left and right when he reached the bottom. "Did you check all the cupboards?"

"Relax the cacks. Everyone who came through that door went out that door before I locked up."

"You still haven't told me what that was about earlier. I asked you to bring Katy — and you brought some guy with a headache. How can I trust you not to blow my cover?"

"You might have already done that yourself."

Billy sat down in front of the teapot and gave a puzzled look.

"Did you see Daisy Rowbottom when you arrived in town?"

"Of course not. And nobody saw me. I was really careful."

"She's been telling everyone she saw you."

"Why would that dozy old cow be out at that time of the night anyway?"

Paddy shrugged. "I'm just saying what she's been telling

everyone. The problem for you is the more people believe you're alive, the greater likelihood someone will figure out where you hid the model of the hunter."

"I don't follow you."

"If you're not lying in that coffin, something else is. Otherwise the pallbearers would have noticed it was empty."

The sweat was building on Billy's forehead. "Meaning?"

"You know what I mean. And if I'm smart enough to realise you buried the evidence in the coffin, someone else is bound to twig, too."

Billy clenched his eyes shut.

"I can't believe Dave the undertaker went along with the faked death, too?" Paddy said. "It's one thing for him to buy a takeaway shop, it's a big step up for him in the criminal world to aid and abet a fake burial, and hide evidence at the same time."

"You won't tell?"

"Of course I won't tell." Paddy sighed. "I've got enough problems of my own. But the fella I brought upstairs is the least of your worries. Why would he suspect anything? As far as he's concerned, you're my cousin from Ireland."

"And you reckon he swallowed that codswallop?"

"Why wouldn't he? You've never met him before, have you? Besides, I couldn't have left him downstairs with Wish-Wash and Oodles."

Billy looked around the foyer. "You sure no one's going to come through that door all of a sudden?"

"Chill. I locked it when Oodles and Wish-Wash went home. I expect you're dying to stretch your legs."

Billy looked lovingly at the teapot. "And I've also worked up a thirst."

"What? Not you too? I suppose you like dunking your biscuits, too?"

"How did you know that?" Billy scratched his head. "So, when is Katy coming over anyway?"

"Wednesday night after work."

"You told her I was alive?"

"No, I told her I dug you up from the graveyard. Of course, I told her you were alive."

"Why Wednesday? Didn't you tell her my need for money is urgent?"

Paddy sighed. "Look, she's doing you a favour, roight? Wednesday is the night she's free."

He handed Billy a feather duster. "I'll make a pot of tea when the work is done. In the meantime, make yourself useful."

"You're joking?"

"I was joking about the $19 entry fee," Paddy said. "But you can clean the gallery for free. You'd know which cupboard to look in to find the vacuum cleaner?"

"The museum gallery never got particularly dusty when I ran it."

Paddy sighed. "Well, now it need vacuuming. You'll see not much has changed though. The only big difference is the new exhibit in the glass box where the model of the hunter used to be. If you want to see what used to be there, you'll need to get an exhumation order."

"Very funny," Billy said. "And where will you be while I'm doing all this slave labour?"

"Out here, settling the till, then tidying up the foyer."

————

As Paddy was tallying up the day's takings, there was a knock on the door.

The Irishman looked up. He had forgotten Oodles was dropping by with the leash.

FIFTY-SEVEN
HELLO, AGAIN!

IT HAD TAKEN years for James to feel comfortable about visiting Roses Supermarket but he had finally settled into a ritual every Monday morning.

He now walked Howard to the shop, tied him up outside, and bought himself a small carton of skim milk. Today, as usual, he turned off his hearing aids before going into the shop. What people said behind his back, he just didn't want to hear.

But when Daisy Rowbottom came down the aisle, he turned them back on.

"Good morning, Miss Rowbottom."

"Morning, Mr Mayor." No matter how many times she addressed him like that, it always brought a smile to his face. She was one of the few people in town whose voice wasn't laced in sarcasm when she used the title. It wasn't her fault her brother was such a recalcitrant nancy boy.

As James leaned into the fridge to find the carton with the best use-by date, he was conscious Daisy had stopped behind him.

He turned around.

"Something else you wanted to say, Daisy?"

She pursed her lips, like she was framing her words, then blurted: "Do you think it's wise to let that new chap at the museum walk your dog?"

"I've done nothing of the sort."

"I did see it with my own eyes."

"Impossible."

"It was dark, but I know what I saw — that new giant and your dog were walking along the High Street about one-thirty this morning."

"What the dickens were you doing up at that hour?"

"I couldn't sleep," Daisy said.

"At that time, Howard would have been tucked up asleep in his basket." The Mayor pointed to the front window beyond which the tiny collie was tied to a post at the edge of the footpath. "Do you think he'd be as keen for a walk now if he had been up all night?"

"But haven't you got the only dog in town?"

That's the moment when James saw red.

If Daisy was right (and why would she make the story up?), there was an illegal dog in town!

He should have known nothing good would come of the bog Irishman's arrival in town. There was a high degree of likelihood he was being aided and abetted by those two geriatric misfits, who had approximately the same level of sophistication as the assorted misfits from that godforsaken country.

Grasping the milk carton in one hand, he brushed past the others in the checkout queue. "Out of my way, I'm in a hurry." He threw coins on the counter as he passed.

He quickly untied Howard and picked up the pooper-scooper and plastic bag.

He set course for the museum, knowing there was no time to waste.

On the other side of the street, however, he caught a glimpse of the Irishman's back as he went into the Wind

Tunnel. What luck! Now witnesses would be on hand when he made a citizen's arrest.

James changed course, crossed the road, and tied Howard to a post outside the cafe.

It was only when he reached the door he realised he was still holding the doggy things in his left hand. But it was too late to put them down.

He opened the door and saw the back of the Irishman. White shirt, blue waistcoat, dank ponytail.

He was sitting at a table with four other men. James recognised Gordo Bennett, whose mouth glistened with wire; Freddy Cuthbert, who had one arm in a sling; and the skinny Dutchman, but he couldn't see the face of the chap sitting next to Paddy.

"I've got a bone to pick with you, you big Irish layabout," James said.

The man turned around, and James realised he had made a terrible mistake.

It was actually Moose Routley and he was wearing that sinister smile again. "Look who we have here?" he said. "My old mate Jimbo."

James was acutely aware of five sets of eyes shining on him like headlights, including those of Tiger Kowalski who had turned around to see the Mayor holding the pooper-scooper and the bag of doggy doo-doo.

FIFTY-EIGHT
MOOSE ON THE LOOSE

James Northan started jumping to conclusions about Moose Routley in 1991 when he heard he was squatting in an abandoned farmhouse. He loudly declared to anyone who'd listen that Moose was unwashed, lazy, and dangerous.

Furthermore, he was probably defrauding taxpayers by claiming unemployment benefits when in fact he was working as a Tasmanian Tiger hunter, which, in the Mayor's mind, was a quite ludicrous pursuit.

Moose and his equally undesirable friends had occupied the boarded-up farmhouse out on Blackstump Road, which was evidence enough for the Mayor that he had committed at least one crime.

But police sergeant Randolph Birtwistle's preference was to apply a strategy of containment. He said if Moose and his friends didn't bother the townsfolk, it was better not to stir up a nest of bullants.

Who knew that when Moose signed up with the Windy Mountain Football Team, it would lead to him stirring up the self-appointed king of the ant hill.

TWO DAYS BEFORE THE 1993 GRAND FINAL

Moose guided Windy Mountain to the 1993 grand final —
and only Slutz Plains seemed to stand between them and the
elusive premiership.

But no one had anticipated Mayor Northan spoiling
things.

For years, his family had owned an apple orchard close to
town.

But now he wanted to rip out the trees and build a wind-
sock factory on the site. He had read it was a looming
booming industry, a virtual licence to print money.

The town's festive mood turned hostile.

A group of conservationists claimed the orchard needed to
be protected because Tasmanian Tigers had been seen there
eating apples.

This claim was widely regarded as a fabrication but many
people lined up behind the greenies because that orchard was
where they got their apples from for their businesses.

Chief among them was the Applecart Hotel, which only
sold cider, not beer.

But there were others.

Two of them were teammates of Moose.

Hoo-Chung Loo's ancestors had come from China in 1851
during the gold rushes. They never found much gold, and
ended up moving to Windy Mountain and setting up a
general store. Over the years that had evolved into a green-
grocery, and when in season apples were big sellers. Loo was
a handy utility player.

Jimmy McMartin's family came out from Scotland much
more recently, so recent that Wee Jimmy, as he was called, still
spoke in a strong Scottish accent. Short, nuggety and with
powerful legs, he played mostly out on the wing. He was a
renowned baker. His speciality at the Windy Mountain

bakery were apples pies, which were so good people would travel from far away just to smell where they had been before they had sold out.

The final training session before the grand final was on a Thursday night, which was when Loo and Wee Jimmy walked into the footy sheds late wearing the same style of beanies worn by the greenies.

"Nice of you blokes to turn up," coach Tiger Kowalski said. Then he cocked his head. "What's with the beanies?"

"We want people to take us seriously," Loo said.

Tiger laughed. "I'd take you more seriously if you were wearing your guernseys and shorts."

"We're not staying for training," Loo said. "We just wanted to tell you something else has come up."

Tiger's jaw dropped. "What?"

"We're going to the protest."

"What protest?"

"Didn't you read about it in the newspaper today? The Mayor has hired some workmen to cut down his trees tonight. We're answering a call to arms to stand in their way. We've got to protect our livelihood."

"Fuck's sake, why do your apples even need to come from that orchard?" Tiger said. "Lots of other orchards grow around here."

"We've always got our apples from that orchard. You're too new to this town to understand the importance of the tradition."

Moose couldn't have cared less about the orchard. He knew Tasmanian Tigers didn't eat apples. What a stupid thing to claim!

But Tiger sent him along to the protest to keep an eye on Wee Jimmy and Loo because he didn't want them doing anything silly and risking their availability to play in the big game.

Moose's blood only started to boil when the Mayor

demanded the protesters vacate his property or he'd have them all thrown in jail.

It irked him that the Northans had been lording it over the locals for generations.

"You can't tear down this orchard," one of the protesters said. "It's our heritage."

"Nonsense," the Mayor said. "It's my heritage and I can do what I like with it."

"I'm not sure you can," one of the greenies said. "Everyone knows this is the natural habitat of the Tasmanian Tiger."

The Mayor just laughed. "Only morons like you can't accept the Thylacine is extinct. And even when it was alive, it never ate apples. Only meat!"

Nearly every set of eyes locked on to Moose, urging him to use his authority to contradict the Mayor. It was hard to think clearly in that cauldron. But he felt he had to do something.

So he grabbed a rope and tied the Mayor to a gum tree.

As he pushed James Northan's face into the trunk, he said, "So you won't mind spending the night here, Jimbo? If you've still got all your limbs come morning perhaps you can back up your extinction claim with some evidence."

The Mayor did survive the chilly night, albeit with his dignity in tatters.

It was no surprise to Moose when the coppers came to arrest him at dawn.

What surprised him was the reception he got when he arrived at Risdon Prison. No other man had ever been imprisoned for tying a mayor to a tree, which gave him cult-hero status among the inmates.

Still, he wasn't sad to farewell that place five months later.

He came to regret going back to Windy Mountain though.

ONCE MORE WITH ILL-FEELING

Moose Routley turned up at the football club again in March 1994 looking like he had done nothing but lift weights and get more tattoos during the off-season, and he was welcomed back as if he were the prodigal son.

Club president Fred Furlong had looked as happy as a man who had just won the lottery. "Let's forget all about last year," he told Moose. "You won't have to worry about running into the Mayor, either. He doesn't even like football."

Windy Mountain made it to the final day again.

The biggest crowd for years turned up for the grand final, despite the day being wet and cold. The game was played at a ferocious pace, and ebbed and flowed.

The ball became a cake of soap in the slippery conditions but Moose handled it as if he were playing in a different dimension.

With seconds left, he coolly kicked the long-range goal that gave Windy Mountain a one-point win and ended a century of disappointment.

He was chaired off by delirious supporters who had jumped the fence and swarmed on to the field.

The players gathered on the wing in front of the grand-stand and beer cans were passed around as they watched the presentation area being set up.

Sponsorship signage was erected around the microphone, and the premiership cup was placed on a trestle table.

The voice that came from the microphone startled Moose. Surely not? It was James Northan. What was he doing here?

"I think I speak for everyone when I say my great-great-great grandfather would have been proud of the game played here today." His voice reverberated around the ground. "So it is my great pleasure to present the Colonel Richard Northan perpetual trophy." He glanced down at his notes. "I'd like club president Fred Furlong, captain Tiger Kowalski and the player of the match Bruce Routley, to come forward."

"Me?" Moose was standing with his teammates in the shadows near the presentation area. He was confused because even his mum didn't call him Bruce any more. He was propelled forward by pats on his back.

The Mayor didn't recognise him as he came closer. Perhaps it was all that mud?

When James saw Moose close up, however, he stepped back with his mouth open.

Moose just smiled, flashing what teeth he still had left. Then he grabbed one handle of the heavy silver trophy, which was still on the table, and Tiger took hold of the other, and they hoisted it for the crowd to see.

Moose shouted to the roaring crowd, "Let's party. Finally, Dick is ours."

The Mayor whispered into Fred Furlong's ear, "What did he just say?"

"Dick," Furlong said loudly so he could be heard above the noise. "That's our nickname for the trophy. Isn't it, Tiger?"

"Yes, three cheers for Dick," Tiger yelled into the microphone, and the crowd chanted 'Dick, Dick, Dick'.

The Mayor grabbed the microphone and shouted into it, wisps of froth spraying from his mouth. "Now listen here, you rabble. My distinguished ancestor was never called Dick in his life. He was Richard. Colonel Richard. Get it. Richard."

Tiger let go of his end of the trophy and grabbed the microphone from the smaller and weaker Mayor, and he egged the chanting crowd on by waving his arms about like a demented orchestra conductor and shouting at the top of his voice. "Dick, Dick, Dick, Dick, Dick . . ."

James Northan tried to wrestle the microphone back — but Moose cut short his protest by slamming the silver trophy down on his head.

The crowd went even more berserk.
But this time the jail sentence was much longer.

FIFTY-NINE
THE OFFER HE CAN'T REFUSE

James disappeared out the cafe door like a rancher backing out of a saloon in the wild west.

Van Gogh looked at Moose, who was smirking. "You seem to have some history with him?"

"You might say that," Moose said.

Freddy laughed. "Just as well he has that pooper-scooper because I reckon he might need it. He's probably worrying what you're going to do with him next?"

"Nothing." Moose held up both his hands as if he were surrendering. "I'm only back here for the footy reunion. I'm getting too old to do any more jail time."

Van Gogh looked down at his hands, which were locked on the table. "So you fell into a good job when you came out?"

"Can't complain. It's only contract labouring — digging holes, pushing wheelbarrows and carrying bricks, things like that — but there's always work around. Cash in hand, too."

"Long may that last." Van Gogh smiled as he looked up. "If you don't mind me asking, how old are you, Moose?"

"I'll be 47 next birthday. But contractors know they'll get a good day's work out of me."

"Pleased to hear that." Van Gogh paused for a moment. "But can you really see yourself doing that type of work in, say, five, 10 years' time? Do you wonder if the phone will be still ringing when you're 60? And what about sick leave and superannuation? Will you be able to afford to retire if you do your back in?"

The Dutchman pulled out a roll of banknotes from the inside of his jacket. "Are you sure we can't persuade you to join us?"

Moose's eyes popped. He hadn't seen that much money in a long time.

"Thing is," Van Gogh said. "We have a couple of little things you can help us with during your short stay. We'd make it well worth your while. Wouldn't you rather have a wheelbarrow full of money or a wheelbarrow full of wet concrete?"

"If you put it that way, I guess it'd be wrong of me not to at least listen."

"Glad to hear you have an open mind," Van Gogh said. "Have you heard about the new guy at the Tasmanian Tiger Museum?"

Moose shook his head.

"Big man, about your size." Van Gogh looked around at the wounded men at the table. "These guys don't want anything to do with him again. You can probably guess why from looking at them."

"What makes you think I'd fare any better?" Moose said.

"I've heard you have forged a certain reputation." Van Gogh smiled. "How many guys came at you in Risdon? I heard 11. I'm surprised they let you out at all, given all the GBH charges they must have had against you?"

"Hey, every fight I had within those walls was in self-defence. But luckily, no one ever sees anything in jail anyway."

"This wouldn't be self-defence though."

"How much money would that pay?"

"Depends. If you wanted to earn the whole wheelbarrow full we'd also need you to make him disappear. Think you can do that?"

"Maybe. What's the other thing you wanted done?" Moose said.

"You remember Billy Gumboots?"

"I heard that he died not long ago?"

"That's what he wanted us to believe. But he's alive."

"Really?" Moose looked Van Gogh in the eye, then turned to Tiger Kowalski, who just shrugged like it was news to him, too.

"Do you think you can help us lure him out of hiding?" Van Gogh said. "Then scare him enough so he'll give up some information?"

"That's a tougher gig," Moose said. "The only thing I have against Billy is he's annoying. That's probably not to warrant hurting him though."

"Even for another wheelbarrow full of money?"

Moose's voice went up half an octave. "*Two* wheelbarrows?"

"You drive a hard bargain. Three, if you finish the job."

"That much?" Moose thought fleetingly about the new lifestyle he could afford, and decided there was no harm in asking further questions. "Where do you think Billy is?"

Van Gogh shrugged and looked left and right again. "If we knew that, these two pussies here could probably manage to take care of him. If that old woman is right about having seen him, we need to find out where he's hiding so we can have a little chat with him." He smiled. "That's when you'll earn that third wheelbarrow."

SIXTY
CRIES FOR HELP

Sergeant Stretch glanced at the clock on the charge room wall. He had worked all night and he was counting down the minutes until it was time to go home to his bed.

He had been at this station almost forever. He had cut his teeth as a junior constable walking the beat with Constable Smith and being growled at by Sergeant Birtwistle. When Birty retired, Smithy took command and when Smithy moved on, Stretch was next in line.

When he heard the doorknob on the front door turning, he looked up and saw a pale-faced James Northan enter. The former mayor slouched over the high counter and opened his mouth but nothing came out.

Stretch stood up and came nearer.

"Are you all right, Mr Northan?" He examined his face for clues. "What's happened?"

"It is what's going to happen." It came out as not much more than a squeaky gasp.

"Sorry, sir, you'll need to explain. Take your time."

James threw his hands in the air and found peak shrill. "I have just seen Moose Routley in the Wind Tunnel Cafe so you will forgive me for thinking there is no time to waste."

"He's probably back for the footy reunion." He leaned on the other side of the counter. "Moose did serve his time, you know?"

James pinched the bridge of his nose. "Sergeant Birtwistle would never have allowed a terrorist to run amok in this town."

"He's hardly a terrorist, Mr Northan. Was he doing something illegal in the cafe?"

"Not that I could see, but that does not mean he was not thinking something bad. You should arrest him, so you can find out what he is up to?"

"The law doesn't work that way. We have to act on evidence." Stretch locked his fingers. "Now look. What you need is a strong cup of tea."

"Do NOT tell me what I need!" James roared. "Sergeant Birtwistle used to know what was going on. But you? I bet you know nothing about the illegal alien in town either?"

"Illegal alien?"

"Well, an illegal dog. I knew nothing good would come of the Tasmanian Tiger Museum, and now the Irishman who has started running the place has a dog. Ask Daisy Rowbottom."

————

After leaving the police station, James Northan went to the council chambers.

When he came through the revolving door into a public foyer, he didn't even bother to look who was on the other side of the wide oak counter. "This is urgent, girly. I have something important to tell Maddie."

The council-clerk stopped writing, and looked up from his desk behind the counter to see who was speaking. "Your daughter is not available right now, sir. But if you tell me, I'll pass on the message."

James was startled to hear the deep male voice. Where was the dizzy young secretary who was normally there?

Tom Vance was a former sergeant in the army who had served as a medic in Timor. He wouldn't have picked him as being gay, but wonders never ceased. In four or five months in the job as council-clerk, Vance had become an obstructive nuisance.

"Better I speak to her myself, Tom." James lifted the gate in the counter to go into the inner sanctum. "I don't know how high your security clearance goes."

Vance rose from his desk and stood between James Northan and the real Mayor's closed door, with his arms crossed. "You can't see her right now because she's in a meeting."

"With whom?"

"I'm not at liberty to say, sir."

James had laid awake in bed at night lately wondering if Maddie had hired a Rottweiler like Vance just to keep him at bay. She might have inherited that nasty streak from her mother.

James turned around and cringed when he saw the hard plastic chairs in the waiting area. If he had known that one day he'd have to sit here, he would never have got rid of the soft, comfortable chairs during his tenure as mayor. It made sense at the time. He had done it to deter time-wasters. "I will wait." He sat down.

Vance resumed his seat and picked up his pen. "Please yourself, sir." He started writing and spoke loudly to the page in front of him. "But it'll be a long wait. The meeting is in Hobart. Maddie won't be back until Thursday."

James Northan bounced back up. "A likely story! Do you not think she would have told me if she was going away for that length of time? I only live behind her house!"

"I know. You occupy the granny flat."

"Do I look like a granny?" James screwed up his face. "Would it kill you to call it a studio apartment?"

"You can call it what you like, sir. I'm just using the term that's on the council plans."

"Why would she not have told me she was going away?"

Vance shrugged. "I don't know how high your security clearance goes, sir."

This was just typical. Vance was more interested in engaging in diversionary tomfoolery than finding out about a crisis that threatened to rip asunder the very social fabric of this town. Who did he think he was, anyway? He was a mere ex-sergeant and that was a long way down the ladder from a colonel or even a former mayor.

James started walking towards the exit but he stopped and turned. "I do hope you kept up your weapons training, Tom, because we happen to have a wild man and a wild dog on the loose in this town."

SIXTY-ONE
DOG CATCHER FOR LIFE

Wɪsʜ-Wᴀsʜ ᴡᴀs ɴᴏᴛ the first person to claim he had seen a Tasmanian Tiger.

But he was probably the first town drunk to do so.

For two weeks in 1967 Wish-Wash told anyone who would listen how a Tasmanian Tiger had woken him up from a nap in a bus shelter.

An initial report on the front page of the local rag caught the attention of mainland print and electronic media, who despatched their best news crews to find Wish-Wash. They came from all over to interview him, usually in his familiar spot in the back bar of The Applecart. One film crew even came from as far away as the United States. Wish-Wash had never had so much attention.

"Yeah," he'd say, after taking another swig of his cider. "The Tasmanian Tiger is alive and kicking here in Windy Mountain."

James felt this egregious deviation from truthfulness reflected poorly on the town. Windy Mountain was becoming the laughing stock of the world.

Wish-Wash's fertile imagination was probably fuelled by those books he liked to read — spacemen and time-travel and things that could not possibly be true. He could not help himself. Every time he told a story he embellished it just a bit more until finally it bore little resemblance to the original version.

If Wish-Wash had been a political adversary, James would have come at him with a tried-and-true tactic: discredit him, undermine him, and/or create a diversion by suggesting he had a questionable past. But he felt that wouldn't work in this case. For some reason, the locals seemed to like the town drunk.

So he could not believe his luck when he heard that a wild dog had been seen mauling and menacing sheep on farms near the township.

The Machiavellian streak in him sensed immediately he could kill two birds with one stone if he could propel the young council dog catcher, Douglas Dougal, into action.

Doggie, as he was known, worked out of the council depot, which was at the opposite end of town to the orchard.

Mayor Northan seldom went to the yard because it was both grimy and dangerous with all those tools and machinery in the sheds. In the corner stood at least half a dozen cages which were sometimes occupied by ferocious dogs. So he usually sent a more expendable underling.

But given the urgency of this issue, this time he had to make an exception and go himself.

"This must be important," Doggie said when he looked up to see James walking nervously towards him.

"It is," the Mayor said. "The safety of the townsfolk depends on your marksmanship."

"Say again?"

"I have a special job for you."

Doggie's role was normally to catch the canines. If they had to be put down, that was a job for the district vet. But James said the wild dog mauling the local sheep warranted a shoot-to-kill policy.

Doggie pointed out that shooting wild dogs wasn't in his job description.

"You are correct," the Mayor said. "But this town is at crisis point. Tell you what, you do this one thing and I will see to it you have a job for life."

"Can you do that?"

"I am the Mayor, am I not?"

Doggie's eyes lit up. "Well, in that case . . . "

"Just one other thing." The Mayor lowered his voice. "This is just between us, right? No need to parade the carcass when you kill this mongrel. Just take it to the tip and incinerate it."

Doggie did as he was asked, and James came good on his promise to honour the town's new hero.

He made Doggie the town's dog catcher for life.

Some years later he enacted the town's only-mayors-can-have-dogs policy, and covered it in enough red tape to bamboozle any dissenter.

He stood down as mayor near the end of 1994 after nearly 30 years in the job. His run-in with Moose triggered a nervous breakdown, then Prue walked out on him. He was a mess.

But Doggie stayed on. He didn't retire at 65 because he calculated he didn't have enough money to fund his retirement, and decided his job for life was a better deal, especially now he only had one dog to keep an eye on.

———

After failing to raise any alarm at the police station and/or the council chambers, James walked briskly to the works depot.

He found Doggie snoozing in a rocking chair in front of six empty cages.

The Mayor shook him. "Wake up, there's not a moment to waste."

Doggie opened his eyes. "What's the hurry? You haven't

found another piece of dog shit that couldn't possibly have come from your dog?"

"Very humorous! I have a witness this time. There really is an illegal canine in town. Quick, if you come with me, I'll show you where he is."

"Oh, no. It doesn't work like that these days. You'll need to fill out a form."

"A form? To tell you what?"

"We need to know what kind of dog we're dealing with, for a start."

"I don't know that! All I know is that it seems to belong to the Irishman who's taken over the Tasmanian Tiger Museum."

"Can't you even give a vague description?"

"Of whom? The canine or the Irishman?"

"The dog, of course. If, say, for argument's sake, it only has three legs, that can be a useful thing to know when I'm trying to follow its tracks. But there is a question on the form about the owner, too. From memory, I think it asks whether you know if he's a former mayor."

James stamped his foot. "This whole thing is ridiculous. It is red tape gone mad. If we go now we can catch the Irishman in the act."

Doggie's eyes widened. "Are you trying to get me into trouble, Mr Northan? We have to follow procedure these days, or else."

"Or else?"

"Or else the council might get sued."

"Over a dog?"

"I'm afraid that's the way it is these days. It'll only take you 30 minutes to fill in the form, and then we can do this thing properly."

"Good heavens! 30 minutes?"

"Forty minutes at the most."

"We do not have that kind of time to waste."

"What's the hurry? The dog will still be there tomorrow, won't it?"

"Tomorrow?" James's face dropped. "I thought if I filled in the form you could check it out today."

"Oh, no, I couldn't possibly do anything today." Doggie leaned back and started rocking. "I always knock off early on Mondays to make up for any extra hours I work over the rest of the week."

SIXTY-TWO
FLOWER OVERPOWER

THE OLD MEN were still catching their breaths after transferring Wish-Wash's big surprise from the back of Oodles's ute and arranging it around the foyer.

Wish-Wash had just slumped into his seat behind the counter when he heard a crackle of wheels on gravel outside, and looked up to see a delivery van parking. "Christ Almighty. I've just flamin' sat down."

The van was emblazoned on the side with Smith's Catering Supplies. The driver got out and opened the back.

"He's bringing a box in." Wish-Wash started rising from his chair. "You better go and tell him he's got the wrong place, Oodles."

"Don't you dare," came the voice from the top of the stairs, which was followed by a rapid cascading of footfalls that made the structure vibrate. Paddy appeared at the bottom, with bare feet, wet hair and a shirt he was still buttoning up. "I'll take it from here. Our catering supplies have arrived."

Wish-Wash sat back down. "What do we want with flamin' catering supplies? If people want a cuppa, why can't they go to the cafe up the road like everyone else?"

"I'll explain later." Paddy finished buttoning as he crossed the foyer and opened the door.

He smiled at the delivery man carrying the box past him, and pointed. "Put it down over there . . . um . . . " his voice trailed off, ". . . next to those yellow flowers."

Wish-Wash wondered when he'd notice. Did he think his cologne was the source of the lovely smell? The foyer was flooded with red roses, yellow roses, blue roses, long stemmed roses, short stemmed roses . . . it smelled like a florist's showroom

The delivery man pulled a piece of paper out of his pocket and, still puffing, looked at it over the top of the glasses balanced on the end of his nose. He touched the box. "Five dozen mugs here. I have a box of cups and saucers in the van, an urn and, um, a coffee machine." He looked at the paper again. "For Professor O'Brien?"

"That's me."

The man handed Paddy the invoice.

When he had left the building to fetch another item, Paddy said, "Where did all the flowers come from?"

"You said you liked the other ones I got for the vase?" Wish-Wash said.

"I did. And I do like these, too, I really do. But you can't afford all these?"

"Just don't you worry about what they cost, Professor. All you need to do is enjoy them."

His partner in crime scoffed. "He nicks them from the Colonel Richard Northan Memorial Rose Garden early in the morning when there are no witnesses."

Wish-Wash glared at him. "No one can flamin' prove that! Besides, it's not always early in the morning." He looked out the window towards the delivery van. "How much hard-earned are you paying for those?"

"I'm just doing what Sally Hopkins recommended."

"And you reckon she knows what she's talking about, do you?"

"Relax the cacks! This will have dual benefits. Aside from providing customers with cuppas, it'll keep the drivers and guides out in the foyer, which means they'll have no chance to put the scat under scrutiny."

"Did Sally Hopkins say who she thinks will run this show? If you're not here, that just leaves Oodles and me — which is OK if you don't mind a bit of spillage on the floor but you're asking for trouble if you expect us to operate a flamin' coffee machine. I've just taught myself how to drive the cash register, you can't expect me to become a flamin' barista overnight."

"Whoa," Paddy said. "You're getting all worked up for nothing. I told you yesterday, I've hired some help."

"Where did you find someone with those skills around here?"

"You'd be surprised what the younger generation can do with a decent coffee machine."

"Who?" Wish-Wash said.

"One of the Korean twins."

"Which one?"

"Vicki. Katy says she hasn't got enough work for her at the salon at the moment so I'd be doing her a favour."

"Does Jimbo know?" Wish-Wash said.

Oodles nodded towards a car that had pulled up next to the delivery van. "I think we're about to find out."

SIXTY-THREE
OUTING FOR AN OUTING

TWO MEN ALIGHTED. One was James Northan.

"Who's that with him?" Paddy asked.

"Trouble," Oodles said. "He's only brought the blinkin' dog catcher!"

Paddy opened the door again for the delivery man, who was carrying another large box, but James and Doggie Dougall cut in front of him.

"Gentleman." James nodded slightly at Oodles. "And others." He shifted his glare from Wish-Wash to Paddy.

He had both hearing aids in today, which is why he turned like the rest of them he heard a car pulling up outside.

A young Asian woman with green hair got out of the little red sedan and started walking towards the door.

James watched her enter. He looked shocked. "Velda? What are you doing here?"

"Granddad!"

He rolled his eyes and lowered his voice to a hiss. "I have told you before, do not call me that in public."

"Oh, sorry, Mr Northan. I've come to work here. Didn't Dad tell you?"

Oodles walked over to Paddy and said quietly, "I thought we were getting Vicki."

"So did I."

"That's definitely Velda," Oodles said. "Vicki has purple hair and Velda has green hair. It's the only way anyone can tell them apart."

Velda must have heard them because she said to Paddy, "I hope you don't mind I swapped jobs with Vicki. She's working at the takeaway today."

"You sure you know what to do?" Paddy said. "I don't want you driving my customers away because you don't like the provenance of my coffee beans, or something like that."

She pulled out a pair of latex gloves from her handbag. "As long as no one gives me their germs, I'll be fine."

James waggled his finger at the Irishman. "It is not fine with me."

Paddy looked down at him and scowled. "I'm not sure it's any of your business. She's an adult, probably a future mayor from what I've heard."

"A future mayor?" James choked on a gulp of air. "Over my dead body."

Wish-Wash threw his hands in the air. "Yessss, bring it on."

The Mayor looked around at all the flowers, and re-aimed his finger at Wish-Wash. "Have you been at it again? It is high time somebody reports this."

During all this commotion, no one noticed the other man come in. The door was opening and closing anyway with the delivery man coming in and out, so it's no wonder they didn't see him.

But when Paddy saw the stranger standing there listening, he said, "Can I help you, sir?"

He cleared his throat. "My name is Peter Rowbottom." His voice rose. "I've come to pick up my dog."

Paddy gave Oodles and Wish-Wash a puzzled look.

Oodles broke into a grin. "Excellent timing, Pete. Gough is around the back. His leash is hanging next to his kennel."

Out of the side of his mouth, Oodles said to Paddy. "I'll explain later, OK?"

James looked from face to face. "You named your dog Gough?"

"Don't look at me, Jimbo," Wish-Wash said. "That was Oodles's idea. I wanted to call him Trotsky."

"Is this right, Mr Rowbottom?" James said. "You allowed these reprobates here to name your dog?"

"You know me, James. I've only ever been good at naming cats. You can't call a dog Tiddles, can you?"

"Oh, my dizzy aunt! Since when did you decide to start owning dogs?"

"I'm allowed, aren't I?" Rowbottom said. "Under the statute, I'm entitled to do so as a former mayor."

James's face was ablaze. He stamped his foot. "I get it? You are all conspiring against me."

He turned on Doggie Dougall. "*You* must have told this old fairy about this? You were the only person who knew we were coming here this morning."

Rowbottom stepped between them. "That's right, he did tell me," he said. "In bed last night, if you must know."

"I beg your pardon!" James spluttered.

"You heard it here first, OK?" Rowbottom said. "We've both come out of the closet."

"The closet! I never thought you even went *into* the closet. But him?" James pointed a trembling finger at the dog catcher. "I remember when he had the eyes of all the young girlies around town!"

"Obviously you don't know where he got his nickname from?" Rowbottom smiled at Doggie and moved closer to him. "He's rented out his place to his washing lady and moved into my house. There, I'm glad it's out in the open. It's been a chore going discreetly from house to house all these years."

James's face was like a red balloon about to burst.

"You can't blame Doggie for seeking my advice," Rowbottom said. "Yesterday he had one dog to worry about; now he's suddenly had his workload doubled. Is council going to raise his salary commensurately? I don't think so."

"This is preposterous," James said. "It was bad enough having one queer in town! But two! No, three if you count the council-clerk! As if Maddie didn't have enough to worry about with Moose Routley showing his face in town again!"

Oodles pointed towards Paddy. "You know as well as we do, James, that was a case of mistaken identity."

The Mayor stamped a foot. "I saw Moose with my own eyes in the Wind Tunnel Cafe yesterday. His beard is a bit greyer than it used to be, but it's him all right. No telling what he'll do this time."

With those words, he unplugged his hearing aids.

If he heard the screech of brakes and flying gravel outside, he showed no signs of it.

He marched past the tour bus and continued up the street.

Among the people who got off the bus was Sally Hopkins — which meant she could see the new catering setup in action.

The last person to get off the bus was a large, bald man with a spider-web tattoo on his neck.

Paddy gulped. Things had gone arseways again!

SIXTY-FOUR
CHANGE OF PLANS

PADDY SCAMPERED to the other side of the counter and crouched down below it.

Wish-Wash was still in the chair.

Paddy looked up at him and spoke in a panicked whisper. "Tell me when they've all gone into the gallery."

A few minutes later, he heard Sally Hopkins's voice on the other side and it sounded like she was writing a cheque. "I see the catering supplies have arrived. I'm looking forward to morning tea." Then she was gone and Paddy heard a scuttling of feet and the swing of a door.

"Is everyone gone?" he said softly.

Wish-Wash looked down at him. "Christ Almighty, what's going on?"

Paddy started to rise slowly "Do you mind sitting in for me for a bit longer? I need to go upstairs."

"You still haven't told me what's going on?"

Paddy turned to Oodles who was on the other side of the counter. "Change of plans. Are you OK to take me fly-fishing today?"

"Today? It's the grand final of the pub trivia night tonight. They're relying on me."

Paddy pondered this for a moment. "Guess I'll have to go on my own then. Can you point me in the roight direction?"

Oodles shut his eyes for a second. "I can't let you go to Bing Bong Mountain alone. Even if you made it up there, you'd never be able to find your way back. If the tiger snakes didn't get you, the Tassie Devils certainly would. You'd feed a whole family of them, perhaps two families."

"So you will take me?"

"I said I would, didn't I? A promise is a promise."

"Hang on," Wish-Wash said. "When you asked me to mind the desk a bit longer, just how long were you talking about?"

Paddy patted him on the shoulder. "Would you mind looking after the museum for two days? You did such a good job yesterday."

"You didn't flamin' think that then."

"I was having a bad day, OK? But today suddenly got worse, and I really need you to cover for me."

"But two days! That's asking a lot."

"I know. But please. I can't explain right now but you'll just have to take my word that it's a life-and-death situation."

"That urgent, eh? Well . . ."

Paddy turned for the stairs. "I can't tank you enough, Wish-Wash. When I get back, I'll find a way to start paying you. Promise."

On the way, he said. "You're a star, too, Oodles. You know I wouldn't impose on you unless it was important."

The old man sighed. "Last year's champions probably have the wood on us again anyway. I mightn't have made a difference."

The stairs trembled again as Paddy started bounding up.

"We should be back Thursday lunchtime, Wish-Wash," he shouted as he went around the first bend. "Go home now, Oodles, and pack the things we need."

Then his voice came from near the top of the stairs. "Oh

tanks Doggie. Tanks Peter. I'm not sure yet how you fellas fit into all this, but tanks heaps."

He bellowed from the top. "And tanks for coming, Velda. I'm sure you'll make a big difference."

Wish-Wash looked at Oodles, searching for further explanation.

But Oodles shrugged. "You know as much as me, old cock."

"Does he know how important the flamin' trivia grand final is to you? You've been practising for months."

Oodles shrugged again. "They'll have to do without me. You heard Paddy. It's a life-and-death situation."

SIXTY-FIVE

BOOT'S ON THE OTHER FOOT

BILLY WOULD NEVER FORGET Moose kicking that winning goal in 1994.

Even though selectors had sacked him from the team, they couldn't prevent him being a spectator.

The recollection helped him forget he was bored out of his brain hiding in the sitting room.

In reality, he was lying on the couch, hands locked behind his head.

But he only had to close his eyes to rerun the memory of watching that glorious grand final on a rainy Saturday in September.

He was standing by the boundary fence with a good view of the Tigers' half-forward line.

He could even smell the pie he was munching into during those exciting, final minutes.

The crowd held its collective breath as Moose gathered the ball on the grandstand wing with the clock counting down.

Cool as you like, Moose ran 10 or 11 steps, bounced the ball, ran eight more steps, then sank his boot into the water-logged football.

It didn't seem possible anyone could kick that far in those

conditions. But the ball tumbled end-over-end through the air and sailed through the goals, and Windy Mountain went from five points behind to one point up.

Then the final siren blew, and wild applause erupted as everyone breathed again.

Billy threw away his half-eaten pie, and joined hundreds of people who vaulted the fence and ran on to the ground to congratulate the players.

He was one of the first to reach Moose and he helped chair the big man off the ground. Moose stank of mud, sweat and liniment, but it didn't worry Billy. He was elated. Moose had unwittingly forced Billy into an early, enforced retirement. But he had been wearing Billy's boots, and one of those boots had scored the goal that ended such a long premiership drought.

Billy savoured the memory as he stretched back on the couch.

He could hear movement downstairs, and lots of muffled chatter.

So this was what solitary confinement was like?

Still, it would be worth doing the time just to see the look on everyone's face when he turned up at the reunion.

Would a news photographer capture the moment? His mum would like that. Marta had cut out every article that had mentioned him since he had started playing football.

SIXTY-SIX
WHAT COULD POSSIBLY GO WRONG?

PADDY HAD BARELY STARTED OPENING the door when he heard Billy say, "Have you brought me something else to eat?"

"No, I have not," Paddy whispered as he opened wider. He stepped inside and closed the door gently behind him, trying not to make a sound. "I just need to get away from that lot downstairs for a while. Anyway, you should wait to see who's coming through the door before starting with your blathering. Jaysus! If it's someone who you don't know, you're supposed to be a deaf mute."

"I recognised your heavy footsteps."

"If I'm such a dead ringer for Moose Routley, how'd you know it wasn't him?"

Paddy sat down in the armchair opposite. "He's back in town, you know?"

Billy beamed. "Is he?"

"According to James Northan, he is."

"Him?" Billy said. "Moose could have done us all a favour by hitting that bloke a bit harder and actually killing him."

"That's a bit harsh, isn't it?"

"Maybe, but what's a few more years in jail for a bloke like Moose."

"I didn't mean you were being harsh on Moose, I meant it was a bit harsh saying that about James Northan."

"Have you even met the man?"

"Didn't you hear him shouting downstairs?"

"He hates this place. So you must have made him pretty mad for him even to visit."

Billy seemed to be waiting for the full story, but all Paddy said was, "He's gone now. Thank God."

"So why are you hiding up here?"

"I'm not hiding," Paddy said. "I'm resting, that's all."

"Resting for how long?"

"It depends how long the group that just arrived stays in the building."

"That could be an hour."

"Maybe two, now we're serving coffee and tea."

"You're serving drinks?"

"Not me. Velda. Do you know her?"

"The Green Wiggle? Oh, yeah, I know her. Not as well as I'd like to, mind . . . " Billy's mind looked like it was somewhere else.

"You really are a sleaze-bag, Gumboots."

"Thanks."

"That wasn't meant to be a compliment."

"So did you bring a pack of cards with you?"

"Cards?"

"What else are we going to do for two hours?"

"Dunno," the Irishman said. "Talk? Do you know anything about fly-fishing? Oodles is taking me up to Bing Bong Mountain."

"I thought that silly old bloke gave up that caper when his missus was killed."

"He did," Paddy said. "But I've persuaded him to come out of retirement."

Billy shook his head. "When?"

"Today."

Billy plunged his head into his hands. "Sheesh. You said Katy was coming around to cut my beard off?"

Paddy blinked slowly. "Would you mind putting it off?"

"Fair dinkum, it's not just about looking good for Friday. I've got to get some money in my pocket before I go to the reunion. The drinks there will probably be free, but what if we kick on to somewhere expensive? Do you even know how long you are going for?"

"Two nights. We'll be back on Thursday afternoon. So tThere'll be plenty of time."

Billy rubbed a hand over the right side of his thin beard. "What if something goes wrong?"

"We're going fishing, not jumping out of planes! What could possibly go wrong?"

SIXTY-SEVEN

COMING CLEAN

PADDY WATCHED Oodles lay down the equipment and provisions on the back patio.

Two fishing rods, a tackle box, two sleeping bags, two rolled-up foam mattresses, a small spade, a dozen cans of assorted food, packets of tea, salt and sugar, a frying pan, a billy, two chipped enamel mugs, two even more chipped enamel plates, two sets of rubber waders, two oilskin coats and two backpacks . . .

"Do we really need all of this?"

"Too right we do," Oodles said. "And you'll need to pack at least two sets of clothes so you're prepared for the worst weather." He patted his pocket. "And don't let me forget the matches — unless you like your trout raw, *if* we catch some."

"What do you mean *if?*"

"It's not a lay-down misere, old son. Sometimes the fish don't bite."

"Really? You mean we go to the trouble of hiking in with all this stuff, all for nothing. That's not very sporting of the fish!"

"Lesson No. 1 is to have low expectations." Oodles tapped Paddy on his upper left arm and smiled. "Don't look so worried though. I might be a bit rusty, but hopefully I haven't lost the touch."

Then his face creased up. "Are you sure you want to go on this trip, old son? I wouldn't think any less of you if you changed your mind."

Paddy waved his finger. "Don't think you get out of this that easily?"

"I'm honestly not trying to squib out. It's just all this is happening so quickly. And another thing . . . " Oodles turned sideways and lowered his voice so Wish-Wash couldn't hear. "What about your cousin?"

"My cousin?" Paddy had momentary amnesia.

"Won't he get lonely upstairs in hiding?"

It came back to Paddy, almost. "Shaun?"

"I thought you said his name was Nigel."

"Did I?" He had to think quickly to cover his faux pas. "How rude of me to call him by his surname! But you don't have to worry about him because he's moved on."

"Where's he gone?"

Paddy shrugged. "You know what these illegal immigrants are like? They don't like to leave tracks or forwarding addresses."

Paddy pointed to the rolled-up blue plastic parcel on the ground. "I heard that rattling when you put it down. What is it?"

"It's a two-man tent, hopefully with all the pegs." Oodles sighed. "It might be a bit of a tight fit for both of us but it'll have to do."

"Why do we need a tent at all?" Paddy said.

Oodles looked at him as if he were stupid. "Where else are we going to sleep?"

"Isn't there a hut?"

"Jesus wept, Bing Bong Mountain is the heart of the wilderness." He pointed to the spade. "Did you think we're going up there to do a spot of gardening?"

"I hadn't really thought about it. But a tent . . . ?"

"I know what you're worried about? You're worried your snoring will keep me awake? Well, perish the thought. I'm betting my snoring is much louder than yours."

"Can't I sleep outside?"

"Perhaps." Oodles looked up at the clear sky. "But the weather changes quickly up there."

"But if it's noice, I could sleep outside?"

"Up to you, old son — but you run the risk of being eaten alive by mozzies, or a tiger snake crawling into your sleeping bag."

———

Their aim was to set out straight after lunch, and leave Wish-Wash with the dishes.

But Oodles had time to swing a tea towel, after all, because Paddy said he had to go make a phone call.

When they did hit the track, Oodles took one look at him and said, "Strewth, anyone would think we're going to the beach judging by all the sunscreen on your face."

"My fair skin burns in this sun."

"You smell like a coconut. You'd better walk behind me till the pong disappears."

Then he said, "Who were you talking to on the phone?"

"Katy."

Oodles's voice came out strained. "You still don't get it, do you?"

———

Paddy started with the heavier of the two backpacks, and it just got heavier as they traipsed up the narrow, uneven paths to Bing Bong Mountain.

This was because they stopped every half an hour to transfer stuff from Oodles's pack to Paddy's.

"I can cope," Oodles protested every time. But he fell further and further behind, and Paddy had to stop regularly to let him catch up. The further up they went, the more the old man listed, and his walk became a shuffle. Paddy was worried Oodles would stumble and hurt himself.

Oodles was puffing as he handed over yet more gear. "I just don't remember it being this steep."

They arrived at the upper reaches of the river before darkness fell, but the journey took nearly five hours rather than the three they had planned for.

Oodles said they should get the camp site set up pronto.

"You're the boss." Paddy was glad to put down his heavy cargo so he could wipe off the sweat that was running down from his brow and stinging his eyes. "What do you want me to do?"

"Since you've got the tent, why don't you go and put that up over there." Oodles pointed back the way they had come. "We don't want to be too close to the river. Running water doesn't play well with my bladder overnight."

"Ah, one snag." Paddy mopped his forehead with his handkerchief. "I'm not sure where to start. I've never had to put up a tent before."

"Never? You must have gone camping as a little tacker?"

"I never got the chance." Paddy stared at his feet.

The colour had returned to the old man's face, but it drained again when he heard what Paddy said next.

"I think the time's come for me to come clean. You'd better start calling me Joffa because that's my real name."

SIXTY-EIGHT
AN ARSONIST CALLED JOFFA

OODLES AND JOFFA sat cross-legged around the campfire.

"I'll say this: you know how to build a good fire." Then Oodles realised what he had said. "Oh, I didn't mean it that way, Paddy, I mean, er, Joffa."

The Irishman stared into the flames, transfixed by the flickering yellows and reds and the occasional blue tips.

"I still can't believe it." Oodles shook his head. "You? An arsonist?"

———

When Joffa was eight he had set light to his primary school in Dublin. He didn't know a janitor was inside. But that poor fella died and Joffa was sent to a youth correctional centre for three years. It was there his name morphed from Jerome O'Fury to a nickname based on his initials.

A year after his release, his family emigrated to Australia to make a fresh start.

Joffa made a name for himself as a schoolboy swimmer. But when he was 15 he was beaten by a bitter rival in a race, and took out his frustrations by trying to set fire to items in his locker at the pool. He was caught in the act and, worse, he was accused of lighting a spate of fires he had nothing to do with. This time he was incarcerated for much longer.

He couldn't blame his parents for moving back to Ireland in shame. But they could at least have left a forwarding address.

As Joffa elaborated on his story, Oodles's head shook from side to side on the other side of the fire. "I don't know what to say, old son. I can't for the life of me understand why anyone would deliberately light fires?"

Joffa hung his head. "I can't explain why I did it. All I can say it's a long way in my past now, and I've honestly moved on."

"Wish-Wash and I did wonder about you. But we didn't suspect you had been in jail. Heck, you don't even smoke?"

"What's that got to do with it?"

"I thought every one in jail smoked."

"That's a stereotype. That and the fact that they took away my matches."

He had tried six times to win parole.

He finally cracked it with the help of Johannes Tomasch, who worked for a voluntary organisation that went into bat for the prisoners that the legal system gave up on.

Joh had let him live at his place in Paddington until he got back on his feet.

He even found him a job as a dishwasher at a restaurant.

Joffa just did his job, and said very little as he wrestled with pots and pans.

Most of the conversations around him were conducted in a different language, anyway, and it took weeks for him to twig something else was going on.

He worked out the kitchen was actually the command centre for a people-smuggling operation.

When he told Joh about this, the lawyer had informed the federal police and got Joffa straight out of there.

He didn't want the authorities to suspect Joffa might be involved, too.

Now he was a key witness, Joh said he wanted to get the Irishman well away from the felons until the police could gather enough evidence to arrest them.

The job at the Windy Mountain Tasmanian Tiger Museum presented itself as the perfect cover. All Joffa had to do was pretend he was someone else, sit tight for a few months and return to Sydney to testify.

"I wasn't scared of them." Joffa watched the billy begin to hiss and boil. "You know I can handle myself. But Joh insisted. And everything was going to plan until a fella I was in jail with got off that tour bus this morning."

Oodles's leathery face creased. "And you're sure it was the same bloke?"

"No question. Bruiser Brown. Big, bald fella with a spider web tattoo on his neck."

Oodles exhaled, making the flames bend. "Did he see you?"

"I don't think so. But I didn't want to take any chances because he knows what I look like. I put him in the prison hospital once and the next time I saw him he was on duty behind the serving counter handing me a plate with a smirk. I knew then he had just gobbed in the gravy and stirred it in."

He smiled at the memory. "It didn't go to waste though. Bruiser's best mate was at our table and when he saw I wasn't eating, asked if I minded if he ate it."

Oodles laughed. "So this Bruiser Brown knows the blokes who might be looking for you now?"

"I doubt it. *His* kind wouldn't give *their* kind the time of day. But some of the bad fellas he mixes with *do* mix with those other ones, and I didn't want to take any chances of my whereabouts getting back to them."

SIXTY-NINE
IN THE DRIVING SEAT

For the first time in his life, Wish-Wash wished he had a wife to look him over before handing him his lunchbox and waving him off to work.

What do you think, honey? Does this striped blue tie I bought at the op shop go well with my Hawaiian shirt?

As he came around the front of the museum just before 7am, he felt a bit guilty. He wished he had sounded more grateful. The Professor didn't have to hand him the key to the front door, not after he had breached his trust by snooping around upstairs and then banning that tour guide.

Wish-Wash took the key out of his pocket with the reverence normally reserved for handling religious icons. He looked around, hoping to catch a glimpse of a person or three gobsmacked by the sight of him performing this door-unlocking ritual while dressed up to the nines.

But no one was milling around the street at that time of the morning.

Even Velda wasn't expected until 8am, shortly before the first of the three buses were due.

She had done a sterling job yesterday, making the various coffees and tea for all those people. Who knew there were so many types of coffee? Cappuccinos, expressos, lattes, macchiatos, doppios, mochas, flat whites . . . even tea came in different varieties. One bloke even wanted peppermint tea. Left to his own devices, Wish-Wash would have asked him if he wanted one squirt or two of the toothpaste tube into his cup of hot water.

Wish-Wash carefully put the key back in his pocket and walked over to the desk as if he owned the place.

He sat down with a feeling of satisfaction. It was like the old days when he had his own stool in the back bar of The Applecart, and other drinkers knew not to sit in his spot. The main difference was he wasn't surrounded by flowers then. This was *his chair* for two whole days.

He looked at the cash register and wondered why he had ever been frightened by it.

A few days ago, he had probably been regarded as the town's least socially upward mobile person.

But now he was operating the till, being entrusted with amounts of money he had never dreamed of handling, and using a range of social skills he didn't even know he had. And it was all because of this young Irishman. Bless him.

Wish-Wash swivelled around. The clock on the back wall said it was five past seven.

The first bus of the day was an hour away and he wondered now why he had come so early?

He heard a noise upstairs.

He pricked his ears. It sounded like creaking floorboards. But that didn't make sense because Paddy couldn't possibly be up there.

That's when Wish-Wash realised he had an even greater responsibility. Protection trumped privacy.

He crept up the stairs.

It was a toss-up who got the bigger shock when he opened the living room door. Him or Billy Gumboots?

SEVENTY
SPILLING THE BEANS

Roger Dykes cringed when the bus pulled into the car park.

He was sitting in the jump seat next to the driver and had a good view into the museum. It looked like the old bloke was behind the desk.

This was all he needed!

Dykes was on his last warning.

Twice now he had returned to base at the end of the day with one passenger fewer than he had left with, he had been hungover at work too many times to mention and he had been late three times and missed his bus.

Sally Hopkins had stepped in for him twice in a few days, which had infuriated her.

This morning she had read him the riot act. Someone had accused him of being drunk on duty. When he complained back to her that no one should have to tolerate being called names such as Big Nose or Roy Orbison in the course of work, she just told him to grow a thicker skin. One more mistake, and he'd be back in the job queue.

Dykes could not prove Wish-Wash had complained but you didn't have to be Einstein to join the dots.

What had the old man said? That he'd be reporting him if

he didn't leave the premises right away? It wasn't his fault the Irishman had invited him back.

He spoke into his microphone. "If I can have your attention, ladies and gentlemen. Here we are at our first stop of the day, the Windy Mountain Tasmanian Tiger Museum, where you will get to see a very recent remnant that challenges the claim the last Thylacine died in 1936. Please disembark and go through to the museum. Our driver will accompany you in. Afterwards, there will be complementary tea and coffee in the foyer."

The driver glared at him and whispered. "Bad enough I have to cover for you when you're late. Now you want me to do your job for you, too."

"Just this one time, please. I really can't go into the museum."

Inside, about all Wish-Wash could see against the morning sun was a big bus parked in the car park.

He got a better view as people started alighting.

Big Nose was second-last off, holding what looked like a cheque book.

Dykes was last off. As he descended the steps, Dykes had a full-on view through the museum window. The Irishman was no where in sight, nor was Killer.

"I'm just walking up the road to that cafe," he told the driver, who was directing passengers to the door. "I need a coffee."

"You can get a cuppa in the foyer," Big Nose said. "That's what I'm going to do while the group is in the gallery."

"Have you seen who's behind the desk?"

"We don't even have to talk to him."

But Dykes was already walking away.

———

When he walked into the Wind Tunnel Cafe, both tables were occupied.

Three men sat at one table, and an elderly man and woman at the other.

"Ye're welcome to take a seat here," the old chap lilted. He wore a priest's collar and when he poured the last drops of tea into his cup, his liver-spotted hand quivered. "We'll be leaving soon. Won't we, Daisy?"

"You sure?" Dykes said. "I don't want to intrude."

The man pointed to a spare chair. "Get away with ye, take the weight off yer feet."

"Thanks." Dykes sat down. "Are you any relation to the two Irish blokes at the Tasmanian Tiger museum?"

"Two? I only know about the *one* from Dublin."

"You didn't meet Paddy's cousin from Dingle?"

The priest and his lady companion looked at each other.

One of the men at the other table turned around. He looked a bit like a head on a pogo stick.

"Excuse me, but I couldn't help overhearing." He spoke with a European accent. "Paddy has his cousin staying with him?"

"Sure does," Dykes said. "His cousin is a deaf mute."

The man turned to his companions. Judging by their expressions, they had never met Paddy's cousin either.

The big, blond man said something, but he was terribly hard to understand because he hardly opened his lips.

"What Gordo is trying to ask," the head on the pogo stick said, "Is what does this deaf mute look like?"

Dykes pinched his nose and closed his eyes as he tried to summon up the image. "He was sitting down, but I guess he is fairly tall with a scruffy beard. Oh, and he has a big silver earring."

"Interesting," the priest said as he rose from the table. "So Paddy has a cousin here? Haven't been dis many Irishmen in dis town since transportation."

Daisy got up, too. She smiled at Dykes. "Nice to meet you."

The pogo stick turned to the man at the table who had his left arm in a sling. "I think we've fallen on our feet here. I just knew those photos would come in handy."

Father O'Rourke and Daisy were only half a block away when they heard footsteps running behind them, and turned.

"Can I have a word, Father?" the man in the sling said.

"Of course, Freddy," the priest said. "What did ye do to your arm?"

"I cut myself shaving."

The priest laughed. "Do ye want to talk here or back at the church?" He laughed again. "Dis better not be about the Titanic. She was fine when she left our emerald shores."

Freddy stepped towards and held out the A4 yellow envelope he held in his good hand. "No, here's fine. This concerns you both."

SEVENTY-ONE

FATHER O'ROURKE, THIS IS YOUR LIFE

FREDDY HANDED over the envelope on the footpath.

"What's dis?"

"Father O'Rourke, this is your life." Freddy laughed. "Go on, open it."

The priest unsealed the top and slid out the contents. They were photographs of him and Daisy walking together, dining together, and sitting on the bench together eating jellybeans.

The priest looked up. "I don't understand."

"On their own they're quite innocent," Freddy said. "But they do tell part of a very interesting story." He reached inside his jacket pocket with his good hand and pulled out another photograph he handed over.

Father O'Rourke took one look and said, "Oh good lord. How did ye get dis?"

Daisy leaned over to see, and the colour drained from her face.

The photograph had been taken through the bedroom window of the presbytery. But how was that even possible? The bedroom was upstairs.

"Who do you suggest we should send these to?" Freddy said. "The archbishop? The Vatican?"

"If you're trying to blackmail me, you're wasting yer time," Father O'Rourke said. "I haven't got any money. In case ye didn't know, I've taken a vow of poverty."

Freddy snatched back the photo and held it up to the priest's face. "You took a vow of chastity, too, so how does this fit in?" He pointed. "What's Daisy doing in this picture? Praying?"

Both Daisy and the priest looked ashen-faced now.

But Freddy said, "This is your lucky day because no one else has to see these pics. All you have to do, Father, is hear a confession from one of the lost sheep from your flock . . . and tell us what he says."

SEVENTY-TWO

THE TRUTH ABOUT BILLY

OODLES WAS like a contented dog sniffing the breeze. "Didn't I tell you it was lovely up here?"

The first night of camping had gone well. The Irishman had been quite happy to sleep in the tent, as it turned out. If Oodles had snored, Joffa didn't say. The young bloke seemed happy to zip up the tent and seal them in.

They had hit the river early on Wednesday morning when the sun was just starting to rise.

Oodles spent the first hour explaining how to cast, the best flies to use, where to stand, etc. He had then planted a large stick in the bank of one of the biggest basins on this stretch of the river. "You can roam anywhere downstream of this stick."

"Where will you be?"

Oodles pointed upstream. "My part of the river is up there. Don't worry, I'll check on you once in a while to make sure a snake hasn't got you."

When Oodles returned two hours later, he was carrying two fair-sized rainbow trout. Joffa had caught nothing but snags.

As Oodles cleaned his catch, Joffa sat on a nearby rock, staring into space.

The sky was blue, with not a cloud in sight. The mountain water trickled down the slope, forming little crystal-clear ponds at the bottom of babbling waterfalls. The branches on the trees barely quivered in the gentlest of breezes. And an orchestra of birds chirped and warbled.

"These will make a mighty fine breakfast." Oodles continued to scale the fish with his pocketknife. It was the same knife he used to carve notches into the bench, the same knife Madge had bought for him all those years ago. It had gone through half a dozen blades since then but it had the same bone handle.

The former owner of the Wind Tunnel Cafe had done more than get him a job in 1972.

He had sown the seed that would get him hooked on fly-fishing.

Oodles would never forget what the man had done when he returned from the kitchen with their tray on which were two fine china cups, a teapot covered with a bright red woollen tea cosy, a plate of succulent scones, two little porcelain tubs which contained dollops of strawberry jam and cream, three side plates and assorted cutlery.

He set the tray down, then sat down at the table. "You don't mind if I sit here, do you?"

"Ah, no . . ." What else could Oodles say? The man was already seated.

The man reached out for one of the five plump scones on the tray and waved it under his nose. "Mmmm. Hope they taste as good as they smell."

Oodles and Madge looked at each other.

"I know what you're thinking." The man lathered his scone with jam and cream. "Three people, only two cups . . . But you're not to worry. I'm not having tea. I just wanted to try one of these beauties. That's why I put an extra one on the plate."

He took a large bite, leaned back in his chair, and closed his eyes for a moment. "Oh yes, I can die happy now, Beryl."

He opened his eyes and licked his lips, and wiped his hands on his apron. "Beryl's my wife. She's the cook around here."

He threw out a still-sticky hand to Clarrie to shake. "Bill Watley. I don't suppose you want to buy a cafe, do you?"

"Ah, no . . ." His voice trailed off, then gathered pace again. "Clarrie Noodle, glad to meet you."

Bill turned to Madge "And, this is Mrs Noodle, I presume?"

"Madge," she said. She always hated being called Mrs Noodle. Or worse, Mrs Clarrie Noodle.

"Where have you come from, Clarrie?"

"Melbourne."

"On holiday?"

"Nope," Oodles said. "I hope to get a job down in Hobart. Is there much work down that way?"

"Depends what you do?"

"I worked for a council back in Melbourne but I'll turn my hand to most things. Except for running cafes, sorry."

"Can't say I blame you." Bill munched back into his scone. "I've been trying to offload this place for nine years. Law of averages says I've got to hit on the right passers-by sooner or later. It's like fishing, eh? You can sit on the riverbank for hours without a bite. Then suddenly: ZZzzzzzzzzzzzzzzzzzzzz."

The comparison was lost on Oodles. "I've never actually been fishing."

"This might be your lucky day, then. I hear the local council is hiring. They'd probably kill for an experienced codger like you. You could try some trout fishing, too, in your spare time."

Oodles inspected the fish he was cleaning to be sure he

had got all the scales. He glanced across to Joffa, who looked like someone had died.

"It took me weeks to catch my first trout."

"It's not that," the Irishman said. "It's what's waiting for me back at Windy Mountain that worries me."

"Relax. Your secret is safe with me." Oodles walked over and held up the gutted fish. "Cheer up, these fish look happier than you do. And you also need to gather some wood for the campfire."

Joffa chewed his lip. "You sure you're fine with me building a fire?"

"You can put a match to it, for all I care. I reckon a bloke deserves a second chance. And if push comes to shove, I reckon most folk around here will feel the same. You've built up some brownie points."

"You don't know the people looking for me. These are bad bastards, and if they find me. . . "

Then he said, "There's something else I haven't told you, Oodles. The people-smugglers I am hiding from aren't the only people-smugglers in my life."

The old man's facial wrinkles doubled.

"Turns out the Tasmanian Tiger museum is just a front for smuggling Tasmanians to the mainland."

"What *are* you talking about?"

"Biggs and Sons smuggle people to Victoria."

Oodles laughed. "Who told you that nonsense? Tasmanians can move to the mainland freely. They'd have to be stupid to pay people smugglers good money."

Joffa shrugged. "I'm only telling you what Billy Gumboots told me."

"Billy Gumboots? Not you too? I saw him being lowered into the ground."

Joffa shook his head. "All you saw was a coffin. He faked his death and hid a diary that would incriminate the people-smugglers." He hung his head again. "I lied when I told you I had my cousin staying with me. It's Billy Gumboots, and he's still there."

"I'll be." Now Oodles stared into space. "Are you sure it's him?"

"I'm sure," Joffa said. "He plans to crash the football reunion on Friday."

Oodles whistled tunelessly into the air.

SEVENTY-THREE
'WE KNOW HE'S THERE'

WISH-WASH ANSWERED the phone all business-like. "Tasmanian Tiger Museum, how can I help you?"

"Wish-Wash, me old cocksparrow, where's the big Irish git?"

"He's gone fishing with Oodles. Who is this?"

"I thought you would have recognised my voice. It's Freddy. Freddy Cuthbert."

Wish-Wash spluttered into the mouthpiece. "I thought Paddy told you not to come near this place."

"If I had known he wasn't actually there, Gordo and I would have come in person. I guess it's your lucky day, old man."

Wish-Wash heard another bus pull up outside and looked up to see its door open.

"Look, I have to go," he said. "What is it you want?"

"Be nice. I was hoping to go through the Irishman, let him know he only won round one and the fight's not over yet. But I guess you'll do."

There was a long pause on the line. Then Freddy said, "We know Billy Gumboots is hiding there. I need you to pass him this message."

SEVENTY-FOUR

CONFESSION IS GOOD FOR THE SOLE

THE MESSAGE WISH-WASH relayed to Billy Gumboots was that Moose Routley wanted to meet him at the church first thing on Thursday to work out some kind of deal.

But when he got there, he found Father O'Boring waiting in the dimly lit interior, dressed in a long-sleeved white linen garment with a purple stole hanging around his neck.

"Ye all roight, Billy? Ye don't look yer normal self," the priest said.

"Where's Moose?"

"Moose?"

"The message I got was he wanted to see me. I was hoping he's ready to let me have at least a share of the glory."

Father O'Boring shook his head. "I don't know anyting about dat. I was tol' ye want me to hear yer confession."

He pointed to the confession box. "Shall we? Dis is a first for me. I usually hear people's confessions *before* dey die."

SEVENTY-FIVE
HEADFIRST

"TOUGHEST FISH I EVER HAD," Oodles said as he scraped up the last remnants of George from his enamel plate.

They were back at the campsite, sitting around the fire.

Oodles rubbed his stomach. "Probably the best fish I ever tasted though."

"That sounds warped to me," the Irishman said. "Remind me not to come back as a fish so you can hunt me down and eat me."

"You caught him, old son. Didn't I see you eating him, too?"

"Yes. But you ate the end with the head. I think you'd better see a psychiatrist about that."

They had survived their second night together in the tent, and had hit the river at dawn.

Joffa got a strike on his first cast. Oodles had barely started walking to his spot upstream when he heard the splashing of water and Joffa's whoop of excitement.

He got back to the clearing in time to see the big Irishman land the monster, his very first fish.

"You reckon this is the fish you told me about?"

"Without a doubt. It's George, all right."

"Can I get him mounted on the wall?"

"Be buggered. I've waited a long time to get even with this fish." He handed Joffa his knife. "Kill him quickly before he jumps back into the water."

They grilled George over the coals and ate him greedily for breakfast.

Oodles looked up at the trees swaying. "The weather is turning a bit nasty. We better start packing up to head home."

"It's a warm wind though." Joffa looked skyward, too. "No rain clouds I can see."

"Still, we'd better make tracks soon if you want to be home by lunchtime."

"What's the hurry?"

Oodles shrugged. "It's not the kind of walk you want to do in the dark, but I guess we have a bit more time. Just try not to catch such a heavy trout this time though. It'd be more weight to carry home."

SEVENTY-SIX
FIRE AND BRIMSTONE

Henk van Gogh knew Billy wouldn't give up his secret easily. That's why he told Freddy and Gordo to go to the church to soften him up, persuade him to tell the priest everything they wanted to know.

"What is it you want us to do exactly, boss?" Freddy said.

"Use your imagination. The less I know the better."

The three of them were sitting at a table at the Wind Tunnel Cafe. Freddy, his head swathed in bandages and his left arm in a sling, looked at Gordo, hoping he had some kind of idea but all he got was a blank look straight back at him.

"Goodness me! How hard could it be to come up with some fire and brimstone? Do I have to do every fugging, little thing myself?"

"No, boss." Freddy staggered to his feet. "We'll think of something, won't we Gordo?"

Once outside, Gordo said, "What exactly is brimstone anyway?" (It sounded more like *Fhat fexactly fis frimstone anyfray?* Having his jaw wired up had caused this new speech impediment, though Freddy had no problem decoding it.)

"No idea," Freddy said. "But the fire bit gives me an idea.

You'll have to drive though because I'm not sure I can manage it."

First stop was Freddy's place. Freddy got out and opened his garage door. A few minutes later he emerged carrying a jerry-can, which he put into the boot. When he got back in the passenger seat, Gordo asked him what was in the can.

"Petrol."

Gordo pulled a face. "I fope you know fhat you'f doing?"

"Just giving the boss what he wants. The plan is to give Billy a bit of a fright. This will make him think he's about to meet his maker so he spills his guts and the priest gives him a clean slate."

"Fhat if the fire gets out of fontrol?"

"Chill out, will you?" Freddy motioned for Gordo to do a U-turn and head back towards the church. "Does that wire go into your brain, too? That church has been standing for more than 160 years and hasn't burned down yet."

They parked out the front.

"You reckon they'f in fere?" Gordo said as they walked up the path.

Freddy was carrying the jerry-can in his right hand and stopped to look at his watch, which wasn't that easy with that sling. "Should be by now."

They arrived at the door and opened it to listen.

Freddy pointed to the confession box and whispered. "I can hear a couple of voices."

He splashed petrol around the entrance. Then Gordo lit a match and threw it.

———

The reason the old church had never burned down is no one had ever splashed the portal with petrol before.

But people had been saying for years it was an accident waiting to happen.

The church had been built by the Catholics in 1855 on the same site as the lean-to that in the early days of the settlement served the spiritual needs of the Irish convicts. The stone Church of England church across the road originally only had one door, too, but a second door was opened up years ago to satisfy fire regulations. How the little wooden church escaped the same regulation was anyone's guess. Over the years, many a candle had toppled over but they were either seen in time or burned out harmlessly.

But that bit of accelerant made all the difference today.

The timber building had dried out over 161 years, and once the fire took hold at the entrance, the flames rose higher and higher until the roof caught ablaze, too, with a mighty roar. Smoke billowed out of the doorway and the building started hissing and cracking. It was starting to get breezy outside, too.

It all happened so fast.

Freddy, in his blue denims, and Gordo, wearing his chef's trousers, stood wide-eyed. The only thing that stopped Gordo's mouth from dropping open was the wire holding it shut.

"Fhat are we goingf to tell the bossf?"

When they heard screams inside the church, Freddy and Gordo guessed the men inside were goners.

No one would think any less of them if they passed up the chance to be heroes. Heck, if they had wanted to rescue folk from burning buildings, they would have joined the fire brigade.

Gordo could hear the trees around him groaning and swishing in the strengthening wind.

"Let's get out of here," Freddy said, and they turned and started bounding down the path.

Coming in the gate was Sergeant Stretch and his two constables.

"Detain those men," Stretch shouted to his constables. Then he said to Freddy and Gordo, "Is anyone inside?"

Freddy shrugged, Gordo said nothing comprehensible, and Stretch ran to the top of the path and around to the other side.

He could hear screams. He pulled his coat over his head and dashed inside. By the time he came out a few minutes later, carrying one on the figures over his shoulder, more townsfolk had gathered at the top of the steps.

Stretch laid the rescued person down on the asphalt and turned to go back in. But when a large beam dropped in front of him, he stepped back. Then part of the roof caved in.

Arms reached out to hold Stretch back.

He heard someone say, "There's nothing more you can do."

The church was lost.

So was the other person inside.

More people had arrived, and people were tending the rescued man on the grass. He was groaning.

Sergeant Stretch crossed his arms tightly and hugged them into himself as the pain of his burned hands intensified. Then he heard someone else say, "Oh no, the bush at the back of the church has caught fire now."

SEVENTY-SEVEN
SNAKE ON THE WATER

THEY WALKED BACK to the place where Oodles had planted the stick.

Oodles shook his head. "I can't believe you caught George in this pool. I've never known anyone to catch *anything* here."

He was still shaking his head when he turned to go upstream. But something made him turn straight back around, and he fixed his eyes on the horizon.

"You look like you've seen a ghost," Joffa said.

Oodles pointed. "You see that haze? That looks like a bushfire headed this way."

"Shouldn't we run?"

"It'll be upon us in a few minutes. Quick, we need to shelter in the river, wade as near to the middle as we can get."

They weren't the only ones seeking safety. Upstream, a large tiger snake slithered into the water, too.

The water washed the snake downstream, over a little waterfall and into the same basin Oodles and Joffa were in.

They didn't see it. They were too busy picking out the best rocks in the water to walk along. When they reached the middle of the basin, they crouched down low in the water. Day turned into night as the blackness of the smoke engulfed them and the flames raced from tree to tree. The wind roared more loudly than Joffa had ever heard it.

"Keep calm and stay next to me."

"We're in the middle of a fecking bushfire! How do you expect me to keep calm!"

"It'll be past us in a few minutes, old son. But did you see which direction it came from? That's the real worry."

"You mean . . . ?"

"Yep," Oodles said. "It came from Windy Mountain way."

"They'll blame me."

"Why would they blame you?"

"I'm the convicted arsonist, remember?"

"But you were here with me. I'm your alibi."

"It wouldn't be the first time they've twisted the truth against me."

The fire did pass quickly, as Oodles had predicted. The wind vanished and the sky brightened.

"I meant what I said about standing by you. The only thing you've done wrong today is catch George."

Oodles stood up and started wading back towards the bank.

"Time to go check what's left of the campsite," he said. "Look on the bright side. Not only is it mostly downhill going home, we probably won't have much at all to carry."

He was nearly out when the reptilian head appeared. At least, he thought it was a stick. He realised too late it was actually a snake swimming in the shallow water just where he was about to tread.

It struck at his rubber waders and the old man lost his balance. He slipped on the slimy stones in the shallow water, went flying forward and his leg cracked against a large rock jutting out of the bank. He finished up half out of the water with his back half still in the river.

Joffa splashed over to him.

"You all righ'?"

"Not sure." Oodles's eyes were clenched shut. "My left leg feels odd. How's it look?"

Joffa looked down. It was hard to tell through the water and the waders.

He lifted the old man out of the water and put him down as gently as he could on the smouldering bank, and Oodles gritted his teeth.

"Sorry. I don't like hurting you."

"Don't worry about it, it had to be done. I just wish it was a bit cooler on my back." Oodles grimaced as he took his pocketknife out of his top pocket and handed it to Joffa. "You'll need to cut my waders off."

"Really?"

Oodles's eyes clenched shut again. "Shame, eh, to ruin something that probably just saved my life? That snake will probably have the taste of rubber in his mouth all day long."

Joffa sliced down the seam, and gently peeled the rubber back, careful to not to make contact with the leg.

The leg was crooked and swollen. "Oh, feck," Joffa said.

"It *is* broken, then?" Oodles said.

"I think so," Joffa said. "The bone hasn't pierced the skin though, that's got to be a good thing." Then he noticed blood coming from a gash on the old man's head.

"I'll try phoning someone? My mobile phone is back at the campsite."

"Don't get your hopes up, old son. There's no reception up here. But if the campsite is still intact, you can grab the first-aid kit and see if there are some painkillers."

Joffa turned to go. "You sure you'll be OK?"

"Thought I might do a bit of Riverdancing when you're away, what d'ya think?" The old man half-laughed/half-grimaced. "For Gawdsake, be quick though. I'm not sure how long I'll be able to keep the kicks up."

Joffa hop-scotched through the puffs of smoke. Most of the ground in front of him was still smouldering.

He found where the campsite had been. The tent, sleeping bags and most of their possessions had been engulfed in the firestorm and the intense heat had melted the few things still visible.

Joffa returned to the river.

Oodles took one look at his face and knew. "The campsite is gone?" he croaked.

"I found my phone. The downside is it's now a plastic blob so we'll never know if you're roight about this area having no reception."

"Guess I'm going to die up here like poor old Birty. I only wish I hadn't dragged you up here."

"It was me who dragged you up here, remember? Anyway, you're not going to die. I'll go for help."

Oodles blinked. "You don't know your way out of here."

"Can't I just follow the river down to the town?"

"Sooner or later your path will be blocked by rocks and you'll find yourself walking around in circles."

"Then I'll carry you out."

"Don't be silly." Oodles opened his eyes. "We'd *both* end up with broken legs."

"We just wait here for help to come?"

"What choice do we have?" Oodles pointed to a nearby tree. "You reckon you can reach those leaves? Get me a bunch to chew on?"

Joffa had to make three attempts to jump high enough, but he managed to rip off a whole branch he laid down next to Oodles. "What are they? Bush medicine?"

"Buggered if I know. But I've seen people chewing them, so what harm can they do?"

The old man popped a couple of leaves in his mouth and started chewing. The way he screwed up his face suggested the taste wasn't pleasant.

He spoke from the corner of his mouth. "Wish-Wash and

Katy both know we're up here. Mind you, Wish-Wash has been willing me to die for years."

Joffa rolled his eyes. "That's not good. When I told Katy we were bringing this trip forward, she sounded like she was thinking, '*Why do I even care?*'"

"That's down to me." Oodles spat out a mouthful of leaves and green saliva. "I've got a confession of my own to make, old son. Since Katy's dad died, I've felt kind of responsible for her. I just didn't think you were suitable for her. So I lied. There never was a fiancé." He coughed longer than necessary. "I also told her you were gay."

SEVENTY-EIGHT
RAISING THE ALERT

The Town Hall was packed. The meeting had been called to inform everyone about the bushfire crisis.

It was 7pm. Everyone had heard about this morning's blaze at the church and of new concerns the fire could turn back towards the town. They were eager to hear about any contingency plan.

Tom Vance stood behind the lectern up on the stage and motioned for silence.

Sitting behind him was Sergeant Stretch, whose hands were swathed in bandages. He had bare patches where his eyebrows used to be and his lips were smothered in ointment. Normally it would be his job to chair such a meeting but Tom had stepped in.

"Thanks for coming," the council-clerk said. Every chair was occupied and people leaned on the walls to the side and rear. Children sat on the floor in the aisles.

"By now, I think you all know why we're here," Vance said. "Around midnight tonight, the wind could do one of several things. Fingers crossed it will just blow itself out and the fire will burn itself out round the back of Bing Bong Mountain. But it might change direction and head back towards Windy Mountain. If that happens, there will be a compulsory evacuation around one o'clock in the morning. The assembly point is near the bridge. At this very minute, my staff are trying to arrange a fleet of buses to ferry you to a safe haven. Any questions?"

James was the first member of the audience to stand up.

"Has any thought been given to what happened in the Colonel Richard Northan Memorial Rose Garden? I understand it's been denuded."

"Not now, Mr Northan, please. We need to talk about the fire."

"It's just I think I know where those flowers have got to."

Vance gave him the kind of look school teachers give students when they're daring them to keep disrupting the class.

"I said ANOTHER TIME."

Bob Gordon stood up. "Is it true Father O'Rourke was the person Sergeant Stretch pulled out of the church?"

Vance glanced at the policeman, who nodded his approval for him to speak freely.

"Yes, it's true," Tom Vance said. "But he has terrible burns and we don't know if he's going to make it. He was taken by road ambulance to the Launceston General Hospital, and later transferred by air ambulance to the burns unit in Melbourne."

"And is it true a body was removed from the church?" Gordon said.

Vance looked over at the policeman again, and once again he gave his consent.

"Yes, sadly, it's true. But he or she was burned beyond recognition and we don't know who it is."

Nobody made a sound until a voice boomed out, "Most likely it was a Catholic."

When the crowd realised it was James tittering, he was hailed down in boos.

Vance waved his arms, motioning for calm again. When

the noise had hushed down, he said, "No one in the town has come forward to say they have a loved one missing, so until scientific testing is done the identity is a bit of a mystery. Perhaps Father O'Rourke had a visitor from out of town? Two men have been remanded in custody, but neither of them is saying anything."

Katy and Wish-Wash stood up almost together but in different parts of the room.

Vance pointed to Katy, and Wish-Wash sat down.

But Katy's words were incomprehensible as tears rolled down her cheeks, and Wish-Wash stood up again. "What Katy is trying to say, Tom, is that Oodles and Paddy haven't returned from a fishing trip up on Bing Bong Mountain. They were due back after lunch today."

Vance looked around at Sergeant Stretch, who looked equally alarmed.

He turned back towards Wish-Wash. "So they were up there this morning? They definitely were not at the church?"

"No, they left two days ago to go fishing," Wish-Wash said. "The thing is: if they were in the path of that bushfire . . . " His voice trailed off. "Katy and I reckon we should get a search party together, ASAP."

Vance pinched his nose. This was all he needed.

"Of course," he said. "But we're going to have to wait till daylight, presuming we haven't all been evacuated by then." Then he said, "And we're going to need volunteers? I'll leave from the town hall around 5.30am." He looked around the hall but no one stood up. "Anyone? I have search and rescue experience but I'll need someone who knows that part of the bush. Sergeant Stretch obviously can't go in his condition."

Meredith Mayweather stood up. She had a water bottle in her hand. "Where's Moose Routley when you need him?" People looked from side to side and their blank looks confirmed he wasn't present. "That man knows every inch of that part of the bush."

SEVENTY-NINE
'MY TWO MATES NEED MY HELP'

THE WIND DID CHANGE that night. It swung around in a different direction than one that would force the fire back on to the town.

This came as a relief to the townsfolk, especially the anxious ones who had gone to the evacuation area fairly early for fear of missing a spot on the buses. They waited for several hours in the dark, too scared to fall asleep lest they be forgotten.

At 3am, Tom Vance came over to tell them the danger had passed and they could all go home.

This meant they could all go back to their beds, and unpack their bags they had crammed with changes of clothes, their wedding photos and other precious possessions, and release their cats and guinea pigs, which had had such a baffling nocturnal outing in cages by the roadside.

Vance went home, packed his medical kit and dressed in his army reservist clobber.

He was back out the front of the town hall at 5am with his fingers crossed someone with local knowledge would soon be there to guide him.

Eighteen minutes later, that person arrived.

He was carrying a heavy-looking canvas pack on his back and was dressed in clothes that were probably fashionable for bush-walking 50 years ago.

"Christ! I didn't mean for you to volunteer, Wish-Wash," Vance said.

"My two mates are up there, and they might be in trouble," the old man said.

"I appreciate that. But you've really got to put your faith in us younger blokes."

Wish-Wash made a point of looking left and right. "What younger blokes, Tom? All I see is you."

"We've got a few minutes yet. But worst comes to worst, I'm prepared to go in alone. I've trained for this, remember?"

Wish-Wash shook his head. "But how will you find your way?"

"I have a compass, and I can read a map."

At that moment, they heard footsteps and a giant of a man walked out of the shadows.

Wish-Wash did a double take.

Vance had never seen the man before.

"Moose?" Wish-Wash said. "You've changed your mind!"

EIGHTY
SO, HERE I AM

TOM VANCE and Moose Routley travelled quickly.

Both men had packs on their back. Moose carried spare clothes, sleeping bags, several bottles of water, bananas and energy bars. Vance carried a medical kit as well as a fold-up stretcher.

After an hour of walking along fire trails, Moose led them along a well-trodden path to a creek where he knelt and replenished the water canteens.

Vance sat down on a boulder. Sweat poured down his face.

Moose turned and handed him a water bottle. "Used to be blackberries all around here. You never used to be able to see the creek from the fire trail."

The bush around them was eerie. It was devoid of bird life. The fire had consumed most of the ground foliage, leaving behind a carpet of smoking charcoal. A few trees inexplicably had survived virtually untouched but others were blackened and denuded. A few trees had succumbed completely and had toppled over. Smoke still rose from their corpses.

Vance looked around. "Grim, eh?"

"It happens," Moose said, his head turned as he knelt by the water and filled another canteen. "So fast too. You haven't got time to blink in a bushfire." He stood up, and looked around for his own boulder to sit on. "Give it a year or two, though, and most people would be hard pressed to tell a fire had even been through here. Fire is nature's way of rebirth."

"But nature had nothing to do with this. You know the police are holding two blokes accused of setting light to the church?"

"I heard."

Vance chugged down some more water. "You reckon Oodles and Paddy are all right?"

Moose shook his head. "The Irishman he's with probably doesn't know his arse from his elbow. But Oodles knows the bush, and you don't make it to his age without being a survivor."

"What did Wish-Wash mean about you changing your mind?"

Moose stared into space for a bit, then said, "He came to see me last night asking for my help."

"And?"

"And I said no." Moose gazed into space again. "You can't blame me! Truth is, I only really detest one man in Windy Mountain and he's poisoned so many townsfolk against me. About a year ago I got an invitation in the mail to the footy reunion. I replied thanks, but no thanks. Then Tiger Kowalski and a couple of the boys rang me up and talked me into changing my mind. I didn't know Tiger was going to try to hook me up with the blokes who started that fire at the church?"

Vance's eyes widened. "You *knew* they were going to light that fire?"

"I knew they were up to something, but not that." Moose's voice went up in pitch. "You don't think I'd stand by and let them do that?"

Then he said, "I can't say I wasn't tempted when Henk Van Gogh offered me a wad of money to get rid of this Irishman. It would take me months, years even to earn that amount of money. But in the end I said I didn't want any part of it. Tiger said I was mad. He said no one was going to miss a bloke who came from nowhere. But I went back to my room at The Applecart and tried to forget about it. I knew they were trying to flush out Billy Gumboots, too, but, Christ, not kill him?"

"Who told you about Oodles and the Irishman not returning from their fishing trip?"

"Wish-Wash. I had two knocks on the door within 10 minutes around midnight. The first one was the publican who said I had to be ready to evacuate. I told him to piss off, I had paid for my room so I was staying. The second knock came from Wish-Wash. He told me about the church, told me about this situation and asked me to help. I told him it wasn't my problem."

"So what made you change your mind?"

"My conscience, I guess," Moose said. "It wasn't just heat, and the smell of smoke coming in the open window that kept me awake. I worked out who had started that fire. In the end I figured I might as well be out here because all I was doing was tossing and turning anyway. I go back a long way with Wish-Wash and Oodles, and neither of them has done me a bad turn. When I thought it through I couldn't let Wish-Wash come out here — the silly old bugger would probably trip over a cliff and kill himself." He held up his arms in a giant wingspan. "So here I am."

"Well I, for one, am glad," Vance said.

Moose rose from his rock. "We'd better be making tracks again. My guess is we have about another hour of walking."

EIGHTY-ONE
'WHAT? NO PARTY HAT?'

OODLES LIFTED his head when he heard the crunch of footsteps, and saw two figures tramping through the blackened bush. "I knew they'd come."

Tom Vance inspected Oodles's leg and head gash, asked some questions and delved into his medical bag. He handed Oodles a green whistle and told him to breathe in through it.

"What? No party hat?" The old man examined it quizzically before putting it to his lips.

"You're inhaling a drug called methoxyflurane," Vance said. "It'll take the edge off your pain. But seeing as you're in the mood it might also make you feel like putting on your dancing shoes."

He then loaded up a hypodermic needle. "Compared to what you've had to put up with, this won't hurt a bit." He tapped the syringe and stuck it into Oodles's arm. "Let's see if we can make you comfortable, put a splint on that leg and get you to hospital."

Oodles sucked deeply on the whistle and removed it to exhale. "Not sure if I can walk, let alone dance."

"Looks like we'll have to carry you home, then," came a

voice from the other side. Oodles turned and saw it was Moose, who was on his knees unravelling the stretcher.

Oodles, who was getting groggy now, said, "How did you get roped into this, big fella?"

Moose took his wallet out of his back pocket. "Did you forget I owed you $20." He pressed a note into Oodles's hand. "I'm just here to work off the interest."

Oodles grabbed the note tightly and smiled. "Thanks."

"No wucking forries."

Being of roughly equal height, Joffa and Moose took either ends of the stretcher.

They tried not to make the journey too bumpy, and the trip home took more than an hour longer than the trek up. Vance walked alongside the stretcher as much as he could.

Oodles shook his head. "Lucky I'm not a betting man, Tom, eh? I could have sworn these two were on a collision path. Now look at them?"

EIGHTY-TWO
MYSTERY MAN COMES OUT

KATY RAN to meet them when they came out of the bush. She hugged all four men, but the order she hugged them was telling. First she embraced Joffa, then Oodles, then Moose and then Tom.

Oodles had snapped both his tibia and fibula, and surgeons went on to implant a titanium rod to hold his bones together. The gash in his forehead was cleaned up and left to heal itself.

Oodles was still in hospital two days later when word came through Father O'Boring had died.

That changed the voting dynamics for the old men's lottery, and Oodles and Wish-Wash were able to outvote James on the sale of the shares.

"You damn fools," the former mayor said. "I intend to keep my share invested — and you'll be sorry you've sold out, mark my words." He then stormed out of the hospital room.

They weren't sorry though. In fact, they got a good laugh out of it.

Three days after they cashed in, the mining company confessed it had been less than honest in its prospectus, and its share price went tumbling. James had to sell his portfolio before the shares hit zero.

When forensic testing discovered the person who had died in the church fire was Billy Gumboots, Sergeant Stretch got an exhumation order to find out who the heck had been buried in Billy's grave.

Police were stunned to find the model of the hunter in the coffin, and very interested to find the diary and map in the hunter's coat pocket.

The good news for Billy's mother was she saved a heap of money because Billy's body was interred into his recently vacated grave.

This time Wish-Wash went to Billy's funeral, and cried for the loss of his son.

The discovery in the bogus grave helped police build a water-tight case against Mr Biggs and Henk van Gogh, who they had long suspected as being responsible for the reduction of the Tasmanian population. Now they had real evidence, on top of what Freddy and Gordo revealed when they started talking.

The whole lot of them ended up in jail, and the Tasmanian Tiger Museum was put on the market.

Oodles and Wish-Wash decided to use their windfall to buy it.

Wish-Wash moved from The Applecart to the flat above the museum, and became its new manager. By this time, the streetlight had started malfunctioning again but Wish-Wash didn't mind it washing his bedroom in blinking yellow hue because he liked a bit of colour. Besides, sometimes he could just let his sci-fi imagination run wild about Dr Who's Tardis pulling up in the car park or little green men invading earth.

Oodles became a silent partner in the museum. He preferred to keep a low profile so he could avoid forever being pointed out as the man who had chewed on the gum leaves up on Bing Bong Mountain in the hope they had a pain-killing effect.

It was true he had seen a number of people chewing them over the years. But it was probably because all these people had colds. Those kind of leaves were routinely used in the manufacture of cough lollies and elixirs.

Wish-Wash entered into an arrangement with Dave the undertaker to keep the science fiction books in the flat above the museum, which suited them both fine.

Oodles tried to fess up to Katy he hadn't been entirely truthful about the Irishman, but Katy just laughed. "I never thought you meant he was homosexual, I just assumed you meant he was happy and *gay* — old-timer's speak."

The Irishman returned to Sydney to testify against those people-smugglers, and they went to jail, too.

When he returned to Windy Mountain, he came back as Joffa, instead of Paddy, and he moved in with Katy in her tower above the hair salon. When they married, they were the first couple to take their vows in the new brick Catholic church built on the burned-out site.

Oodles, his leg still encased in plaster, gave Katy away, and Wish-Wash was Joffa's best man.

It was the first time Wish-Wash had ever been entrusted with wedding rings, which ratcheted up his self-esteem even more.

It helped that Moose stood beside him as the other groomsman.

James kept his distance from Oodles and Wish-Wash for months.

Just about every other person in Windy Mountain signed Oodles's plaster cast but it had already been removed when James appeared one day and put a new proposition to them in a dialect rarely spoken any more. Shortly after that, he disappeared and someone began stealing local landmarks.

But that's a story for the next book in the Windy Mountain series.

STAY IN TOUCH

Thanks for reading this novel. If my humour amused you, perhaps my FREE (mostly) funny blog posts will tickle your funny bone. Check out all my books too, including Wish-Wash's reviews.

https://johnmartin-author.blog

NEXT IN THE WINDY MOUNTAIN SERIES

WHEREFORE ART THOU, JIMBO?

Oodles and Wish-Wash are supposed to be planning a trip to research family history. How come they become sleuths when the uppity former mayor disappears?

They don't even like James Northan, who was born with a silver spoon in his mouth and now reckons he's a descendant of William Shakespeare.

Things go from bad to worse for them in this black comedy. Important local landmarks start vanishing.

Demolition men try to dismantle the old men's beloved Tasmanian Tiger Museum.

Has the former mayor drowned himself in the stinky sewerage ponds or has he been kidnapped by the unsavoury newcomer to town everyone calls Messerschmitt?

Enter the cow camouflage trousers, walkie-talkies and a

young American who joins them on their mission to rescue Jimbo.

Blokes on a Plane is the follow-up novel to *Lie of the Tiger*.

Whitey and the Six Dwarfs, Blokes in Donegal, Blokes in the House, Who Knew Tasmanian Tigers Eat Apples! and *Who Knew Tiger Sharks also eat Apples?* await with many of the same quirky characters.

EXCERPT FROM BLOKES ON A PLANE

Chapter 1

FOREVER IN BLUE GENES

Huddled together on the bench, the two old blokes were poring over the specials in the Roses Supermarket catalogue when a shadow dimmed their light. Oodles looked up to find the Mayor, of all people, blocking out the sun.

James Northan, briefcase in hand and wearing a pinstripe suit as though he were on the way to the office he no longer had, smiled snidely.

Oodles was flabbergasted. But he knew the big man beside him would react more explosively.

James had avoided talking to him and Wish-Wash for more than 15 months, quite a feat in a town as small as Windy Mountain. They hadn't even seen him at this end of town.

Sure enough, Wish-Wash scowled and thrust out his chin. "Are you lost, Jimbo?"

James sighed loudly as he tilted his head downwards and flicked a piece of lint from his lapel. "Why must thou always have to be so prickly, Bert?"

The reason he called him Bert was that Wish-Wash was his nickname, and James Northan thought nicknames were crass. The big man's full name was Bert Whish-Willson, and he was 82, one year older than James Northan, who had been the actual mayor years ago. People sometimes called him the Mayor nickname because he still behaved like he was.

Oodles's full name was Clarence Noodle. He was 85.

James Northan looked from man to man. "Methinks the time hast just come for us to bury the hatchet."

"Bring it here then, and I'll bury it in your head—maybe it'll stop you from talking funny, too."

James stepped back sharply. "Did you hear that, Clarence? Bert is threatening me with violence."

Oodles sighed. "I didn't hear anything, James. Except, like him, you talking funny."

"I forgot you two are as thick as thieves."

Wish-Wash bounced to his feet with a flash of yellow shirt and the kind of vigour Oodles hadn't seen from him in years. "I'm sick of you calling me thick."

Oodles quickly levered himself up using the armrest and stepped between them, mainly to hold back Wish-Wash.

This wasn't the first time the three oldest men left in the town had nearly come to blows.

Oodles and Wish-Wash were the unlikely owners of the Tasmanian Tiger Museum across the road from the bench where they had been sitting in the sun taking their mid-morning break.

The Mayor had only set foot in that museum once, and that hadn't ended happily for him.

Oodles, dressed in his usual grey overalls, battled to hold Wish-Wash back. "If you've come here to sign my plaster cast, James, you're too late. Doc Jenkins removed it ages ago."

"Thank goodness for that. I don't give my autograph to any damn fool. I'm not about to reward someone careless enough to break his leg. No, I just thought I would buy you both a cup of tea, for old time's sake."

Wish-Wash jabbed a finger over Oodles's shoulder. "I've never known you to do nothing for nothing."

"People change." James tapped his briefcase. "I thought you both might like to see one of the advertisements in this magazine I've come across."

Oodles exchanged a glance with Bert before they fell in line behind the Mayor. James strode ahead as if he were leading them into battle. On the way, Oodles threw the Roses Supermarket catalogue into a roadside bin.

"What's the bet this is another one of his hare-brained schemes?" Wish-Wash said.

"Oh, guaranteed," Oodles replied.

They reached the Wind Tunnel Cafe at the other end of the High Street.

Wendy, the blonde, middle-aged waitress, looked up as they came through the door. "Would you look at this? Someone's put the band back together!"

The Mayor put his briefcase down next to one of the two tables and wrung his hands as he sat down. "Tea for three, Wendy, dear."

Oodles and Bert sat down opposite him as James clicked open the briefcase. He laid a glossy magazine down on the dappled-red laminate table, flipped through the pages, then turned it towards them.

Oodles frowned. "So what's this all about?"

James stabbed at an advertisement. "Did you know scientists can trace your ancestry through DNA?"

"Can they?" Wish-Wash scratched his head.

"Not from dandruff, you cream-faced loon!" James said. "They take a swab from inside your mouth."

"Gawdsake!" Oodles said. "Why would I want to volunteer my DNA anyway? That's how they build evidence against criminals."

James gave him a disapproving look. "Dost thou have something to hide? Like convict ancestry?"

"Oh, I see what's happening here. You want to prove your lineage goes back to someone famous with pure British blood, who spoke in the same stupid way that you are doing now, and you want to out Wish-Wash and me as being descended from petty Irish criminals."

"Are you?"

"Don't know, don't care," Oodles said.

Wish-Wash blew out his cheeks. "I wouldn't mind having a convict in my closet."

"You don't know your lineage?" James asked.

"Are you kidding?" Wish-Wash ran a hand down one side of his unshaven face. "I don't even know who my father was. Not really."

James turned towards Oodles. "What about you? Any idea?"

Oodles shook his head slowly. "Noodle is an anglicised name. But from what, I can't tell you. All I know is my grandparents arrived on a ship. The ship might have left from Ireland, but more likely it came from Ukraine or somewhere."

"I'll pay for the DNA test, if that's what you're worried about."

"You'll also pay for me?" Wish-Wash said.

"That's what I said, didn't I?"

Wish-Wash held up the magazine. "It says here a lucky entrant will win a trip for two, all expenses paid, to the area their ancestors came from."

James snatched it back and scanned it. "So it does."

"So if you pay for me to take the test, and I win the trip, will I have to take you?"

James sighed. "Let's not get ahead of ourselves, Bert."

Wish-Wash grinned. "But what if I do?"

"That is very unlikely, Bert. But if it doth happen, thou mayest take whoever thou willst. Just not me."

NEXT THREE BOOKS

AUTHOR'S NOTE

I WROTE a series of feature articles on the search for the Tasmanian Tiger when I worked as a newspaper reporter in Tasmania.

It was then — and still is now — a contentious topic. Scotland has its Lochness Monster, we have our Tasmanian Tiger.

I received an anonymous postcard after those articles.

On one side was a photograph of the Thylacine; the other side of the card had the scribbled words: "John, this is as near to a Tasmanian Tiger as you'll ever get."

I never did get to the bottom of that postcard. Perhaps it came from a cynical colleague, perhaps it came from a reader I never even knew?

I think I've proven him/her wrong though. With this series of books I've come pretty damn close to the Tasmanian Tiger. More importantly, the Windy Mountain books have winged their way digitally into more than 80 countries. Take that, anonymous postcard sender!

For the record, I'm firmly on the fence as to the Tasmanian Tiger's continuous existence. I reckon we have a better chance than they do in Scotland though.

· · ·

HELP ME

Typos always manage to slip through the net, so by all means let me know if something's out of order.

MY NOVELS

Windy Mountain series

Lie of the Tiger (#1)

He's not who he says he is. Who will rescue him?

———

Blokes on a Plane (#2)

Why is the mayor speaking old English? And where has he disappeared to?

———

Whitey and the Six Dwarfs (#3)

Troupe of Elvis impersonators come to the rescue.

———

Blokes in Donegal (#4)

Three old blokes go to Ireland hoping to discover family history.
The mayor had to take his great, great, great grandfather's head,
didn't he!

———

Blokes in the House (#5)

How the old blokes coped with COVID quarantine (clue: the major didn't).

———

Who Knew Tasmanian Tigers Eat Apples. (#6)

Back to before the beginning. Wish-Wash leads a public revolt.

Who Knew Tiger Sharks also Eat Apples? (#7)

A character from the old days returns in an unlikely guise. It's all about comic revenge.

———

The Life and Deaths of Billy Gumboots (#8)

'His foot, my boot.'

———

Blokes Send in the Clones (#9)

Two old blokes have a crack at cloning a Tasmanian tiger.

To come:

10 — Blokes do the Block

Someone marries, someone dies. Might even be the same old bloke.

———

Funny Capers DownUnder series

The Wrong Magician (#1)

This time he has to make himself disappear.

———

Daddy's Great Escape (#2)

If Mad Bill hates people so much, why does he make it so hard
for them to leave his island?

———

Escape from Mad Bill's Island (#3)

He came seeking to find out what the British were up to on the island in World War 2. He won't like the answer.

———

Standalone novels

Major B.S. comes to the end of his Rope

It all started when he rescued the wrong group of people from a prisoner-of-war camp. It just becomes worse.

———